FOUND YOU

Sarah Jules

To Buster,
who rescued me.

Prologue

His body was bound. Restraints cut into his wrists, the skin puckered and reddened before his eyes. He didn't know how he got there, what he'd done to deserve this. All he knew at that moment was that he wanted the pain to end. For all this to be over, no matter the cost. It was too much for any person to bear. It was weak of him to wish he was dead, but if that was the only way to get the torture to stop, then so be it.

His vision blackened around the edges, blurring and ripping. Flashes of light and slicing agony. It didn't feel real anymore. The man stepped closer to him. Knife in hand. A smile cut into his worn and haggard face. Cameron knew him. The tormentor. He was strangely familiar. A face in a dream that you can't quite place.

The knife was placed delicately under Cameron's fingernail. The smile spread, showing too-white teeth.

"Please, no," Cameron begged, knowing it was futile. A meaningless attempt to stop the abuse. It was the only thing he could do. His body was held fast, no room for even the slightest of movements. Straining against the ropes at his wrists and ankles, veins forcing their way to the surface, he let out a scream of frustration. Breath came ragged in his throat, ripping at his insides.

"You deserve this," the man said, pushing the tip of the blade under Cameron's fingernail, separating it from the nailbed beneath. He grunted against the pain, vowing not to scream. He wouldn't give the bastard the satisfaction.

"What did I do to you?" Cameron gritted his teeth. Each syllable was slow, strained.

"You know, that makes things worse. The fact that you don't know what you did. You get on with your life like it's nothing. Pretending to be a good person, but you're an imposter, hidden behind a mask. None of who you are is real. I know the real you. I see what's behind the guise to the reprobate you really are. I'm going to make you pay for what you did to her."

The fist hit his jaw with unbelievable force, snapping his head backwards. Sparks flew before his eyes. Spit and blood trailed down his chin. The taste of iron filled his mouth. His pulse was a drumbeat inside his neck.

"Fuck," Cameron snarled.

"And I'm only just getting started."

The knife slid into his side like it was butter. Cold and then white-hot. Blinking back tears, Cameron looked down, confusion etched in the lines on his face. It was in that second that Cameron realised he was not leaving that room alive. He started to mumble the words to a prayer, praying to a God that he didn't believe in. *Let this be over quickly. I can't take anymore.*

Cameron

The vibration cut through the silence of the classroom. Looking up from the pile of books in front of him, Cameron shifted around his desk's contents to find the offending item. The phone screen illuminated the room, blue light casting the planes of his face into shadow. It was late. He shouldn't still be working, but he was preparing his year eleven class for their GCSEs, which required providing feedback on their numerous essays, each of which sounded exactly the same as the one before.

Rubbing his eyes, he unlocked the phone, clicking on the text message icon.

An unknown number. The little bubble held only two words.

FOUND YOU.

Blinking, eyebrows furrowing in confusion, he read the message again.

"Knob," Cameron said to the empty space. The words echoed off the cold walls. Shaking his head, he placed the phone back on the desk, turning it over to engage the "Do Not Disturb" mode. Somebody's idea of a joke, or a wrong number. Either way, he didn't have time for that right now. He still had six essays left to mark before he could leave to meet Liz.

As though on cue, his stomach growled. The prospect of dinner flooded his mind. It was date night, like every Wednesday night, and he couldn't be late. She didn't like it when he was late. It was easier not to piss her off, or he'd be in for a frosty night. The woman was drop-dead gorgeous but could also be drop-dead mean.

The clock read 5.30 pm. He had twenty minutes before he had to leave. He wasn't the only teacher left in school at this time by any means, but the halls were so quiet you could hear a pin drop. Everybody concentrated on getting their last bits of work done so that they could be out of the door as quickly as possible and home to their families. He didn't have anybody to go home to, not yet, but the way things were going with Liz, he might not have long to wait. He longed to have that closeness. Somebody to be waiting for you when you got home. Since reaching his thirties, his desire for this had only multiplied.

Cameron stretched out his neck and shoulders. The October weather had turned the afternoon black and the window into a mirror. Even at thirty-two years old, the sight of himself in a suit, looking like an actual adult, never failed to surprise him. Running his hand through his slightly too long hair and suppressing a yawn, he picked up his pen and began to read. All thoughts of the unsolicited text message completely vanished from his mind, as he cast his attention back to *Of Mice and Men* and the literary sensation that was John Steinbeck. It was clear from the essays he was marking that many of his students didn't get what the fuss was about.

Liz was waiting outside the restaurant when Cameron pulled his car into the only free space available on the street. He parallel parked with ease—a lifetime of living in the city will do that to you—and waved to his girlfriend. She was bundled up in an oversized coat, scarf held tightly around her neck. Even after a full day of work, she looked immaculate. He never understood how she managed that. If she were a superhero, that would be her power. Physical perfection.

Cameron loved the attention he got when he was with Liz. They looked great together and people noticed. When she dangled off his arm, people stared. It was like wearing an expensive piece of jewellery that screamed, "Look at me!" whenever he had Liz's hand in his. Heads turned as they walked by. Incidentally, it was the same reason he'd bought the gun-metal grey BMW three series. People looked. And Cameron, despite himself, liked when people looked. Liz was out of his league. He wasn't stupid. He took care of himself, but he only had so much to work with.

"Hi handsome." Liz smiled and drew him into a hug, his arms wrapped around her waist, and he pulled her close, savouring the moment. Her expensive floral perfume was still strangely unfamiliar and enticing. Having only been together for a few months, everything still felt new and thrilling.

They were seated at a table in front of the window. Streetlights illuminated the river, casting it in pools of light and shadows. The heavens opened as they were ordering starters. Sheets of rain hurled themselves at the windowpanes. The tealight at the centre of the table flickered lazily. It was romantic. The lighting, the weather, the restaurant itself, was perfection. It was the entire reason he'd chosen this place. He was desperate to impress Liz, and if that meant pulling out all the stops for date night once a week and going to some fancy restaurant he'd never usually set foot in, then he'd do it without batting an eyelid.

Cameron placed a hand on Liz's knee, feeling the soft fabric of her skirt. She smiled at him and shook her head, never breaking her stream of conversation, giving Cameron a chance to study her perfect features. The gentle curve of her nose. The warm skin, arched eyebrows, and sultry hooded eyes. Long black hair, razor straight, framed her delicate face.

"Cameron?" Her voice, as smooth as caramel, prompted him back to the conversation.

"Pardon?" he said. There was no way he could pretend he was listening. "I got a bit distracted."

Cameron bit his lip and winked, hoping that his cheeky sense of humour would be enough to save him.

"You're such a flirt." Liz leaned forward, pressing her lips to his cheek. He felt the familiar warm glow of longing deep in his stomach.

As she pulled away, Cameron looked out of the window at the scenery and planned to say something romantic about how beautiful it was. But the stark white face, floodlit by a lone streetlight, caught his eye. The face looked like it wasn't attached to a body, the man's dark clothes hiding the bulk of him. From where Cameron was sitting, all he could see was a white, weathered face, and a head entirely free of hair.

His eyes stared directly into Cameron's own. Unblinking. Unmoving. The head slowly tilted to the side and a too-wide smile cleaved his face in two. It became instantly familiar. Cameron knew the man from somewhere. He'd seen him before, but where?

"Liz, look at that man under the light. Where do I know him from?" Cameron said without removing his eyes from the figure.

"Never seen him before." That made sense, given that they hadn't known each other all that long.

"Weird right? That he's just standing there?" Cameron asked, wanting confirmation that he was justified in feeling unnerved.

"He's probably just waiting for somebody." Liz shrugged.

"Yeah, probably," Cameron acquiesced, peeling his eyes from the man, and turning his attention back to Liz.

His face warmed and flushed in embarrassment for overreacting. Something about the man struck a chord within Cameron. It felt wrong. A tingling sensation curled under his skin. After trying to resist looking out of the window, Cameron eventually gave up, slowly allowing his eyes to roam to the glass. The man was gone. The streetlight now illuminated nothing but the puddled pavement. Cameron's eyes searched the rest of the causeway for evidence of the man. He was nowhere to be seen.

Pushing down the feeling of anxiety, Cameron painted a smile onto his face and carried on with date night, wondering why the man had made him feel so uncomfortable. If his discomfort was visible, Liz chose not to mention it, allowing the date night to unfurl in the pattern they'd both become accustomed to. It was strange. The man was no longer there, but Cameron couldn't seem to shake the feeling that he was being watched. His nerves didn't dissipate until Liz was wrapped in his arms, safe in his bed that night.

Savannah

The air was splinteringly cold against her bare legs, sending shivers up her spine. She was already frozen to the bone. The day had been far too long, but she wasn't quite ready for it to be over. A pressure headache was building against the back of Savannah's head, where her skull met her spine. The same place as always. The shift dress she was wearing itched at her neck and under her arms. Her shoes hurt like hell, too. But she looked good, she knew that. Pain is beauty, that's what her friends said. It wouldn't take too long for the pill Gemma gave her to kick in, and then her shoes wouldn't hurt anymore, and she would finally feel comfortable in her clothes. Just a little while longer.

Teetering across the cobblestones, they made their way to the club. Belfry's, their favourite. Cheap drinks, decent music, and plenty of people. They'd probably stay there until midnight when Rain Bar started to heat up. You had to pay to get in there, and Savannah had £3 hidden in the secret pocket of her purse, so she couldn't accidentally spend it beforehand. That would be a major disaster and a premature end to the evening.

Belfry's was warm and sticky. It smelled of spilt liquor and sweat and felt like home. With Gemma on one arm and Penny on the other, Savannah headed over to the bar, ready for the first drink of the night. Jager-bombs. The most alcohol for the least money. That's the way you had to play it in Belfry's. She was served straight away, another perk of coming to Belfry's so often.

With her drink in hand, Savannah fled to the dancefloor, closing her eyes, and allowing the music to wash over her. All feelings of discomfort were quickly forgotten. Amidst the throng of people, moving as one, Gemma slipped another pill into Savannah's mouth. She dry-swallowed it without missing a beat. Bodies pushed against her, and she pushed back, finding herself in the arms of a tall stranger. His handsome, boyish face looked down at her and smiled. Bending his head, he roughly pushed his lips against hers, using his tongue to part her lips. There had been no introductions. None were necessary.

Warmth flooded through her body as she allowed herself to be enveloped by him. They moved together, not quite in time to the music. His mouth traced down her neck, and her body reacted instinctively, pushing her closer to him. Throwing her arms around his neck, her fingers found his hair. Savannah laughed. A perfect moment.

"Let me get you another drink," the man whisper-shouted in her ear.

"Okay," Savannah said, slipping her hand into his and following him to the bar. His palm was warm and wet, slipping in her grasp.

"Four Jager-bombs," he said to the bartender, handing over a note. He didn't ask what she wanted. In Belfry's, it was assumed.

The bartender was about Savannah's age. Unbelievably beautiful. Made-up to the hilt and with red hair that poured to her waist. It made Savannah immediately self-conscious. She looked at the guy holding her hand, to see if he'd noticed the woman behind the bar. His eyes were fixed on Savannah's. Pride built within her. The thought that he found Savannah so attractive that he didn't even want to glance at the bartender, filled her with a sense of pride that only comes from knowing you're more attractive than another woman. She knew it was wrong, and anti-feminist, but that's just the way it was.

"Drink up," he said.

Savannah did as she was told, pouring the sludge-coloured liquid down her throat. She picked up the second glass and did the same. It burned.

"More?" It was a loaded question. Yes, she wanted more. More alcohol. More dancing. More intimacy. More chance to forget the stresses of essays and exams, and what to do with her life when she actually finished university.

"Why the hell not?" Savannah said, biting her lip in what she hoped was a suggestive manner.

The next drinks went down in exactly the same way. They bit at her throat and filled her stomach with warmth.

"Let's dance," Savannah said, grabbing the man's hand and pulling him back to the dancefloor. As long as she had somebody to dance with, to move her body against, and let her inhibitions go, Savannah felt alive. With their bodies pressed tightly together and the bass from the speakers vibrating through the sticky carpet, Savannah felt herself relax. Pushing down the reality that she only ever felt this way when she had her arms wrapped around a stranger, or was on the wrong side of sober, she slid her hands under the back of his shirt, feeling the taut, damp skin of his back.

"What's your name?" She could feel his breath hot against her ear, his body reacted to hers.

"Savannah," she shouted above the noise.

"David," he said, pulling her closer still. "Come back with me?"

The words jarred her. This wasn't how it was supposed to go. The night had barely even started. That would come later, much later. Once sweat had drenched her dress and stuck her hair to the back of her neck.

"Later." She smiled against his ear, kissing his cheek teasingly. She knew she was leading him on. It felt good. She couldn't help herself. Feeling wanted was the ultimate high.

"Come on. Don't be like that. Come home with me?"

Savannah felt David pull away from her just a touch. His body hardened.

“Later,” Savannah repeated herself. “I promise, later.” She tried to pull him back closer to her. “Let's just dance for now.”

“I need another drink,” David said, turning and walking back to the bar.

Savannah found herself abandoned on the dancefloor surrounded by crowds of couples and groups of friends. Penny and Gemma were nowhere in sight. She felt dejected, alone. She had to find them, start the night over. Find somebody else that would make her feel alive, comfortable in her own skin. She took a step forward, and the heel of her shoe stuck in the carpet.

“Fuck,” she mumbled as her knee slammed into the wet floor, hands flying out before her.

“Whey!” the crowd shouted. It was a herd response. One she’d participated in many times. It felt different when it was aimed at you. Savannah pushed back tears. Embarrassment flooded through her body, sending prickles of panic across her skin like electricity.

She stood up, looked at the floor, and pushed her way out of the swarm of people. Their jeers and laughter swirled around her. She hated herself. Really truly hated herself. Continuing to push through hordes of drunks, Savannah lurched around the club. Faces swam before her. Happy, smiling faces. All of them blurred, the edges taken away thanks to the Jager-bombs and the nondescript white pills.

Finding herself at the bar, Savannah decided all that was left to do was buy another drink and wait for her friends to come and find her. They always did eventually. The nights always followed the same pattern.

"Jager-bomb please," Savannah said to the bartender. The same one as before. The pretty girl. The tables had turned. Savannah was now alone.

"Sure," the woman said, pretending like she didn't remember Savannah from before. Savannah could see the smirk hidden under layers of too-pale makeup.

"Let me get that." David's voice cut through the noise. He stood behind her. Centimetres away. The heat of his body radiated against her. She stood firm, refusing to move as a result of him. She had more pride than that.

"No, thank you," Savannah said, feeling the heat once again build in her face. Without looking in a mirror, she already knew it was red.

"I'm sorry, okay? You're gorgeous and I was disappointed. Give me another chance?"

Savannah turned to look at David. He was older than her, a dark crop of stubble across his cheeks and neck, dimples piercing his cheeks when he smiled that boyish smile.

"Fine," Savannah said, pressing her lips into a line. She might have left with him at the very end of the night, once he'd put a bit more work in, but never that early on. It was fair enough that he'd been disappointed. She had led him on, after all. It felt quite powerful that she had the ability to disappoint somebody so significantly.

"You won't regret it. I'll be a proper gentleman from here on out. Bartender, three more!" She couldn't help but laugh at that, the way he beckoned the bartender like somebody out of an old movie. The girl behind the bar definitely remembered David, even if she'd pretended not to remember Savannah. The girl's face was sweet as pie for David, and then she turned and glowered at Savannah. She'd won. It felt damn good.

Fading back into consciousness, the stench of vomit filled the air around Savannah. It was mixed with something sweeter, more clinical. Peeling open her eyes, the harsh lights above her confirmed her suspicions. She was in a hospital. The bleached starched sheets were rough against her skin. Savannah attempted to pull herself upright. The room lurched dangerously around her, a wave of nausea knocking her back down onto the hard mattress. Bile built in her throat. She was going to be sick. Throwing herself onto her side, Savannah tipped her head over the edge of the bed, the tell-tale splashing of her vomit hitting the floor filled her with shame.

Feeling too ill to be entirely embarrassed, Savannah twisted her body so that she was laid flat on her back again. Fog ballooned inside her head, pushing any tangible thoughts away.

“Shit, Savannah!” The words pulled her back to consciousness. Her dad. Somebody must have called him. She braced herself for the incoming barrage of abuse.

“Dad, I’m sorry,” she began. Her go-to response.

“Hey, excuse me, can somebody come in here a minute?” His voice was projecting away from her, out into the hallway. He was finding somebody to come and clean her up.

“Dad,” Savannah said.

“Don’t,” he warned. “I don’t want excuses. I’m fed up with this shit. It needs to stop. How many times do you need to have your stomach pumped before you get yourself together?”

“I didn’t even,” Savannah started. Her voice felt childlike. Too big for her mouth.

“No, no excuses. I’m not doing this anymore. You’re going to stop now. You’re moving out of that fucking house with those stupid girls. Somewhere closer to me. Somewhere with responsible people who aren’t going to abandon you in the street to die.” It went without saying that her dad was mad. His voice was pregnant with anger. She hated herself for making him feel that way.

“I’m sorry. I don’t remember how I got here, Dad,” Savannah said, trying to swallow the sobs that were building within her. It was always the same when he told her off. It made her want to cry. She couldn’t help it. It was her natural response. This night far surpassed the many hospital trips that had come before. She usually remembered how she got to the hospital, but last night was a total blur and completely blank. The absence of anything tangible after the guy she'd been dancing with had stormed off. She didn't want to leave her house, leave her friends. This was the last time. She'd pull herself together. No more drugs. Stick to the alcohol instead and perhaps move to alcopops rather than Jager-bombs. It would be more expensive, but that was the price she'd have to pay.

"You were found in an alleyway next to Belfry's. The bouncer called an ambulance. You were all alone, Sav. You could have died. This isn't a joke. Crying isn't going to help you." He pushed his fingers into his temples, moving them slowly against his skin. She didn't dare to speak, knowing the tirade of anger wasn't yet over. "I'm so fucking angry with you right now. What would have happened if the bouncer hadn't found you? Can you even stop to think about that for a second? I've given you everything you could ever want, and this is what you do. You throw it all away for a night out. I didn't raise you like that. Your mum would be rolling in her grave if she could see you." Her dad's voice was tight, suppressing the emotions he pretended not to feel.

"I'm sorry," Savannah stuttered. What else could she say to that? Once again, she'd broken his heart. But it wasn't her fault. Not really. She must have been spiked or something. She'd not even been *that* drunk or high. Not really.

"I found you a new house. A friend of a friend has some rentals and there's a free bedroom in one. It's close to me. And he said the girl in there is a good person. She doesn't drink or party. You'll move in today."

The prospect of moving all of her possessions when she couldn't even support her own body sent shockwaves of fear down her spine.

"I won't leave. You can't make me leave. My friends…"

"It's already done. You're never going back to that house with those girls. I've asked my assistant to go and get your stuff. She'll be on her way over there now." Savannah knew she must have scared her dad worse than ever before, for him to send his assistant to move her out. He wasn't messing around. He ran a tight ship at work but would never usually ask his assistant to do a personal chore for him.

"Then tell her not to. You can't do that, Dad. Gemma and Penny will think I'm mental if you take my stuff away. I love it there. I'll do better. Give me one more chance," Savannah said. As she ran her tongue over her teeth, she felt the fuzz of last night. It made her body lurch, the bitterness of vomit building once more.

"Here." Her dad held out a cardboard bowl, which she took gratefully. Heaving over it, Savannah began to feel better. Nothing else came up out of her already emptied stomach other than strings of white phlegm, her body's failed attempt to rid itself of the toxins she'd poured so eagerly into it.

"You are going to leave, Savannah. I'm not messing about. If you stay, that's it, I'm done. I can't do this anymore. It's fucking ridiculous. If you don't leave that house, you'll die. That's the end of the story." He looked at the floor as he spoke, unable to meet her eyes.

"Dad, I'm not a kid anymore. You can't make decisions for me."

"That's your choice, I suppose. I won't be around to watch you ruin your life."

"Okay." She sighed, resigned to the prospect of a new life of sobriety. She could be sober around her friends. From the drugs, at least. Perhaps this was the wake-up call she'd needed. If only she could make it stick this time.

The chair groaned as her dad stood up. It was like he'd aged thirty years in a matter of days. The door slammed behind him, the conversation abruptly ending. She'd made her decision. Looking at the rough cardboard, praying that her body would stop trying to vomit, Savannah closed her eyes, and longed to feel well again.

Cameron

It was Saturday night and Cameron was ready for a drink. Preferably something strong. After the date night with Liz, he hadn't quite been able to get rid of that weird uneasy feeling. The smiling man beneath the streetlight had been a regular feature in both his waking thoughts and his dreams. Yet he still couldn't quite place him. It was driving him mad. Liz had become very quickly annoyed at Cameron's repeated mentions of the man and so he'd started keeping it to himself, far easier than dealing with the annoyed exhales that usually resulted from a disagreement.

One Saturday every month, Cameron met up with his friends from university, those that still lived around that area anyway, for a meal, drink, and possibly some dancing. Tonight was that night. It was something he'd always looked forward to, and it prevented him from feeling like the stereotypical uncool teacher he'd turned into.

The busy streets of Leeds felt like home to Cameron, despite having moved a little further afield since his university days. For the first time, Liz was joining them on their regular night out. He was excited, if not a little apprehensive, for his friends to meet her. She was obviously stunning, so he knew the men would be jealous of him, and their partners would be jealous of her.

Their one night a month was dress-down, or "jeans and a nice shirt," as they'd come to call it. He'd given Liz the same instructions, but he'd never once seen her in jeans, so he wasn't sure how that would work out. When she knocked on his front door, Cameron was not disappointed.

Liz wore figure-hugging jeans and a white blouse, an oversized blazer draped over her shoulders like it was made to measure.

"Ready, handsome?" she smiled as she walked in.

"You look amazing," Cameron said, pulling Liz close to him. After seeing her in those jeans, painted onto her body, the last thing he wanted was for her to leave the house.

"You don't look so bad yourself." Liz pushed him away playfully.

"I can't wait to show you off." He grinned, deciding that they didn't have time for what he had in mind. Instead, he followed her to the car, admiring the view.

"This is Liz," Cameron said by way of greeting to his friends. "Liz, this is everyone."

"Hi," Liz said, dropping into a seat beside Cameron's oldest friend Reese, who he'd met while studying English Literature all those years ago.

"This is Reese, and his partner Wendy." Cameron gestured to the pair of them. Wendy looked exhausted. Many moons ago, she was always put together. Now, she looked like she'd rather be anywhere else. Having three kids under four would do that to you, he supposed.

"And this is Mitchell and Rose." The eldest of the group, Mitchell and Rose had always been dowdier than the rest. Rose had been a mature student, but only by a few years, and she'd met Mitchell at Freshers. The rest, as they say, was history. They now had two kids of their own, five and seven, if Cameron remembered correctly.

There were a few stragglers too. Dan, Joe, and Helen, all still single, and so tended to sit together. Usually, Cameron was relegated to their side of the table, but now, thanks to Liz, he was able to sit with the couples and not feel like a fifth wheel. It felt like a promotion.

The group descended into friendly chatter, Liz holding her own. When Dan and Joe gave him a thumbs up and a wink, he felt a rush of pride, but shrugged it away. He didn't want to be the kind of guy who defined his worth based on his friends' opinions of him, or the person he was sleeping with. But it didn't hurt that they thought he'd done well.

Cameron dipped in and out of the conversation, watching in awe as his friends fell in love with Liz.

"I think it's our round, babe," Liz said, breaking his train of thought. Liz had fallen into conversation with Wendy and Reese, about what, Cameron wasn't sure. But the two women were sitting as close as possible, their knees pressed tightly together. She fit right in.

"Sure, you're right." Cameron barked out a laugh, amazed by how well she'd slotted into their tight-knit circle. "Same again everybody?"

He was met with nods of assent and so he made his way to the bar. The queue was a few people deep, reminding him of his clubbing days, when the best part of the night was spent queuing at the bar trying to get served. The pretty girls, all dolled up, wearing heels they could barely walk in, had always been served before the men, no matter who'd joined the queue first. The experience was different now, at least, given that most of the people at the bar were men, sent there at the behest of their partners.

After ordering from a sullen-looking bartender, Cameron pulled out his phone to check the time. 6.15 pm. The night was only just beginning for most of the revellers. His phone was still in his hand when the photo came through. A text message, with no text, only a photo. The same number as the text he'd received at work, "FOUND YOU," a text he'd all but forgotten about. A blurred photograph filled his screen. He squinted to try and make it out, only to be interrupted by the bartender.

"That'll be fifty-seven, ninety, please, sir."

"Oh, sorry," Cameron said, pulling out his wallet and tapping his card on top of the machine.

“Thanks mate,” the bartender said, leaving the tray of drinks in front of Cameron.

Stuffing his phone in his pocket, Cameron walked back to his friends, disseminating the drinks, before taking his own. The gentle Stella bubbles glided down his throat as he retrieved his phone from his pocket to take another look at the message.

The photograph was obscured beyond recognition, like it was taken through drunken and half-closed eyes. A misty, vague shape sat at the centre of it. On a chair, possibly. If Cameron squinted, the photograph looked like a man strapped to an old-fashioned electric chair. Bizarre.

“Hey look at this.” Cameron passed his phone to Liz, and she tilted her head to study the photo.

“What is it?” she asked.

“I don’t know. An unknown number texted it to me.” Cameron watched as Liz’s face contorted with confusion, trying to figure out what she’d been handed.

“What a strange thing to text somebody. Have you asked who it is? Maybe they sent it to the wrong number by mistake.” It sounded reasonable. A likely explanation, but it didn’t sit right with Cameron. His intuition was telling him that something was off.

Liz didn’t know about the text from the other day. He hadn’t thought to mention it; maybe that information would sway her judgement. At all costs, he wanted to avoid coming off as paranoid or insane, so soon into the relationship. He and Liz were still at that point in their relationship where he'd like to pretend to be normal, and sharing weird texts didn't fit into that narrative. Couple that with the fact that he'd kind of freaked out about the man watching him from under the streetlight the other day, and Liz was bound to think he was mental. No, he wouldn't tell her about that. Not yet.

Cameron took the phone off her. "You're right, probably just a wrong number. I'll message and see what they say."

Liz looked at him quizzically, like the conversation wasn't quite over, but didn't say anything.

'WHO IS THIS?' Cameron quickly typed out, hoping that Liz was right, and it was all some kind of weird misunderstanding. He chanced another look at the photograph and now that he'd seen it, he couldn't unsee it. It reminded him of the magic eye books he'd had as a child where an image was hidden within a swirling and unfocused pattern. The photograph was of a man strapped into a chair, head lolling to one side. The fact that it was blurred seemed to make the whole thing more unsettling.

Reminding himself that he was a grown-ass man and shouldn't be letting a couple of random text messages get to him, Cameron turned his attention back to his friends.

"What do you think?" Liz said to Wendy. "Cameron's got a photo from a random number he doesn't know. It's blurred. Show them, Cam."

Unhappily, Cameron gave his phone to Liz, and it was passed around the circle. The general consensus was that it was strange, but of no concern.

“Hey, you might have a stalker?” Mitchell slapped Cameron on the shoulder as he spoke.

“I’m not pretty enough to have a stalker.” Cameron laughed, but something about the words caused his stomach to chill. It was unsettling, uncomfortable.

“You don’t have to be pretty to have a stalker,” Rose said, laughing. “I knew a girl at uni who was stalked, and she was pretty ordinary looking.”

“I think you’re gorgeous, Cam.” Liz laughed along.

“It’s more common than you’d think, you know,” Reese said. “It seems like everybody and their mother has a stalker these days.” He winked at Wendy as he spoke, clutching her hand in his. They’d always been touchy-feely people, ever since university. They were forever attached to one another. At least one part of their bodies had to be touching. It made Liz feel miles away, even if she was only a couple of metres from him. He resisted the urge to go and grab her hand, showing the world that she was his.

The eyes met him across the room.

Cameron blinked, and they were gone. The man from the streetlight melted into the crowd.

"Are you okay?" Reese said. Both he and his partner Wendy were looking at Cameron with concern etched on their faces.

"Yes, I'm fine, sorry." Cameron's words bumbled out of his mouth.

"You've gone all pale," Wendy said. "Do you feel ill?"

"Honest, I'm fine. Just a dizzy spell I think." Cameron's attention was on the space where the man had stood only seconds before. Near the toilets and cloakroom. The blank space was too obvious to have been a trick of the eye.

Without giving himself a moment to change his mind, Cameron excused himself to visit the toilet. He could feel his friends' eyes on his back as he walked away, wondering what the hell was wrong with him. Cameron's body felt hot and cold at the same time, flushed yet like he'd swallowed ice. Now he knew he was definitely being followed. It was too much of a coincidence to see the same man twice in the same week and smiling at him in that god-awful way.

Other than the smile, he'd looked like a regular man. Older than Cameron, and bulkier, but otherwise normal. That stare, and the grin—something wasn't right about him. Cameron didn't believe in coincidences. He had to know if he was being followed for sure. He had to find the man.

Pushing his way through the crowds, Cameron swung open the door to the toilets. All four cubicle doors were open, and two men were standing at the urinals, their backs to Cameron. Neither was the man. Spinning on his heels, he turned and walked out. The cloakroom was the only other possibility.

A bored-looking girl stood at the desk. "Are you here to collect your coat? Ticket please."

"No, I'm not. Sorry, did a man come this way?"

As soon as the words were out of his mouth, Cameron realised how stupid he sounded. *Did a man come this way?* In a club full of men, of course a man would have walked past at some point.

"Excuse me?" the girl said, looking up from her phone, her right eyebrow arching comically high.

"I'm looking for a friend. Bald, six-foot, wearing a black coat, I think." Cameron hadn't got a good enough glimpse to describe the man anymore thoroughly. The only thing he vividly remembered was the smile twitching on his face. Too wide. Too many teeth. It reminded him of the Big Bad Wolf. *What big teeth you have, Grandma.*

"You've just described like a quarter of our clientele." The girl shook her head at him, turning her face back to her phone.

"Fair enough, sorry." Cameron walked away before he could say something else incredibly stupid.

His friends all looked up at him when he approached.

"You feeling better, babe?" Liz asked, patting the empty seat beside her.

Cameron dropped into the space she'd left, and she grabbed his hand, giving it a squeeze.

"Yeah, I'm fine now." He was suddenly embarrassed by his behaviour. It would have looked bizarre to both Liz and his friends, and that was quite literally the last thing he wanted. "Just went dizzy. I'm totally fine now."

"We can go if you want? You still don't look right," Liz said.

"I'm fine," Cameron snapped and immediately regretted it. "Shit, sorry. I'm fine." He attempted to smile at her but knew that it didn't reach his eyes.

"Okay." Liz smiled back, her face as tense as his own.

"Don't be upset about the stalker, mate," Joe said. "People would kill to have one. It means you're popular!" He always teetered on the edge of what was a decent thing to say. In all likelihood, none of the group would have realized just how much the text had impacted him.

The group descended into laughter. Cameron tried to keep up, laughing at his own misfortune.

After that, the conversation never felt quite right again. He felt his friends looking at him and knew that they were wondering what was wrong with him.

His phone buzzed in his pocket. He couldn't bring himself to pull it out and check what it was. It remained there for the rest of the night, burning against his skin.

Savannah

Savannah walked home alone. The only clothes she had were the ones she'd been admitted to hospital in. The dress was agonisingly short, the heels stupidly high. It would have been like any other walk of shame except for the fact that her stomach was entirely empty from the poison being pumped from it. The drip had hydrated her. It was a strange sensation to be both achingly hungry, yet completely hydrated. She'd texted Penny and Gemma as soon as her dad left, asking for one of them to come and pick her up. They both had cars which they parked too far onto the curb at the front of the house. Neither replied, likely still in bed in the fugue state induced by the hangover. Their typical way to spend a Sunday. The house was a silent spectre when she walked in. Not even the sound of her roommates' gentle snores could permeate the walls. Savannah walked the long corridor to her bedroom, threw herself into her bed, and tried to fall into a merciful sleep. After an hour, she gave up and decided to shower.

The hot water burned her skin, washing away the feeling of grime and dirt accumulated over the night before. Her entire body was sore to the touch, even lathering in the sickly sweet shower gel made her body ache. Rubbing shampoo against her scalp made tears press against her closed eyes. Everything hurt, yet she stayed there under the stream of water, allowing it to fog up the room, until the hot water ran out and the shower began to cool.

Wiping down the full-length mirror, she surveyed the damage she'd done. Her body was entirely battered. Mottled bruises covered her knees and forearms. Her face was gaunt and sunken.

"Fuck," she muttered to herself. Shame filled her. Had she no regard for her own safety? She had to be more careful. God only knew what would happen the next time around.

"There you are!" Gemma sauntered into the living room. It was 4 pm and the first time Savannah had seen her roommate since they went to the club last night.

"Where else would I be?" Savannah said, barely able to pull her eyes from the TV she wasn't really watching.

"You didn't come home last night. So, what was he like?" Gemma threw herself onto the sofa beside Savannah, putting her slippered feet onto the coffee table.

"Who?"

"The guy you went home with?" Gemma tilted her head like a confused puppy.

"I didn't go home with anyone." Savannah felt anger flood through her.

"You didn't come home?" Gemma prompted.

"I went to the hospital to have my stomach pumped. A bouncer found me passed out. Where did you guys go?" Almost unable to contain her resentment, Savannah tried to reason that her friends probably hadn't left her on purpose. She'd been the one who'd been dancing with somebody else, after all.

Gemma's eyes widened. "Again?"

That was the last straw. Savannah felt her resolve snap. "Yes, again. What were those pills, Gem?"

"Hey! Don't blame me. I had as many as you did, and I'm fine. Whatever happened to you is nothing to do with me. I'm not your babysitter." As much as it pained Savannah to admit it, Gemma had a point. She'd been fine, Savannah hadn't.

"But you left me." She was mortified when she began to cry. The tears felt like acid, burning behind her eyes.

"No, you left us. God, you always cry about stupid shit, Savannah. The world doesn't revolve around you. It's not my job to watch you. I'm your friend, not your carer."

It was at this exact moment Penny walked into the room. Savannah prayed for the sofa to swallow her whole. "What's going on?"

"The usual." Gemma rolled her eyes. "Savannah is blaming us for her nearly killing herself."

"That's not—" Savannah began to protest but was cut off.

"Don't lie. You know what you said. You said I gave you bad pills, and that we left you. Neither of those is true. You're a liar, Savannah."

"Did you really blame us?" Penny stood in the doorway as she spoke, hands on hips like a drill sergeant.

"I…" She couldn't find the words and so Gemma intervened.

"You know what she's like."

"Honestly, Sav, you really need to sort your shit out. I'm not sure how much more of you I can take."

Together, the two of them walked out of the room, leaving Savannah completely alone. It felt like an eternity before she could force herself to stop crying. She'd never felt so alone. Curling up into a ball, she closed her eyes and willed sleep to come.

Cameron

Cameron was back home before he could bring himself to look at his phone. The thought that somebody out there was toying with him, and he didn't know who it was, made him feel incredibly vulnerable. Like a teenage girl running through the forest to escape her killer in a horror film. He couldn't think why anybody would want to text him weird messages, or stalk him for that matter, but wasn't that always the case? In the movies, the detectives always asked if the victim had any enemies, and every time their family said no, that they were well-liked, until suddenly they weren't.

Liz sat next to him on the sofa, her legs curled up underneath her, and her back pressed against Cameron. The warmth from her body felt good against the chill in the air. It was time to start turning the heating on.

"WE'VE MET BEFORE," the text read.

The phone slipped through Cameron's fingers and onto the floor. Landing on the corner, the screen splintered, like a spider web. The crack only covered the top centimetre of the screen, but anger flooded through him.

"Fuck!" he snarled, pushing Liz off him so that he could bend to pick the phone up. The cracked screen teased him mercilessly.

“Careful,” Liz turned to him. It took her only a second to register the real anger on his face. Cameron watched as her demeanour changed. “What’s wrong, Cam?”

“I dropped my fucking phone. It’s smashed, look!” Cameron stood up, thrusting the phone into Liz’s face.

“That’s nothing to worry about. You can still use it, or get it fixed. Why are you so upset? This isn’t like you. Have I done something wrong, or are you mad about something else?”

At the gentle tone of her voice, Cameron softened. He felt terrible for snapping at her. “I’m sorry, I’m having a weird moment. I’ll be fine. I think I’m just tired.”

Cameron sank into the sofa, placing his elbows on his knees and his head in his hands.

“Oh Cam, you work too hard.” Liz placed her arms around his shoulders and pulled her to him. He pushed his forehead into her neck, breathing in her perfume. He felt safe in her arms. Unfolding himself, he pulled Liz closer to him.

“I shouldn’t have snapped at you. You must think I’m a dickhead,” Cameron said into the warm recesses of Liz’s shoulder.

“You are a dickhead, but not because you snapped at me.” Liz laughed. “You’re a dickhead for pretending to be okay when you need a break. You need to tell me when you’re feeling like shit. It’s what you do when you’re a couple. You never know, I might even be able to make you feel better.”

The words were suggestive. Cameron felt warmth pooling in the pit of his stomach.

"And how would you make me feel better?" Cameron pulled away so that he could see the smirk on Liz's mouth. The way she was biting her lip made him want to take her right there.

"Let me show you." At those words, Liz moved so that she was straddling Cameron. Her hair fell over his face like a waterfall, tickling his chin. She bent slightly so that her lips met his. Gently, at first. She began to force his lips open with her tongue, deepening the kiss. Before long, Cameron could no longer fight the urge to carry her to the bedroom. It didn't take long for him to feel completely better, thoughts of the broken phone lost in the curves of Liz's body.

Lying there in a tangle of sheets, Cameron's chest rose and fell rapidly. He felt better. A hell of a lot better, actually. Liz was curled into his side, her head resting on his chest and arm placed over his stomach.

"Thank you," Cameron whispered, pressing a kiss to her hairline.

"Did you just thank me for having sex with you?" Liz laughed and buried herself in the crease of his armpit.

"I didn't mean thank you for the sex, although now you mention it, that was pretty great too. No, I meant thank you for being there for me. For breaking me out of my mood. I was an arse to you, and you still made me feel better."

"Like I said, when you're in a relationship, you have to tell the other person when you need them. We've been together a decent amount of time now, not ages I know, but enough to know each other and want to help the other when they are feeling shitty. The more time you spend with a person, the more you get to know the real them, warts and all. I like that I've seen a different side to you. It means we're getting comfortable together." Liz's wide eyes looked up at him. Her cheeks were stained red with the embarrassment of saying something so personal.

"You make me very happy," Cameron said. His words felt inadequate compared to Liz's speech, but he'd never been able to express himself very well. Ironic, given the fact that he taught English for a living.

"I enjoyed meeting your friends last night. It made me feel like we're a proper couple." Liz's body was warm against his own. The tart scent of wine clung to her breath.

"I enjoyed you meeting my friends." Cameron nuzzled against her, wanting to be as close to her as possible.

"I do have a question though," Liz said.

"Oh yeah?"

"Yeah. Don't get cross but what's going on with Reese and Wendy?"

"What do you mean?" Cameron moved so that he was propped onto his shoulder, looking down at Liz.

"The way he speaks to her. The way he always has to be touching her. I don't know, it just felt a little, excessive, maybe?"

"I've never noticed anything before. They've always been like that." Cameron couldn't stop himself from wondering what Liz was getting at. It seemed strange to mention that now, upon the first time of meeting his friends. He hoped that she wasn't about to try and stop him from seeing them, like so many girlfriends from his past had done and failed.

"It just doesn't sit right with me. She looked unhappy, don't you think?" Liz stared into Cameron's eyes in a way that made him want to agree with her. But he couldn't. Wendy and Reese were just the kind of couple that bickered all of the time.

"I thought she looked fine," Cameron said. Wanting to keep on Liz's good side, he decided to add, "But I'll definitely look out for it. Reese is my oldest friend. He was my roommate in uni. If something is going on, he'd tell me."

"Men don't really do that, do they? Talk to one another about relationship problems? I thought that they just compared women's boob sizes and complained about how much money they spend." Liz tried to crack a smile, but there was an edge to her voice.

"We talk about a lot of stuff. Especially because I've known those guys for so long. We've been through a lot together, you know?"

Cameron felt the shroud of defensiveness come over him. Mitchell and Reese, particularly, had been a huge part of his life. They'd shared everything from cars to girlfriends over the years.

"I didn't mean anything by it. I just wanted to learn more about their dynamic, I suppose. I've had friends who have been treated terribly by men in the past. I think I'm just over sensitive to it. I'm sorry."

Cameron softened at her apology. He pulled her close to him, allowing her head to rest on his shoulder. As she began to trail kisses down his neck, Cameron immediately forgot the terse words that came before. He allowed himself to get lulled away by her touch.

"Do you ever think about us moving in together properly?" Liz asked, her words innocent, but her timing was too good to be a coincidence. She continued to kiss him lightly in between her words.

"You'd want to live with me?" Cameron was amazed that even after his behaviour, the stunning woman lying next to him still wanted to be with him, never mind anything more than that.

"Yes, of course. Wouldn't you want to live with me?" She narrowed her eyes as she spoke. Cameron knew that he didn't have the time to think carefully about what he said next. Any pause would give her room to jump to other conclusions.

"I would love to live with you. Are we talking now, or in the future?" Cameron traced his fingers down the curve of her spine as he spoke. There was something just so intoxicating about her body.

“Well, there’s something I’ve been meaning to mention. The lease is up on my apartment, and I can renew it, if I want to. But then I’m trapped into it for another twelve months. That means that if we do want to live together in the future, we’d have to wait another year, or pay two sets of bills.” Liz rested her hand gently on his lower stomach, moving it backwards and forwards. The movement was very distracting.

“I see. You think we’re ready to live together?” Cameron asked, trying to weigh up his options while also buying time. He thought Liz was amazing. She was out-of-this-world stunning, and funny, and smart, and kind. But living together was a huge commitment, something he’d never done before. He hadn’t lived with another person since his university years, and that was very different. That had been a group of single lads.

“Why not? We like each other, right? We spend as much time together as we can. We practically live together anyway, so why not live together?” Liz waited a beat before continuing. “If you’re not ready, that’s totally fine. I think we could have done with another month or two too, but that doesn’t seem to be an option.”

“Let’s do it,” Cameron said, the heat filling his face as he spoke. He wasn’t going to be able to get anybody better than Liz. The thought of committing in such a significant way made him incredibly nervous, but she was right. It was the only real option. He couldn’t foresee them not being together in a year anyway, so why not move in together now? It made sense. Plus, there was the saving on bills and all that other boring stuff too, which was an added bonus.

"Really?" A smile broke across Liz's face. She looked like a kid on Christmas morning. Cameron felt a rush of justified pride that he'd made her feel that way.

"Yeah. It makes sense, like you said. And I kind of like the idea of waking up beside you every morning." Cameron couldn't help but smile too. His life was about to change significantly. It was daunting, but also exciting.

"Yay! I'll tell my landlord tomorrow," Liz said, pulling Cameron on top of her and pushing her fingers into his hair.

"Again?" Cameron said trailing kisses down Liz's neck. She didn't answer, but her body did.

The vibrating of his phone woke Cameron the next morning. It was early. Too early. The alarm clock flashed 5:34. He screwed his eyes closed before blinking them open again.

Reaching for the phone on his bedside table, Cameron unlocked it. The blinding white light of the screen awakened him fully. The crack in the top corner brought his early morning amnesia crashing down. The text yesterday. How could he have forgotten about it?

WE'VE MET BEFORE.

The night had unravelled into something else entirely in the moments after he'd received the text. Something beautiful and distracting. But in the dim light of morning, the text was uncomfortably real.

Another text.

This time there were no words. Only a photo. It was a close-up of a hand, slick with blood. Browns and reds marred the white hand. It was a man's hand, the fingernails blunt and rounded. It could belong to anybody. There were no distinguishing features other than the knife blade prying the fingernail away from the finger bed.

Savannah

Things had gone from bad to worse. Gemma and Penny both refused to talk to her, a frosty silence filling the house. It was painfully awkward. Even when Savannah tried to make friends with them, starting conversations or making cups of tea, they didn't bite. They gave one-word answers and walked away snickering. The worst part was that they were spending all of their time together, holed up in one another's rooms. Their laughter made Savannah's stomach knot and spasm. It made her hate herself more than she ever had done before. They were her only friends, the ones from college had drifted away all over the UK, and so Savannah literally had Penny and Gemma. That was it.

It was a random Tuesday morning when the air shifted and thawed. Penny walked into the room. Her pink pixie cut was the first thing Savannah noticed, as it had been blue that morning. Gemma trailed at her heels, the exact opposite of Penny in every single way. Preppy and neat to Penny's grunge. They shouldn't be friends, and yet, there they were.

"How was class?" Gemma said, flicking the kettle on.

Savannah looked for a moment before realising they were talking to her.

"Oh, good, thanks. The usual, you know."

"Good. We're going to the pictures later if you want to come."

It felt forced, wrong, but Savannah was entirely sick of living in silence, and so pounced on the opportunity to make things right again.

"Yes, definitely! What are you going to see?"

"The Crazies, it looks good, really scary." Gemma smiled in a way that didn't reach the creases of her eyes. They knew Savannah detested everything horror related. They were testing her. She wouldn't rise to it.

"Sounds great," Savannah said, decisively. She'd just shut her eyes if it was too much. They'd never know. It was an olive branch that she wasn't going to let slip out of her fingers.

The film was terrible. Terrifying and too disgusting to put into words, but her friendship with Gemma and Penny seemed to be right back on track, so all was well. As they left the cinema, Savannah trying to blot out the most graphic scenes of the film from her mind, she noticed a group of lads laughing and gesturing towards her.

"That's her," she thought she heard one of them say. A pocked face boy with too much gel in his hair.

"Are you sure?" another one said.

When Savannah turned to look at them, raising her eyebrows in a silent question, they averted their gaze and giggled like children.

"Are they laughing at us?" Savannah asked her friends.

"I don't think they're laughing at *us,*" Gemma said, a snort erupting from her mouth and turning into laughter that she did nothing to try and conceal.

"What do you mean?" Savannah asked, facing Gemma head-on.

"Oh, I thought you'd know already. I thought that was why you'd been sulking." Gemma smiled at Penny, completely bypassing Savannah's look.

"What the fuck are you on about?" Savannah said, exasperated.

"The Facebook page?" Penny said like her answer was the most self-explanatory thing in the world.

"What Facebook page?" Savannah felt the tell-tale prickles of shame across her cheeks. Something was happening that involved her, and she was well and truly in the dark.

"She doesn't know about it." Penny tried to hide the smile stretching at her lips.

"What?" Savannah shouted. The boys across from them began to laugh harder. They were congregating around a phone and occasionally looking at Savannah.

"I think you should show her," Penny said to Gemma.

"Yeah, it's only right she sees it from her friends and not some stranger." Gemma pulled her phone from her pocket and tapped on the Facebook app. Into the search bar, she began to type 'Dru…' The rest of the phrase came up in the recent search history. 'Drunken Slut Savannah.'

It felt like white hot liquid had been poured down her throat. Gemma passed the phone to her, and she could barely grasp hold of it, her hands were shaking so badly.

The page was full of Facebook posts, each containing a photograph. Each photograph was Savannah.

Collapsing onto the bench behind her, Savannah began to scroll down the page. The first photograph was of her sitting on the toilet in a club, the door open, pants around her ankles. Her head hung to her chest. You couldn't see anything, but the photo was bad enough. *Almost* pornographic.

The second photo was just as bad. Somebody, out of the frame, was holding Savannah's hand in the air, forcing her to look at the camera and smile. Vomit crusted her face in clumps, sticking to the ends of her hair. The more she looked at the photo, the more she couldn't breathe. Who would take a photograph like that and post it online?

"Did you?" Savannah mumbled to her friends.

"Of course we didn't! We weren't even with you. You ran off and were slutting it up with some guy. We found these later." Gemma was indignant, shaking her head like Savannah had suggested something totally out of leftfield.

"Have you reported it?" Savannah looked to both of them. When they shrugged, she took that as her answer. "We have to report it, now."

“Fine, whatever.” Penny took the phone out of Savannah’s hand and tapped on the icon that led to the report feature. “Done. Happy now?”

“Not really.” Savannah wanted to cry, to kick and scream, but what good would it do her? “But I want to see the rest of them.”

“You sure about that? They’re not flattering?” Gemma leered. Savannah wanted to rip her throat out.

“Give it to me.”

The photographs went from bad to worse. Not only did the majority of them contain her face, but they also had captions scrawled across them. SLUT. SLAG. THICK BITCH. The last one Savannah scrolled to had a speech bubble protruding from her mouth. It said, “I suck dick for cash.”

“Why didn’t you tell me about this sooner?” Savannah couldn’t hold her anger anymore.

“We didn’t want to upset you.” The look on Penny’s face told Savannah it was more than that.

“You should have told me. You should be defending me, not smirking about it! I should go to the police. This is cyber-bullying, or something. Whatever it is, it’s got to be against the law.”

“Don’t be stupid. Taking pictures of someone and posting them online is not against the law.” Gemma and Penny sniggered and rolled their eyes. Savannah almost couldn’t breathe.

“It has to be against the law.” Savannah was certain it had to be.

“It’s not. Plus, do you really want to bring more people’s attention to it? Just report it and move on. Jesus. You’re so dramatic.”

“Are you fucking kidding me? I can’t… I can’t believe you two. What the fuck? How am I being dramatic? There are photos of me online, disgusting photos, that I can’t remember being taken, with captions that make me look like the world’s biggest slut.” In exasperation, Savannah threw the phone down. It bounced once on the floor before settling.

The three of them stared at the phone.

“Well, you kind of are a slut,” Penny said, breaking the silence.

Mouth hanging open, Savannah had no way to answer.

“I can’t do this anymore. I’ll report the page too. But I’m leaving. You two are twisted. I can’t believe…”

“Can’t believe what?” Gemma raised her eyebrows in a challenge.

“I can’t believe I thought you were my friends.”

“Do you know what? I can’t believe you thought we were either.” Gemma picked the phone up, slipped her arm through Penny’s and walked away, leaving Savannah to consider what choices she had.

Savannah

Her body melted into the overstuffed sofa. It reeked of leather and sweat; a combination that made her feel sick to her stomach. A headache pounded at the base of her skull and Savannah gritted her teeth against the pain. She'd taken as much paracetamol as she could, and so she'd have to deal with the pain that remained. It was withdrawal. She wasn't stupid. She didn't need a therapist to tell her that. Not even twenty years old yet and an alcoholic, that was about as embarrassing as it got. Her dad liked to remind her that at least it wasn't "harder" stuff. That it was just booze. He didn't know about the pills, and she intended to keep it that way. But the withdrawal symptoms felt like she'd stopped taking heroin or something. Not that she'd tried heroin, but she couldn't imagine withdrawing from that being any worse than how she was feeling now.

"How are you feeling?" the therapist asked her. Not a psychiatrist. A *psychologist.* Her dad had insisted that he'd done his research, and that Amanda was one of the best there was when it came to teenagers acting out. He'd actually said "acting-out." Her actions had quickly been reduced to something you'd say about a toddler. At that moment, Savannah almost wished she'd tried harder stuff. Done something worse. Then this whole situation might have been worth it.

"Not great," Savannah answered truthfully. As much as she resented being forced into therapy, she intended to take it seriously. Waking up in the hospital having completely blacked out was not something she intended to repeat again. The fact that she had no idea what happened that night needled at her, constantly buzzing just below the surface. Until that point, she hadn't known the complete disregard she'd had for her own safety. That, in itself, was terrifying. The photographs on Facebook had been the final straw. To see how vulnerable she looked, and how somebody, she still didn't know who, could manipulate them and post them online in order to make her feel like shit, well, it wasn't something she ever wanted to experience again. Thankfully, the gods at Facebook had taken down the page after she'd reported it. There had been no need to go to the police, which she was very much thankful for.

"Tell me about that," Amanda said. She had a kind, motherly face that made Savannah feel at home. Not entirely comfortable, but safe.

"I have the worst headache ever."

"And why do you think that is?" Amanda reached forward and poured some water into a glass, placing it next to Savannah.

"Because I haven't had a drink in a week." A whole week. Something that hadn't happened since she was in high school. Alcohol was her coping mechanism. It made her into the person she wanted so badly to be. She'd figured that out a long time ago, without the help of a therapist. It was common sense. Her dad had hidden all of the alcohol in his house and stripped her of any and all independence since she'd gone crawling back to him with her tail in between her legs.

"And how do you feel mentally? Has not having a drink changed anything there? Have a drink of water, it'll help with the headache." A sad, caring smile spread across Amanda's face. It made Savannah want to cry. Instead, she gulped down the water, swallowing the lump in her throat too.

"Drained. Tired. I have assignments due, and I can't concentrate on them. I still have to move into my new student house, and meet my roommate, which is difficult when you feel like shit. Add that to the fact that I'm absolutely terrified she will have seen the Facebook page about me. I know I would judge if I were in her shoes. A new roommate who got so drunk that she allowed people to take photos of her when she was doing stupid shit. People she probably didn't even know because they posted them online and thought it was hilarious. Fuck, I'm sorry. I shouldn't swear."

"You can swear all you want. If that's the right word, then say it. There's no judgement here. What happened to you was awful, but it wasn't your fault. I have to urge you to go to the police, though. Whatever that person, or people, did to you was wrong, and it was a crime. You don't have to let them get away with it." The way Amanda looked at her made her want to curl into a ball. She hadn't wanted to tell her about the Facebook page. It had slipped out.

"Facebook took it down. It's sorted now. I don't want to dredge it all back up." Her stomach filled with dread whenever she thought about the photos resurfacing. The page had been taken down. That was all that mattered.

"Well, that's entirely up to you. I can't make you do anything you're not comfortable with. So, you're moving in with a new roommate. Your dad sorted that for you, right? But you're also struggling with classes. We need to consider how we're going to move forward. Let's come up with a plan, okay? Having a plan, a fluid one that can change as your goals do, helps us to feel more in control. But I want you to remember something… You've been through something scary and traumatic, and you need to recover from that just like you'd recover from the flu. It sounds like you have a lot on your plate, so maybe we try to take it steady and just do a little at a time."

The tears forced their way out of the corners of her eyes. Amanda was being so kind and so reasonable, and Savannah didn't deserve that. She'd brought it on herself. How could she rest and recover from something self-inflicted? It hadn't been a broken leg, or life-threatening surgery. It had been an alcohol (and pills) induced blackout.

"Tell me what you're thinking," Amanda said.

"You're being so kind to me, and I don't deserve that. I did this to myself, why should I get to take it easy?"

“Hey, you’re not taking anything easy. You’re recovering, and sometimes in recovery, we have to slow down and heal. You need to heal, Savannah, and that’s what I’m here to help you do, okay? We’ll do it together.”

“Okay,” Savannah said. She didn’t agree with Amanda, but she’d said it in such a way that made her sound wise, like she had all the answers.

“My first plan is to send an email to your tutor explaining your circumstances…”

“No, please don’t tell them what I did.” Savannah sat upright, dread filling her body. Her tutors were the ones to grade her, to decide if she passed or failed. If they knew what she’d done, what she did in her spare time, how could they ever grant her the first she so badly wanted? Needed, if she was going to get a decent job in the future.

“I won’t tell them anything you don’t want me to. How about I tell them that you’re having some treatment for your mental health, and would benefit from an extension on your deadline?”

“I don’t know.” Savannah weighed up the proposition in her head. On the one hand, she could really do with the extension. The words just wouldn’t come to her when she attempted to do her assignments. The cursor blinked at her aggressively from the blank page every time she attempted to write.

“Just think about it, okay? I won’t do anything you’re not comfortable with. But if it gives you a little time to heal and focus on the future instead of the past, then I think it would be invaluable to you.”

Amanda was right. Savannah knew it. She didn’t want to admit that she needed help. She’d always been self-sufficient, and now a therapist was fighting her battles for her.

“Okay, do it. I think I need a break.” Savannah barely whispered the words.

“Great, you’ve made the right choice, Savannah. Well done. Right, so on with the plan…” Amanda pulled out a sheet of paper and a pencil and wrote: SAVANNAH’S PLAN, in block capitals at the top of the page.

“Tell me what you want your life to look like.”

Cameron

"Fuck!" Cameron exhaled, unable to pry his eyes away from the phone. He couldn't help but study the photograph. The fingernails were torn from the nail beds, the raw red skin beneath them seeming to throb.

He couldn't see anything else in the photograph. Not really. A close-up of the man's hand, hovering above what looked to be his trousers, but he couldn't be sure. All the clarity was focused in on the hand, the flash illuminating it and casting the background into a blur of nothingness.

What kind of a sick bastard would text a photograph like that? The possibilities ran through his mind. A student who thought it was funny? A friend playing a prank? A stranger who typed a random number into their phone and decided to torment them by sending them graphic images? Something about it felt very, very wrong. Cameron wondered whether it might be time to go to the police with this, but not until he'd given them a chance to stop. One more chance to stop.

THAT'S ENOUGH. I'LL TAKE THIS TO THE POLICE IF YOU CONTINUE. I'M GOING TO BLOCK YOUR NUMBER. DO NOT CONTACT ME AGAIN.

Cameron studied the words, wondering if he was overreacting. His response sounded out of the realm of reasonability, an overreaction at its finest. He'd had enough. He didn't care whether he looked crazy or showed the other party that it was getting to him. It had to end.

After waiting a few minutes to see if he got a response, Cameron was quietly optimistic that his authoritative text had done its job. He blocked the phone number and laid his head back on the pillow, attempting to crawl back into the deep sleep he'd been awoken from.

As sleep began to draw him in, images flashed across his mind's eye. A bloody fingernail falling from the tip of a finger and onto the floor. It made a clattering sound too loud for the light object. Then another fell. The same noise rang through his mind. Another and another until whole fingernails, still caked in blood and dirt, rained from the sky and around Cameron. He was looking through his own eyes as he threw his head back to the sky, the clouds breaking overhead and flooding the world with separated nails.

Within the cloud, he saw a face he recognised, and pulled himself back to consciousness. Waking himself up from the nightmare, he threw his body over his legs and took deep breaths, attempting to steady himself. He was going crazy. Maybe he needed help. What kind of grown man had nightmares?

The face he'd seen set his whole body alight, prickling with sweat. That macabre smile, too wide, didn't reach the man's eyes.

How Liz had remained asleep through his ordeal remained a mystery to Cameron. He wanted to talk to her about it, but how did you bring something like that up, especially with the person you'd just agreed to move in with? The commitment was still shiny and new.

The alarm clock blinked at Cameron, reminding him that it was too early to be awake. 6.04 am. Sleep was out of his reach now, the prospect of closing his eyes too much to bear. Pulling himself out of bed and deciding to make the most of his early weekend morning, Cameron shuffled into his running gear and headed out of the door, leaving a softly snoring Liz in his bed.

The rest of the day was uneventful, if slightly stressful. Liz had been online shopping and had ordered a multitude of new things for his (*their)* house. Working at a magazine, she always had her eye on *aesthetics,* as she liked to call them. And his place needed a "woman's touch," she'd said, excitedly. Ordering huge house plants, pampas grass, and throws, Liz spent most of the day with a smile attached to her face. Deciding not to mention anything about his home's extreme makeover, Cameron focused on his planning and marking, getting ready for the week ahead.

He hated the fact that when his phone buzzed on the table, a shiver of apprehension ran through his body. Picking up the phone,

Cameron looked at Liz to see if she was watching him. His nervousness was not something he wanted her to pick up on.

YOU THOUGHT BLOCKING MY NUMBER WOULD WORK? TUT TUT.

Gritting his teeth, Cameron tried not to react. He wouldn't let this bastard, whoever it was, get to him. The new course of action was not to respond. Surely the guy would get bored eventually and leave him alone. And if not, then it was time to visit the police station and let them handle him.

Cameron felt the unfamiliar twinge of embarrassment as he recalled the frantic message he sent last night. That wouldn't help his cause by any means, and now whoever it was knew that it was impacting his life. They were achieving what they'd set out to do.

Placing the phone back on the table, Cameron caught Liz's eye and smiled, rolling his eyes and feigning derision at the mountain of work he had to do.

"Let me help with that," Liz said, walking over to him. She placed her hands on his shoulders and began to massage out the cricks and knots. It felt so good that he almost slumped over the table. Knowing that reaction was a sure-fire way to not get any work done, he leaned his head back, kissing Liz on the cheek.

"You're amazing," he said as he picked up his pen and threw himself into planning his Year Seven creative writing module.

The second vibration was unexpected. Liz smiled and picked up his phone, beginning to type in his passcode to unlock it.

"Are you cheating on me?" she joked. The joke was coated in something more than humour, a genuine fear, perhaps, that he was being unfaithful. Why did women always think men were cheaters?

"Give it here." Cameron stood to take the phone out of her hand, not the smartest move in terms of convincing her he wasn't a cheat but what if it was the stranger sending him bizarre photos again? What if Liz saw his terrified reaction to last night's message?

"Okay," Liz said, allowing the phone to be removed from her grasp.

Just as he feared, the message was from his tormentor.

IT HURTS MY FEELINGS WHEN YOU DON'T ANSWER.

Following the message was another photograph. It took a minute to load, and Cameron held the phone so tightly that his knuckles turned white. Liz was silent, as though sensing something wasn't right.

The photograph was worse than any other. Cameron's blood froze within his body. His eyes widened and his stomach protested its contents in disgust.

"What the hell?" Cameron mumbled.

He was vaguely aware of Liz asking what was wrong. The photograph drew him in. It grabbed him by the throat and wouldn't let go. It was taken from further away than the last one, meaning that the whole man was in the shot, rather than just a hand. He was tied to a chair and slumped over. His hands and ankles were bound with blue rope. His head lolled forwards like a puppet with sliced strings. The body of the man was covered with blood, like it has been poured over his head from buckets. A scene from a slasher film. It disguised the body too much for Cameron to be able to tell anything further about him.

The more he stared at the photograph, the more things he saw that he didn't want to. The pool of drying brown blood on the floor at the man's feet. The slits across his arms and tears in his jeans.

Cameron clicked on the photograph, his heartbeat loud in his ears. It drowned out everything else around him. The man had been put through hell, tormented to within an inch of his life.

Zooming in, Cameron looked at the fingernails, or lack thereof. The man's fingers were bloody stumps.

"What the fuck is that?" Liz's voice slapped him back to attention. He turned and saw her looking over his shoulder.

"Nothing," Cameron said, without thinking. Another lie to add to the list. He tried to cross off the photograph, but Liz was too quick. She snatched the phone from his hand.

"What the fuck are you looking at, Cam? Who sent you this? Are you some kind of sicko who likes this kind of thing? I thought you were fucking normal!" Liz's voice spiralled out of control, reaching peaks Cameron didn't know were possible.

"Liz, listen to me. It's not like that at all. Let me explain." Cameron tried to place his hands on her shoulders to steady her, holding her close to him, while he explained.

"Let go of me," she said, fear saturating her eyes.

"Somebody has been sending me messages, okay? Fucked-up ones. Threatening ones. This isn't the first one like this. They're getting worse, Liz. Somebody is doing this to me. I'm not fucked up. This isn't me. I'll show you, okay? I'll show you."

Cameron studied Liz's face to try and gauge her reaction. She gave a slight nod, handing Cameron back his phone.

"Sit down. I'll show you."

Liz did as she was told and sat at the table next to him. He placed the phone between them and scrolled through the messages from the number he blocked, before moving to the latest messages from a new number.

Silent throughout the whole process, Liz took the phone in her hand and studied the messages again, re-reading them. Cameron couldn't decipher her expression. It was an unsolvable puzzle to him.

"This is messed-up. Who'd do this to you?" Liz asked, placing the phone back on the table and pushing it away from her as though it was infected.

“I don’t know. I really don’t know. I’m hoping it’s some kind of prank.” Cameron watched Liz carefully before placing his hand on hers.

“What are you going to do?” Liz asked.

“I’m going to ignore it. None of this is real, obviously. It’s just some stupid prank, right?” Cameron said, hoping that Liz agreed with him. If there was a chance that the photograph was of a real person, and not a scene out of a film or a staged photograph, then he should go to the police. If somebody was hurting another person in this way, they should be stopped. And quickly.

“It’s definitely not real. Who’d take photos of somebody they’re torturing and send them to a stranger? It makes no sense.” Liz nodded, as though trying to convince herself that she was correct in her assumptions

“You’re right. It looks fake anyway!” Cameron tried to laugh, but it came out as a barking cough.

“Yeah, there’s no way it’s real,” Liz said, squeezing Cameron’s hand.

The phone filled the empty, silent space in the room like a spectre. Whatever was happening wasn’t over. It was clear to both of them that there was more to come.

Savannah

The question spun around her head incessantly on the car ride home. Savannah's dad was taking her to and from every therapy appointment to make sure she went, at least until he trusted her again.

"Tell me what you want your life to look like."

What do you say to that? Savannah had no idea what she wanted her life to look like. All she could think to say was she wanted to be sober for it. To not repeat what had happened last weekend. But other than that, she honestly had no idea at all.

"You're very quiet," her dad said, taking his eyes off the road to study her face.

"Just a lot to think about, you know," Savannah said. He wanted more information from her, that much was clear. He wanted to know everything, and she couldn't bring herself to do that. She couldn't tell him that she'd slept with more people than she could remember. That she'd allowed these boys to do things to her that she definitely didn't want to do. That every single time she'd been drunk, or worse, she did things that sober Savannah hated herself for.

"You can do this, Savannah. We'll get you sober, properly, and you won't go back to how it was before. No more blackouts and stomach pumps, okay? You owe me that much. And now that those stupid girls are out of your life, you can focus on you. You're a good girl, Sav. Without them egging you on, making you drink and make bad decisions, you'll come into your own again." Her dad didn't look at her when he said those words. He'd always been the same. Unable to make eye contact during difficult conversations, especially when he was emotional himself. A typical "man" from that generation. Emotions were a sign of weakness to him. They had no place in his world if he could help it.

Savannah hated that she made her dad feel this way. He'd always been this big, strong man who'd protected her from everything, and the second she'd got a taste of freedom, she'd done everything in her power to be unsafe. How spoiled was that? It was the kind of girl she didn't want to be.

"I'm sorry, Dad, I really am."

"I know you are, so let's make it stick this time. No going back. You're free from the bad influences. And, from what I've heard, your new roommate is lovely. Not at all like the old ones. You'll be fine here." He pursed his lips and nodded his head slowly, as though confirming his own thoughts.

"No going back," Savannah agreed. The only issue was that she didn't particularly like who she was when she was sober, or when she was drunk for that matter, but at least when she was drunk, she was confident. Sober, she was nothing. If she could find a happy medium and drink a little, without going overboard, then she'd be fine. But she couldn't. She'd never been able to manage that. Which is how her photos had ended up plastered on that god-awful Facebook page. It was something she hoped to never have to suffer through again.

"Here we are, home sweet home," he said as he slowed his car to a stop outside of the Victorian terraced house. Savannah's room was on the top floor, with a view over the city. She loved it and couldn't help but think that if she'd been there originally, then none of this would have happened. She'd have been happy. It was now a week since the *incident.* She'd lived with her dad until last night. This would be her first night in her new home. While she'd been therapized, her father's assistant had moved all of her things from her dad's home to here.

This was it. The new start.

"Come on, let's get you settled."

Nerves prickled at her stomach. It was the first time she'd meet her new roommate, El. What if she was like Penny and Gemma, who had seemed lovely at first, but had turned her down a wrong path and then abandoned her? Worse, what if El didn't like her? She wouldn't blame her, not really. Savannah wouldn't want to be around herself if she could help it anyway. And if she's seen the Facebook page, or worse, liked it, then this wasn't going to work out. It was near impossible to have so much faith in a person you'd never met. Especially one who could have seen you in some compromising positions.

Taking a long, slow breath, Savannah turned her attention to the house. The front door was surrounded by stained glass. It was wooden and looked original. Before the door was opened, Savannah could picture the way the light would filter through the glass and leave patterns on the floor below. A smile tugged at her cheeks at the prospect.

"Should we knock?" Savannah turned to her dad.

"No, this is your home now too. You have a key!" He laughed to try and ease her nerves. It didn't work.

Sliding the key into the lock, Savannah peeled open the door.

"Hello, anybody home," her dad shouted down the never-ending hall.

"Coming," a voice shouted down the stairs. Savannah waited where she stood and heard footsteps approaching, walking across the creaky hallway floorboards. Then a person rounded the top of the stairs. The first thing Savannah noticed was the waist-length black hair and olive skin. Hooded, sultry eyes that seemed to smile.

"Hi! I'm El. You're Savannah, and her dad?" El's voice was musical, upbeat like every word was a song.

"Yes," her dad answered on her behalf before she had a chance to speak.

"Nice to meet you." By this point, Savannah was standing in the hallway smiling stupidly. "All your stuff is already here. Your assistant is very nice, Mr…"

"Windsor. You can call me Mick. You're making me feel very old!"

"Are you going to join us for a cup of tea? I think me and Savannah have some getting to know each other to do, and is there a better way to do it than over a cup of tea?" El winked at Savannah, who couldn't help but smile back. Already, she liked El. The relief of that almost made her knees buckle.

"I'll leave you to it. I don't want to cramp your style." He laughed. Turning to Savannah he said, "I'll ring you later on, okay."

Pressing a kiss onto Savannah's forehead, much to her embarrassment, her dad turned to El and said, "I'll be seeing you."

"See you later, Mr Windsor!"

The door pressed closed behind him. Savannah was right. The mid-day light poured through the stained glass of the door surround. It reminded her of the magnificent windows in churches. It was soothing.

"Gorgeous, isn't it? Come on, let's go get a cuppa and you can tell me all about yourself."

White-hot dread filled Savannah's stomach as she followed behind El. She'd have to tell a version of the story that didn't make her sound like a complete lunatic.

Savannah

Savannah woke up with a banging headache drilling against the inside of her skull. She hadn't slept at all, well, maybe a little bit. Each hour that passed signified her failure. Another hour less of sleep, and another hour closer to the day ahead. The day she was dreading. Her first day back in lectures since the *incident*. The night had been filled with "what ifs" and "I can't do this," her mind playing out scenarios that she prayed wouldn't come true. The worst part was wondering just how many people had seen the Facebook page before it had been taken down. If the cinema trip had been anything to go by, then plenty of people had seen it. Each evening, she checked to see if a different variation of the page had been created. It hadn't. Whoever created it in the first place had obviously gotten the message. That what they'd done had been wrong.

She couldn't think of the page without thinking of Penny and Gemma. Their faces swam in front of her eyes whenever Savannah closed them. She couldn't believe how cruel they'd been to her. How they'd laughed instead of rushing to her defence. She hadn't spoken to them since that night. They hadn't reached out to her. And she hadn't reached out to them either. Savannah made the mistake of checking their Facebook profiles, only to learn that they had both either blocked her or deleted their profiles. It shouldn't have upset her, they were terrible people, but it did.

Savannah could only imagine how annoyed they'd been when her father's assistant had showed up to their house to remove her things. Under no circumstances had she wanted to set foot in there. Her father had offered, but Savannah was scared of what he'd do, what he'd say. She couldn't cope if he'd lost his temper with them. It wouldn't have ended well. The fact that Savannah's belongings had been removed from their house, without any explanation, would have definitely stirred up some unpleasant feelings. She only hoped that they didn't put those feelings to use, spreading rumours or making her life miserable. She'd seen a different side to them, and now wasn't sure what they were capable of.

With her head pressed firmly into the pillow, Savannah pulled the duvet over her head and prayed to whatever god was listening that she wouldn't bump into them today. She just couldn't face it. She couldn't even begin to think about what she might say to them.

It was unlikely that Savannah would see her ex-roommates and ex-friends, given that they did different courses in different buildings, but there was still a chance she'd see them in between lectures, and that caused acid to bubble in her stomach.

"Savannah, you up?" The knock came at the door. El had taken on the role of matron and caregiver since Savannah had moved in a few days ago. She'd told her almost everything, brushing over a few of the gorier details. As it transpired, El hadn't seen the page, and she hadn't heard anybody talking about it. So it must not have been quite as far-reaching as Savannah thought. Perhaps only a few of the university's students, rather than all of them. Savannah knew that it was likely her dad had asked El to take on the supporting role, but Savannah wasn't going to second guess that. It was nice to know somebody had your back.

"I'm just getting out of bed," Savannah called in response, her voice paper-thin. Once she climbed out of bed, the day officially started.

"Cool, I'll get the kettle on," El said, her footsteps trailing behind her and down the creaking wooden staircase, worn spongy with age.

After plunging herself into the shower and putting on fresh clothes, Savannah caught a glimpse of herself in the mirror, something she usually actively avoided. Her waist-length hair was darkened with the water. The moisture held onto the usual pale blonde, almost-white, hair so that it became a mottled and mousy brown. Her hair was Savannah's favourite part of herself. Since the start of university, where the excessive drinking and moderately excessive intake of recreational drugs had taken place, Savannah had looked perpetually tired. Her already skinny face was sunken and grey. But today, it wasn't. There was a pink tinge to her skin, and despite the bags under her eyes from the lack of sleep, she looked healthy.

The realisation that she looked better than she had in a long time, even without makeup or the consumption of something to make her feel confident, made a smile prick at the corner of her lips. Things were looking up for her. After sweeping some blusher on her cheeks, and some mascara across her eyelashes, Savannah went downstairs, ready for the day.

El was sitting at the kitchen table, an old sturdy thing that looked straight out of pre-war England. It had likely been in the house since it was built. El's hands were wrapped around a steaming cup of coffee. Savannah's mouth watered at the prospect and went over to the kettle to make her own. To her surprise, a mug was already there, curls of vapour rising from it.

"You're an angel," Savannah said, turning to El and taking the seat across from her.

"I could get used to hearing that," she said, taking a long sip of her coffee. "So, it's your first day back today?"

It wasn't so much a question as a statement of fact and so Savannah simply nodded.

"Well, lucky for you, I don't have class today, so I'm going to tag along, do some work in the library, and we can go for lunch together. How does that sound?"

Mixed emotions flooded Savannah. The prospect of having somebody by her side, should any awkward encounters occur, was beyond incredible, but she also didn't need a babysitter. Savannah had never needed anybody and needing somebody to walk her to and from classes seemed excessive. Despite that, she really didn't want to be alone today. If she did happen to bump into Penny and Gemma, or anybody else who had seen the page, then it would be nice to have a friendly face by her side.

"You don't have to do that," Savannah said, hoping that her voice didn't betray her true feelings.

"I know I don't. But I want to. We all need somebody from time to time, and I know this is difficult for you. Don't worry, I'll get you back when I need you!" El reached a hand across the table and gave Savannah's a squeeze. They'd only known each other a few days, but to Savannah, it felt like they'd known each other for a lifetime. El was quickly becoming her lifeline.

Relief flooded Savannah as she saw El waiting outside the lecture hall. The first lecture of the day, on the poetry of Philip Larkin, lasted a grand total of two hours. Savannah was ready for a break. There's only so much doom and gloom a person can take. The last stanza of the poem "Mr Bleaney" swirled around Savannah's consciousness.

"That how we live measures our own nature,
And at his age having no more to show

Than one hired box should make him pretty sure
He warranted no better, I don't know."

Now she had something to tell her therapist. This was what she didn't want. She didn't want to wind up as a person with nothing to show for their life, just a string of failures and embarrassments. When she died, she wanted to be surrounded by family and friends, people whose lives she had made better. That was what she wanted.

"What on earth was your lecture about? Everybody looks miserable as sin!" El exclaimed when Savannah pushed her way through the crowd and over to her.

"Poetry," Savannah said, not sure how to explain the enigma of Philip Larkin.

"Ah, that explains it!" El said chirpily and dragged her off to the café around the corner from campus.

The Grind was a popular place with students, and was, therefore, slammed when Savannah and El walked in. After scanning the room, they found a two-seater table in the corner, next to the toilets. It wasn't the most ideal spot, but it would do.

As they ate, El chatted away about her latest assignment, a paper in which she had to define her approach to photography. Savannah checked the faces of the other patrons for any sign of recognition on their faces, that they knew she was the girl from the Facebook page. There were a few people whose gaze lasted perhaps a millisecond too long, but other than that, Savannah remained as anonymous as she had hoped.

"How the hell am I supposed to know that? I take photographs of things that are beautiful, or ugly, or real. They're just there. Urgh, it's so irritating. Why do we have to define everything? Why can't things just be?"

El's tirade continued until they'd both finished their lunch and were drinking the dregs of their cappuccinos. It wasn't until there was a noticeable silence, that Savannah realised she'd not been listening. She'd been too busy casing her surroundings. What she'd do if somebody recognised her, she didn't know, but she couldn't physically prevent herself from searching their faces.

"I'm sorry, what did you say?" Savannah asked, hoping she hadn't been too rude.

"Nothing important, just ranting, you know. It's good to vent!"

Savannah laughed, catching El's eye. The door chimed as it had been doing incessantly during their lunch. For some reason, this time Savannah looked at the door. She couldn't explain why. There was simply this inexplicable need to look in that direction. In walked the most beautiful boy she'd ever seen. About her age, maybe a touch older. It wouldn't have been right to call him handsome—he was beautiful, but in a masculine way. Square jaw, but no stubble on his chin, the opposite of most of his peers. Behind him trailed a group of other boys. They were all laughing and joking, making their way to the tills.

Suddenly, his eyes were pressed against Savannah's. He'd caught her looking at him. The intensity of his gaze took her breath away. Did he know her from the page, or was he just into her? It had to be the first one, surely. People that looked like him weren't ever into people that looked like her.

Fixing her gaze on the table, Savannah didn't dare look up. Instead, she pretended to laugh at something El said, that may or may not have been funny.

There was something about this stranger that made Savannah feel like her stomach was on fire. Taking a deep breath, she looked up again and caught his eye once more. Twisting his mouth into a wry smile, like they shared a secret, he winked at her before taking his coffee to go and walking out of the shop.

"Did you see that?" Savannah said, probably cutting El off mid-sentence, she wasn't entirely sure.

"See what?" El asked, turning and following Savannah's stare.

"Nothing, it doesn't matter," Savannah said, her mind filled with the image of the handsome stranger. The fire in her stomach was replaced with eager butterflies.

Cameron

It was that time of year when things were crazy in schools. The run-up to Christmas. The short days, coupled with children buzzing with excitement made his job so much harder. None of them believed in Father Christmas anymore, but that didn't mean Christmas had lost its magic for them. Quite the contrary, they were obsessed with what gifts they would receive. A new PlayStation, the latest iPhone, designer clothes. That was what made Christmas special to these children. In all fairness, Cameron was the same as a teenager but there's something gross about all these spoilt children running around, bragging to their *friends* about what they're going to trick their parents into buying them that year. Out of his hundreds of students, there was maybe a handful that weren't like that. And they were the ones that got special treatment from Cameron. The ones you knew were going to grow up to be decent human beings.

The year sevens had been particularly difficult. He was certain that many of them still secretly believed in Father Christmas, and therefore the excitement, and the changed timetables, sent them absolutely crazy. He'd caught a group of boys at the back of one of his classes actually scrolling through Amazon on their phones, adding to their wish lists. The utter cheek of it had caused them all to wind up in detention that evening. A particularly snotty, gobby boy by the same of Richard, who had been the ringleader, according to the others who readily pushed him under the bus, had put up a fight about detention, and had therefore earned himself another for the following day. What should have been a nice, if slightly crazy, run-up to Christmas, was turning out to be difficult. Not only was behaviour management taking up the majority of his lessons, thanks to the headteacher's insistence on changing the timetables to accommodate for "fun" stuff, but he felt like his nerves were completely shorn. His thoughts consistently turned back to his phone and his *stalker.*

His phone had grown into an entity, a presence. He could feel it there all the time. In his pocket, or bag, or on the table beside him. It had become weighted. In his last period of the day, Cameron worked through his final marking. Then he had the detention to deal with. After that, it was home time. He and Liz were off to the late-night shopping in the city. Even as an adult, it was something he loved to do. The hustle and bustle, the music, the cheeky Bailey's hot chocolates. Every year he'd done it with his friends, but this time was different. He had somebody to share it with. No longer a third wheel. Or a fifth wheel.

Liz confessed to him last night that she'd never been to the late-night Christmas shopping event, and that made him look forward to it even more. She'd love him for introducing her to it. Christmas was the time for love and romance, and she'd definitely be feeling romantic after an evening amongst the Christmas lights and music.

The clock on the wall said 3.30 pm. It was already dark outside. He'd use the detention to catch up with his marking, while the boys would sit in silence either reading a book or catching up on homework. They arrived separately, having come from different classes. Their demeanours completely changed from their cockiness earlier. They wanted to go home as badly as he did. Richard sat in the far corner. His *friends* Matthew and Ellis, who were clearly too easily led for their own good, sat apart from him.

Just a few more pieces to mark. Student poetry, always as dull as anything. But at least it was quick. The poem in front of him was from one of his favourite students, a member of the elite not-spoiled few. Travis. A quiet kid with a small circle of friends. In spidery handwriting, the poem was scrawled on the page.

They say that absence makes the heart grow
Fonder.
I know that to be true.
The love I feel for her,
She will never know.
A ghost of a memory I cannot
Have.
A loving touch never had.

Young love, it seemed, had filled Travis's mind. It brought a smile to Cameron's lips. Oh, to be young and in love again, when everything seemed like life and death. The study had been on Shakespeare's sonnets, with each student writing a love poem of their own. Instead of grading these poems—Cameron disagreed with grading poetry—he would write a question underneath to hopefully encourage the student to think deeper into their poem and their reasoning for their choices. Cameron wrote, "Why have you chosen to utilize one-word lines in your poetry?"

He kept glancing up at his charges. There wasn't long to go. Only a few minutes. But the way they'd chosen to sit had thrown Cameron, somewhat. His years of teaching had afforded him a radar for when things weren't quite right. And the fact that the usually gobby Richard was sat quietly reading, away from his friends, set his alarm bells ringing.

"Okay boys, all done," Cameron said when the clock eked its way to 4 pm. "Can I have a word, Richard, before you go?"

The boy nodded and watched as his friends left.

"Is something wrong? You seem quiet, and that's not like you at all."

"What do you care?" Richard grumbled under his breath. It was the response Cameron had anticipated.

“Of course I care. I’m a teacher, I care about every one of you. Is something the matter? I can help you.”

When Richard remained silent, Cameron found his suspicions confirmed.

“Look, if you don’t want to tell me, that’s okay, but you really should speak to somebody. The school nurse, another teacher, just somebody you trust.” It was times like this when Cameron wanted to grab hold of the kids and shake them. He couldn’t help if they didn’t tell him what was wrong.

“My dad left,” Richard said to his shoes.

“Oh, I see.” Cameron’s heart sank. “When did that happen?”

“Couple of weeks ago. Haven’t seen him since.” Tears began to fill Richard’s eyes. Cameron wondered if he’d have noticed earlier if he hadn’t been so preoccupied with his personal life.

“That’s a tough thing to go through,” Cameron said. “How are things at home?”

“My mum cries all the time.” Richard spoke as though he’d accepted that this would be his fate. That nothing would change.

“I’m sorry, Richard. I’m glad you told me though because I can help. You can come to me if you need to talk about anything, or if you need me to help with anything. I can get your mum help too if need be. There are services out there to help the both of you.”

Richard nodded his head once. “Thanks, sir.”

"It will get better, you know? My dad left when I was just a little older than you. It was tough for a while, but then it became normal. My mum and sister became happy again too, after a little bit. It takes some getting used to, but I have no doubt in my mind that you'll manage." Cameron never quite knew what to say. He made a mental note to mention this to student services, just so they were aware of the situation. Richard would be monitored a little more closely, just to check all was well.

"Really?" There was a flicker of hope on his face.

"Yeah, and look at me now. I'm living the dream," Cameron joked, winking at Richard. "You'll come out of the other side stronger than ever, okay? I have no doubt about that. And you'll come to me when you need to talk?"

"Yes, sir, thank you."

"And no more phones in class. Go on, I'll see you tomorrow."

"Bye, sir," Richard said, a smile creeping across his cheeks. As the door closed, Cameron allowed himself to feel proud. A job well done. It was one of his favourite parts of the job, being there for students who needed him. Turning back to his marking, Cameron counted down the minutes until he could go home.

The last poems were simply outcries of teenage angst and, as the bell rang signifying that staff were officially allowed to exit the building, Cameron shoved his phone into his bag and headed for his car.

Liz was already standing outside the shopping centre when Cameron parked up, finding a very lucky, and very tight, parking spot on the street opposite. His heart skipped when he saw her, wrapped in an oversized Christmas jumper with Rudolf on the front, complete with a pom-pom nose. In her hand, she was holding a sheet of paper, her Christmas shopping list. All of the people she wanted to buy for. Jealousy flared within him. He'd never met any of her friends or family. It was something he hadn't even considered until now.

"You're looking very festive." Cameron kissed her on the cheek.

"I thought I'd make an effort, seeing as you were so bloody excited about this." Her bright red lips curled as she spoke.

"Is that your shopping list?" Cameron asked, not sure he was ready for the conversation he knew that he was about to start.

"It is." Liz raised her eyebrows at him and flipped her dark hair back over her shoulder.

"And who is on it?" Cameron pushed.

"Not many people. My mum, brother, and nephew." It's almost like Liz didn't feel the weight of the words she'd just said. How didn't he know about her family? Why hadn't he ever asked?

"I didn't know about them." Cameron let the sentence hang in the air, hoping she'd pick it up.

“That’s because they live in Devon. I rarely get to see them. We don’t talk all that often, but I always buy them a gift at Christmas.” She was entirely nonchalant about the whole thing.

Sensing that Cameron was uncomfortable, Liz clarified, “I haven’t mentioned them because I only really think about them when it comes to Christmas shopping. We’re not close. Like, at all.”

“I just thought I’d know about your family,” Cameron said, hoping he didn’t sound like a petulant child.

“I’m sorry, I never thought to mention it. Never crossed my mind. I haven’t met your family either,” Liz said.

“That’s different,” Cameron said, only then realising how cold he was. The conversation was still happening at the doors of the shopping centre.

“How is it different?”

“Because you know about them,” Cameron said.

Liz raised her eyebrows as though making a joke. “I promise, the next time I go and see them, you can come with me.”

She planted a kiss on his lips, wiping off the lipstick with her thumb, after they’d separated. “Come on, we don’t want to miss all the good deals.”

Much to Cameron’s annoyance, she’d made sense and had been able to justify the gap her family left in her life, and so they pushed their way through the shopping centre doors, a warm burst of air cascading over them. The shops were manic, with a constant stream of people heading in and out. The restaurants and coffee shops were just as crazy. There was no respite from the buzz of people. An electric atmosphere filled the space and after visiting at least ten different shops, and purchasing most of the presents they both needed, Liz and Cameron decided to go their separate ways so that they could buy presents for one another.

That evening was the first time Cameron had forgotten about the strange texts, and so his spirits were higher than ever. Watching Liz walk away, hips gently swaying, he made his way to H Samuel's to buy her a necklace. Jewellery was always a good bet for women, and Liz was the kind of woman who liked to wear expensive things. A teacher's salary meant he couldn't spend as much as he would like to, and H Samuel's was having a Christmas sale; a match made in heaven.

After settling on a simple silver necklace with a single diamond hanging genially from the thin band, Cameron stuffed the gift bag into another shopping bag and headed back out to find Liz. He was more than ready for his Bailey's hot chocolate now. He'd earned it.

The man stood before him, still in the middle of a sea of people. They parted as they walked around him. People grumbled at the inconvenience, but nobody said anything to him. Instead, they tutted and adjusted their trajectory. Typical British behaviour that Cameron would find hilarious under different circumstances. He felt like his body was burning cold. He stood, frozen, staring at the man.

He was wearing what looked to be an expensive suit, tailored to fit his body frame perfectly.

The stranger's face tugged at a memory he couldn't quite reach. The man lifted his hand and waved, a smile peeling across his face.

As the man turned to leave, Cameron found himself shouting, "Stop!"

Many of the horde of shoppers turned and looked at him like he was absolutely crazy. As he scanned their concerned, and entertained, faces he lost sight of the man. There was no doubt about it now, he was definitely being followed. Stalked. It couldn't be a coincidence. There was no way.

A newsreel of headlines ran through his mind about stalkers killing the subject of their obsession. But didn't people usually do something to upset their stalkers? An ex-boyfriend or angry employee? Cameron couldn't even place the man, so how could he have done something to warrant this kind of behaviour?

Certainty overcame him. There was no way that the texts and this man weren't connected. They just had to be. It was the only logical explanation. Not that any of this was, in any way, logical. Dropping his shopping bags, he reached into his pocket for his phone, sure that there would be a message there that would make his blood boil.

Nothing.

Shoving his phone into his pocket, Cameron caught a glimpse of himself in a shop window. He was red-faced, breathing heavily.

He had to calm himself down before he met Liz. He had no intention of telling her that he had a stalker if that's what was happening. She'd think he was crazy and leave him, and there was no way he could ever bag somebody as beautiful and smart as Liz again. No, he'd just have to keep this to himself. After nipping to the toilet to ensure he looked sane again, Cameron headed off to find his girlfriend, determined to make the most of the rest of their evening. He didn't plan on letting his stalker ruin their night.

Savannah

"Savannah, there's another one."

El's words sent goosebumps across Savannah's flesh. El had also been checking the internet for other pages dedicated to Savannah's drunken photographs. They'd almost given up on the endeavour. It had felt like all of that was behind her. And then El found it. A blog page. The website address was a mixture of random letters and numbers. Somebody hadn't wanted to pay for a domain name.

"Where did you find it?" Savannah turned to El, who had taken a seat at the bottom of Savannah's bed and passed her MacBook over to her.

"There was a link on the university's Facebook page. It must have been taken down because I can't find it anymore. But this is where it led to. Shit, I'm sorry Savannah."

The photos were new ones. Ones she'd never seen before. She recognised the outfits from nights out in the past. Her favourite shift dress, the t-shirt with the delicate beading, the shorts that finished at just the right length. They were clothes she still had in her wardrobe.

Most of them had captions written across them. "SAVANNAH THE SLUT." "I DON'T WEAR UNDERWEAR." "I'LL SLEEP WITH ANYBODY." In each photograph, she looked drunk, completely gone. But none of them exposed parts of her body. She just looked a mess.

"At least these ones are more modest," Savannah tried to joke.

"Savannah, this is serious," El said. Savannah wasn't listening. She scrolled to a photograph that she recognised. Gemma had taken it. The photograph was of Savannah and Penny. Penny's face was obscured. There was no way you could tell it was her. Savannah was kissing her. Their tongues were visible. It had been a dare. A drinking game.

"You don't think Gemma or Penny could have done this, do you?" She couldn't believe that she'd been so stupid as to miss the obvious. Who else would have been able to coerce her into the awkward poses the photos had been taken in, other than her friends?

"I don't know them, Sav. Do you think they could have?" El pulled the laptop back and shut the top.

"Not too long ago I would have said no, but now, I think it's them. I never considered it before, but it has to be, right?"

"I think so. I can't believe you were friends with them. Jesus, they're such bitches. We need to get this taken down." El's voice was on the verge of hysterics. It was nice, Savannah thought, that El was so protective over her.

"I think I need to ask them if they did it. At least that way I can rule them out, right?" She couldn't see them in person. There was no way on this planet that Savannah would be able to meet face to face and ask Penny and Gemma if they'd created that website and uploaded the photos. Either they'd done it and clearly hated her. Or they hadn't and would be annoyed that she'd asked. Both options were embarrassing as hell, and Savannah had no intentions of putting herself in that position.

"What are you going to do?"

"Text them, I think." It wasn't so much a statement, as a question.

"Or we could just take it to the police and let them deal with it?" El suggested. Savannah wanted to be able to do that. She really did, but she couldn't handle the attention. All those policemen looking at these disgusting photographs of her. No, this was a better option.

"What should I put?" Savannah said, not answering the question El had asked.

"Just say that you've found a website with your photographs on, and that they look like photographs only Gemma and Penny would have had. Be polite, swallow your dignity, and just ask them to take it down. Honestly, you could definitely go off on one and get angry, but I don't think it's worth it. It will get their back up and make it far worse. Just ask them to take them down, say it's making you ill."

It was begging. That much was apparent. She was begging two people she used to consider to be her best friends to just do the right thing. How had she stooped so low?

"Look, you know as well as I do that you don't need to beg. We can take it to the police. But, if you don't want to do that, then I think you'll just have to suck it up and ask nicely. If it was me, I'd want them investigated. They're psychopaths. But I understand why you don't."

Savannah nodded and picked up her phone. She'd decided, at that moment, to message them both separately instead of adding them into a group message on Facebook. Perhaps, if there was anything decent about them, they'd not tell the other about Savannah's message and just do the right thing. It was a long shot, but it was all she had left.

"Okay, here we go. So, I'm going to put, 'Hi, I've come across a website online with photographs of me that I think you took. Did you send photos of me to anybody else, or did you upload them yourself? Either way, can you take them down please? It's not fair to do that to me. I get that it was a joke, but it's not funny. If you take them down, I won't tell anybody it was you.' What do you think?" Savannah turned to El.

"Yes, I think that's probably your best bet."

Savannah held her breath, pressed send, and waited for a response.

Savannah

Unsurprisingly, Savannah gained two fairly vicious responses from her ex-roommates. They both came at the exact same time, which was obviously more than a coincidence. Their texts caused Savannah to flush with embarrassment as she handed them to El to read. She was already being a burden on her new roommate. How long would it be before she went the same way as Gemma and Penny?

El sat there, re-reading the messages, her eyes widening with shock. "Those nasty bitches. What the hell is wrong with them? I'm not being funny, Sav, but you've dodged a bullet getting out of there when you did. Jesus, who knows what they could have done to you?"

Penny's response was bad, but Gemma's was worse.

Penny had written… *Seriously, what the fuck have you been taking? The world doesn't revolve around you. Why would I want to mess with you? You're pathetic. Get a life.*

Gemma had written… *You're an ugly slut with no life. I haven't given you a second thought since you left. You're not worth my time. Do everyone a favour and just die. Thank you.*

"The website has been taken down though," Savannah said. That could have been a coincidence too, that it had been taken down at the same time as she'd messaged Penny and Gemma, but she suspected it wasn't. In all likelihood, they probably hadn't expected Savannah to find the website. It was one of those things to get people laughing at her behind her back. And when she had found it, and they'd been caught, taking it down was the only option. Of course they'd denied it. Who wouldn't? But they would be revelling in the fact that Savannah knew it was them.

"Don't let them get to you. They're terrible people, and karma's a bitch. They'll get what's coming to them, I promise. The world works that way." El raised her eyebrows and tried to get Savannah to smile. "There's no point sitting here moping. We should be celebrating. You caught the bitches red-handed, and the page was taken down. How about I nip out and get us a chocolate cake or something? Perhaps a bottle of some lovely non-alcoholic wine? I'm dying for a Shloer."

Savannah couldn't help but smile at that. Chocolate certainly sounded nice, as did the fizzy pop. "What would I do without you?"

"I don't know. Probably die of starvation from a lack of chocolate cake?" El said, reaching for her purse. "Be back in a minute."

The door shut behind her, leaving Savannah alone with her thoughts. She re-read the messages over and over again. She hated how much weight those words held. With El out of the way, she did a quick Google search of her own name and various scenarios. "Savannah Windsor + nudes", "Savannah + drunk", "Leeds

University drunk slut", and about a million more. When she was satisfied that there were no more photographs of her on the internet, other than the ones she'd uploaded herself, she allowed herself to breathe.

The missed deadlines soon caught up with Savannah. Having missed a couple of hand-ins during the weeks she was incapacitated and had moved house, she now had twice as much work on her plate. Essays, papers, and exams, all to prepare for and all for far too soon. When she wasn't in lectures, she was holed up in her room, textbooks and paperbacks covering her bed. Each time she saw them, she felt the familiar twinge of nerves in her stomach. She did her very best to push them away and concentrate on the writing or revision at hand, but they kept forcing their way back, and worse than ever. It felt like a constant stream of anxiety growing inside of her, never flowing away. It wouldn't be long until the dam would break.

After briefly mentioning this to El, Savannah was convinced to mention this to her therapist, which she did reluctantly. She needed help, but in what capacity, she wasn't sure. If she could find some way to get rid of the nerves, then she'd be fine. Her old coping strategies of cheap alcohol and the occasional pills would no longer suffice. She could only imagine how her dad would feel if she picked up her old habits. In those moments of weakness, when she wanted to scream and hurl her laptop across the room, this is what prevented her from going down to the corner shop and buying a bottle or two of Frosty Jack's. She didn't want to be that person anymore.

The confession had come instantly, as soon as Savannah's body had slumped into the overstuffed chair. "I'm struggling to keep up with university assignments."

Amanda had looked at her, tilting her head like a confused puppy. "What exactly are you struggling to keep up with?"

"I have to do the assignments I missed, plus the upcoming ones. I have exams too." Savannah pulled at the wicks of her fingernails, and watched as Amanda noticed, raising her eyebrow in a way that made Savannah immediately stop.

"Okay. University is tough. Nobody said it was going to be easy, right? Plus, you've had a harder go of it than most, and you're still coping. That has to count for something."

"Yeah," Savannah said, she knew that she wasn't convincing.

"What are you using right now to cope with the pressure?" Amanda asked.

"Nothing!" Savannah said, on the defensive already. As much as she'd wanted to, she hadn't used anything to cope.

"I don't mean like drugs or alcohol, Savannah. I'm sorry if that confused you. What I mean is, when things are getting tough, what do you do to cope?"

“Oh.” Savannah gave a nervous laugh as her cheeks reddened. “I don’t really do anything. I just keep going. The work has to be done, right?”

“Yes, the work has to be done. Your mental health is just as important as completing the assignments.”

“My mental health will be non-existent if I fail the assignments,” Savannah said. She wasn’t trying to be oppositional, but she knew that was how she was coming across.

“Why do you think that? If you fail your assignments, and you fail your course, what’s the worst that could happen?”

The question caused heat to rush to Savannah’s chest, where red blotches appeared. Her pulse quickened and her breathing hitched. Failing her degree would be the worst thing in the world. Her dad would be disappointed. She wouldn’t be able to get a job, and she’d end up on benefits. She would lose her sense of self entirely. Savannah had a plan, to do a master’s degree and maybe a doctorate. To work in academia and publish writing and papers of her own. None of that would be possible if she failed at the first hurdle. Her life wouldn’t be worth living.

“I suppose, I’d figure something out,” Savannah said instead. The missed opportunity to work through some of her issues flashed above her like a neon sign. People never told you how hard therapy was. How draining it was.

"Exactly! Nothing is ever as bad as it seems. I'm not suggesting, for a second, that you shouldn't care about your degree. What I'm saying is that you have to take care of yourself too. So, we need to put strategies in place to help you take care of yourself, while also getting the grades you want."

Nodding, Savannah caught Amanda's eye. The kind smile on the therapist's face made Savannah feel worse. She wanted to cry but forced the tears to remain firmly in the lump in her throat.

"Something that works for many of my clients, is to plan your day out ahead of time. Plan when you're going to have breaks, and make sure you have plenty of them. I would suggest that for every hour of work, you have fifteen minutes off, doing something you enjoy. What kind of things do you enjoy?"

"Watching TV or having a cup of tea. I also like daydreaming. Is that strange to say?"

"That's not strange at all. It's actually kind of like meditation, I suppose. Do you let your mind wander, or do you try to control your daydreams?"

Savannah thought for a second. She'd never considered that before. "I think it depends. Sometimes I decide where the story is going to go, but other times my daydreams kind of do what they want."

"I think you're onto something here, Savannah. How about, when things get too much, you go and have a lie down in bed, set your alarm for fifteen minutes, and just allow your brain to do its thing."

"You think that will help me to feel better?" Savannah was sceptical about the idea. Daydreaming was something she enjoyed, and looked forward to, but surely it was just another form of procrastination and that would make her feel worse than ever.

"I do. I really do. You could just as easily have a cup of tea, do some yoga, or watch a bit of TV too. Just a bit of something every hour for you. Otherwise, you'll get so bogged down by everything you have to do, that you'll just get more and more stressed. Studies have shown that regular breaks make you more productive when you're working too. That's something to consider."

That evening was the first time Savannah put this method into practice. After fifty minutes of work, she pushed her books to the side, clearing everything off her bed and lying down on the pillow. Her alarm had been set and her eyes were closed. She wasn't surprised when her thoughts found their way back to the guy from the coffee shop. The tall, dark stranger who'd winked at her. He'd been the subject of her daydreams since that day, and the fact that she had to carve the time into her schedule to indulge her dreams, was something she found quite invigorating.

In the daydream, Savannah walked over and introduced herself to him. She was confident and beautiful, as was he. Except that he stumbled over his words when he spoke to her. The impact she had on him was exhilarating. So much so that she almost forgot she was dreaming. Her alarm sounded too quickly, and she was brought back to real life, to the mountain of work she had to do. Already counting down to her next break, to see what would happen with the handsome stranger, Savannah began exploring the themes of Philip Larkin, in preparation for her exam.

Cameron

The last day of term had finally arrived, and Cameron was ready for a break. He was exhausted, as he always was at the end of the first term. He couldn't wait to get home, put his feet up, and have a drink. Maybe watch a film with Liz and enjoy a Bailey's. That would be just perfect. His last class was far too noisy and rambunctious, ready to leave for the holidays. Cameron said a silent prayer of thanks when they left the room, and he was free.

"Thank God," he whispered to himself when the door finally closed. No marking. Nothing else to do. He could leave as the children did. Throwing on his coat, gloves, and bag, he practically ran out of the door. When he got to the car park, it was clear that all of the other staff had the same idea. The car park was jammed. People were trying to reverse out of spots and into the line of queueing traffic to leave the site.

He threw his bag into the boot and went to sit in the driver's seat, deciding to let his car heat up, and the queue of traffic dissipate, before he tried to brave the journey home. For once, there was a chance that it would be a white Christmas. However, when you're an adult, all that meant was that the roads would be treacherous, impassable. They were already, but with ice rather than fluffy white snow. The last thing they needed was for the snow to compact on top of the ice and turn the whole village into a skating rink.

The air blew warm on his face from the car's heaters, sending a shiver down his spine. His phone was cutting into his leg in his trouser pocket and so he tossed it into the passenger seat where it immediately made the noise he'd come to be afraid of. Two quick vibrations. A text. Most likely it would be Liz, asking what he wanted to do for dinner that evening. But even so, his breath hitched, and he could only stare at the phone.

Tucked into the crease of the seat, the phone blinked at him. The screen dimmed once more. Still in the parking space, Cameron knew that he had to read the text. What kind of a grown man was scared of his phone?

Grabbing hold of the phone, too tightly, Cameron pressed his finger to the screen. The phone sprung to life, the text there, blinking at him, begging him to read it.

One new message.

The sender's number was unknown.

"Fuck," he cursed under his breath, opening the text message before he could think better of the decision.

Another photograph, no words accompanying it. Only an image that made Cameron want to throw his phone out of the window. Instead, his hand wouldn't let go. The photograph filled the screen. The same chair. The same man. This time, the man was in focus.

His face was bloodied and swollen. Two black eyes bulged against the poor soul's cheeks. Deep purple arches surrounded both eye sockets, pushing them outwards in a way that signified intense pain.

The man's shirt was brown with blood, crusted and dried. Hair hung loosely at his temples, slick with either blood or sweat.

The face. His face. The man in the chair was Cameron. Until this point, there had been some element of uncertainty. But now, there was no question left that it was him. His stomach turned at the grotesque image. For a terrible second, he thought he would be sick in his car.

"What the hell?" he muttered, zooming into the face in the photograph. It was definitely Cameron. Almost unrecognisable thanks to the warped, swollen features. Almost.

By the time he was able to tear his eyes away from the photograph, the car park was empty. None of this made any sense to him. Cameron had never been tortured. Had never been strapped to a chair and beaten black and blue. He'd remember something like that. He'd have the scars to prove it. Yet, the photo evidence was in front of him. There he was. Undeniably so.

Rocking slightly, trying to understand what the fuck was happening to him, Cameron breathed in and out steadily. He knew two things for certain. One, he'd never been tortured. Two, that photograph was of *him* being tortured. Unless he had an identical twin he didn't know about.

Now was the time to go to the police. The decision had almost been taken away from him.

Without thinking, Cameron slammed his car in reverse and headed straight to the police station. He had a vague recollection of where it was, although he'd never been there before. The closest one to his house was on a small estate nearby. The image ate away at him through the Christmas traffic. People trying to get home to their families and friends after the last day of school or work. It was lovely in principle, but it meant that it took him twice as long as it should to get to the police station.

By the time he arrived, Cameron had pulled a chunk of rubber out of his steering wheel, his nerves getting the better of him. He didn't even know what he would say to the police. How did you explain something like that?

Oh, yes, I think I'm being stalked by a bald man in a suit. And somebody keeps sending me torture pictures. Which, as it turns out, they are of me! Even though I've never been tortured before.

He wouldn't blame the officers for thinking he was insane. Hell, he would if he was in their shoes.

The heat was the first thing that hit him as he walked into the police station. The second, was the sad looking tree perched in the corner of the room like somebody awaiting an interview. Fallen leaves littered the floor around it, begging to be swept up.

The police officer behind the desk looked like she didn't want to be there. That was a good start.

"How can I help you, sir?" she said, without looking up from her computer screen.

"Hi, I think I have a crime to report," Cameron said, almost rolling his eyes at his own inability to communicate effectively. *I think I have a crime to report!* Jesus.

"You think you have a crime to report?" The police offer raised her eyebrows at him, echoing his own inadequacies.

"Yes, should I tell you the story? Or…" It felt wrong to tell the story to the officer standing behind the reception desk. On the drive over, he'd pictured himself in an interview room, with a coffee and steel table. With, maybe, two police officers and a detective listening to him.

"That might be a good place to start." She wrinkled her nose as she spoke. It was as plain as day that she was bored with him already.

"Well, here goes. So, a few weeks ago I noticed that I saw a man everywhere. He was really creepy and always seems to be wherever I go. But that's not really the reason I'm here. It is part of it, but not the main part." Sighing and trying to steady his breath, Cameron continued, "I received a text to my phone saying, 'found you', which is weird, right? Since then, they've messaged a few times with strange messages like this. I blocked their number, but they started texting from a different one. They've been sending photographs too. The last one really freaked me out. Here," Cameron said, unlocking his phone and turning it in the direction of the woman.

She scrutinised it for a second before saying, "Is that you, sir?"

"Yes, but the thing is, it can't be me. Do I look like I've been tortured?" Cameron said, pinching the bridge of his nose to try and calm down.

"Then if you've never been tortured, how can it be you?" The officer looked at him like he was wasting her time, although he was sure she hadn't got anything better to be doing.

"I don't know. That's why I've come. It's stalking or something, right? Surely there's something you can do." His voice was desperate, and he hated how infantile he sounded.

"May I take a look at the other messages?" The officer was already scrolling back through the texts as she said the words.

"Yes, sure, thank you," Cameron said, hoping that he was getting somewhere. Once she'd seen the messages, she'd see how crazy this whole thing was.

"Have any threats been made?" she asked.

"Other than the ones in the messages, no," Cameron admitted.

"And do you feel like your life is at risk?" The words were spoken with an air of perpetual boredom.

"Well, I don't know but—" Cameron started and was cut off.

"Look, sir, while this is creepy, I'm not sure any laws are actually being broken. It looks to me like somebody is trying to play a joke on you. And we don't deal with jokes. We're the police. My advice to you is to allow me to log the incident, and then we've got a paper trail if it begins to escalate. You can rest assured, that if you feel at risk, we'll intervene. But it's Christmas. We're busy and, honestly, this just seems like a bad joke to me."

"Okay." Cameron ran his hand over his face. He could see it in the woman's eyes that she thought he was either drunk, high, or crazy. She was humouring him by logging the incident.

"Fill this out and bring it back. We'll be in touch with you afterwards if we need to."

Writing the story again on the paperwork only seemed to convince Cameron further that he was losing his mind. His ramblings sounded like those of a person with some kind of serious problem, not a well-adjusted (and respected) English teacher.

Handing the form back to the officer, Cameron thanked her for her help and retreated to his car, feeling no better than when he walked into the station.

Savannah

"I got a first!" Savannah shouted as she walked into the house. El was somewhere upstairs, her music blaring through the hallways.

"What?" El called, her bedroom door creaking open. Savannah could picture her peering around the door frame.

"I got a first! On my exam! I did it, El!"

Footsteps flew down the hallway and El appeared at the top of the stairs.

"You did it!" El leapt down the stairs and threw herself into Savannah's arms. "I knew you could do it. That's two firsts now, isn't it? Your essay and your exam. Jesus, you're onto a winner here. I'm so happy for you!"

Savannah knew that El meant it. They'd grown close, more like sisters than roommates, even though they'd only known each other a couple of months.

"I couldn't have done it without you," Savannah said, embarrassed as the words flew out of her mouth.

"You bloody could have, but I'm glad to be of help. The magic of the occasional cuppa, eh?" El laughed, letting go of Savannah. "How are we going to celebrate?" El asked, heading into the kitchen.

Her mind immediately jumped to alcohol. That's how she'd always celebrated bad days, good days, Tuesdays. And now, she had no idea how to celebrate.

"Let's go out for a meal? Or we could order in? We have to do something, but not until after you call your dad. You have to tell him, he'll be thrilled." El offered the options as Savannah had remained silent in response to her question.

"You're right. I'll ring my dad, and then shall we go out? What about Pinocchio's? I could go for a pizza right now."

"Pinocchio's it is. I'll phone them now and book a table. Their carbonaras are to die for."

El skipped off to retrieve her mobile phone from upstairs. Picking up the house phone from its cradle, Savannah dialled her father's home phone number. It rang only once before he picked up.

"I did it again, Dad. I got a first on my exam!" She hadn't even bothered to say hello; she was simply too excited to tell him the news.

"Congratulations! I'm so proud of you," her dad's voice came down the line. "I knew you could do it."

"You did?" Savannah said, not strictly believing him.

"I did. I trusted you. Once you got out of that awful house, you pulled yourself together. I'm so proud of what you've been able to do. Not just with school, but with everything else too. You're a strong one. I did a good job with you."

Savannah didn't know what to say to that. Her dad wasn't ever one to talk of feelings and the confession had taken her by surprise. "Thank you," she settled for.

"Any time, sweetie, I love you."

The phone call ended, and Savannah headed back upstairs. She was suddenly very tired, her body and head aching, respectively.

"I'm going to have a nap before we go," Savannah called into El's room on the way past.

"Okay. Table's booked for six pm," El called back.

Savannah expected to sleep as soon as her head hit the pillow. Over the last few weeks, she'd spent more time in bed than she ever had before, daydreaming as a reward for getting her work done. She couldn't entirely believe that it had worked. When she was daydreaming, she wasn't thinking about how many people had seen the photographs of her. It was a respite, and a well-needed one at that.

Amanda was thrilled about it, and so who was Savannah to question her methods? In the time since she'd first started, the storyline with the handsome stranger had developed into a full-fledged relationship. She'd named him Mark. It felt like a manly name and suited him well.

Across her daydreams, she and Mark had gotten to know one another quite well. They'd dated and had even slept together a couple of times. He was exquisite in bed, not like the boys she'd been with before. He knew exactly what to do and exuded confidence in that department. She only wished she could see him again in real-life. After the time at the coffee shop, he'd vanished into thin air. Every time she walked around campus, or went for lunch, she hoped to see him. She kept her eyes peeled, vowing that she would talk to him when she saw him next. Give him her number, or her Facebook information, and ask him out. Hopefully, he hadn't seen the photographs of her. But, even if he had, the Mark in her daydreams would have been more than understanding. He'd have taken her under his wing like a baby bird and protected her from the vicious ex-roommates who had tried to ruin her life.

In the meantime, she had to settle for dream-Mark.

For the first time in the longest time, Savannah was filled with confidence. She was capable, and she was intelligent. She was able to turn away from the bad path she was on and turn something awful into a success. How could you not be proud of that?

As her eyes closed, Mark fluttered into focus. Black hair and a wry smile, eyes that crinkled at the corners when he laughed. He was perfect in every way. Yesterday's daydream had seen Mark invite her on holiday with him. A romantic mini-break to Whitby, where they'd lounge in bed all day, and walk around the cobbled streets hand-in-hand.

Savannah had, of course, said yes. And that was where today's daydream started. Mark picked her up in his arms and kissed her.

Wrapping her legs around his waist, his strong hands holding her against him, Savannah deepened the kiss. As though time had passed, they were suddenly on a white, crisp bed, in the bed-and-breakfast which overlooked the sea. Mark rolled over her, his full weight pressing her into the bed. Moving her legs to accommodate for him, he moaned against her lips. Their clothes were off, and their bodies melded together as one. She replayed the scene until she was happy with it. Sometimes, Mark stripped her clothes from her body, trailing kisses down her stomach. Others, she knelt over him, pulling his shirt over his head and pinning his body down as she unzipped his jeans.

The alarm on her phone pulled her back to real life. She groaned with unrequited desire. A few more minutes would have surely been enough for her to feel satisfied. But it was 5 pm, and she needed to get changed and ready for the meal with El.

Her phone rang the next morning, pulling her out of her slumber. She'd been dreaming of Mark, and how they would have celebrated her first together. Looking at the caller ID, she could see it was her dad.

"Hello," she said groggily into the mobile.

"What's wrong? Are you okay?" her father's voice responded.

"I'm fine, you woke me up," Savannah said.

"Oh, okay." He sounded relieved and Savannah immediately felt guilty. "Are you busy today? I wondered if you wanted to go for lunch? My treat."

Savannah wanted nothing more than to stay in bed, and maybe, okay definitely, revisit her daydreams with Mark. The guilt wasn't enough to convince her to get ready and go and see her dad. "I can't today, Dad. I…" She needed a reason that he'd understand, an excuse that would make him feel better about her cancelling on him. Something that made her seem acclimated and *normal.*

"I have a date." She regretted the words instantly.

"You have a date?" her dad asked. Although the question was simple, it was loaded. He wanted more information.

"Yes, he's called Mark, and he's on the same course as me. It's only our second date, nothing serious yet." Why had she said that?

"Oh, okay. What's he like?"

"He's nice. He doesn't drink or smoke, so please don't worry about me. I won't do anything to undo my hard work." This is what her father had been worried about. She knew him well enough to know that. A little gentle reassurance would go a long way.

"He sounds nice. What are you guys doing?"

"A movie and dinner," Savannah said, knowing she'd convinced him that this was a good idea. Dating was a normal thing to do, and she was trying to be normal again.

"Sounds lovely. Will you let me know when you're home safe?"

“I will,” Savannah promised and made a mental note to remember to do that.

“Great. Enjoy your date.” His voice sounded stable, happy even.

“Will do, Dad. Bye.” Guilt curled in her stomach. She’d lied to her dad after everything he’d done. What a shitty thing to do to him.

Savannah closed her eyes and brought back the image of Mark.

“Your dad would love me, wouldn’t he?” Mark said to her.

“He would,” Savannah said.

Closing her eyes, she allowed herself to get sucked back into the dream, if only for a little longer.

Cameron

By the time he got home, Cameron had riled himself up into a stupor. He was ready to explode. It felt like his body was burning up from the inside out and there was no way to feel normal again. Liz was waiting for him when he opened the door. The first words she said to him were not at all what he needed to hear.

"You're late." She was standing at the kitchen counter with a glass of red wine in hand. "I presumed we were celebrating the start of the Christmas holidays together, but apparently I was wrong."

Cameron's teeth slammed together in an attempt to keep his temper at bay. She didn't know what happened to him. It wasn't her fault that she reacted the way she did to him being late home. Maybe he should have told her he was going to be late, but he'd had other things on his mind.

In a last-ditch attempt to not fall into the rabbit hole of an almighty argument, Cameron headed for the bathroom. He wanted to shower and put on his pyjamas and lay in bed, maybe read his book before falling to sleep at an unreasonably early time. All hope of that vanished quickly when Liz slammed down the glass in her hand, red wine sloshing onto his white countertop. It would leave a stain. The liquid seeped into the porous surface.

"Don't walk away from me." Her words were clipped and cruel.

“This is my home. I can do what I want to.” As he turned to face her, he was too aware of his chest rising and falling as though he’d run a marathon. The resentment he felt towards her at that moment was like nothing he’d ever experienced before. The fuse had been lit at the police station, and by this point, he was ready to explode.

“It’s our home, Cameron. We live here, together. And you do not get to just walk away when I’m trying to talk to you.”

“I’ve had a bad day, Liz. I need to be alone. Let me walk away.” The last sentence sounded too much like a dare.

“No, Cameron. You walk in late and then try to walk past me like I’m nothing. A stranger who just happens to live in your house. That is not how this is going to work. I won’t allow it.”

“You won’t allow it?” Cameron stepped towards her, aware of his height towering over her. “I’ve had a shit afternoon, and you come at me the second I walk through the door. Seriously, Liz, that’s fucking mental! Do you want to know where I’ve been, why I’m late? I was at the police station because I got this…”

Cameron pulled out his phone and navigated his way to the text. Once again, the image startled him. The bulging bloodied eyes, head hanging limp.

“That’s you,” Liz said dumbly.

“Yeah, I know. That’s why I went to the police. And then I get home and you have a go at me. I can’t even look at you right now.”

Cameron left the room and within minutes he was in the shower. Hot water cascaded over his body. He felt more human the second the water touched his skin. Leaning his hands against the wall, he allowed the water to wash over him. When he closed his eyes, he saw the image again. The broken man. None of it made any sense at all. The more he tried to explain it, to rationalise it, the crazier he felt. Somebody had a photograph of him being tortured. Somebody was stalking him, trying to push him over the edge. If they were trying to send him towards a breakdown, they were heading the right way. If only he could explain the photograph. Honestly, it would feel better to know he'd been tortured, to remember it. That way, the photograph wouldn't be evidence of his steady mental decline.

The fact of the matter was that he had never been tortured. He hadn't been subjected to what the man in the photograph had. You'd remember being tortured, or at the very least, you'd have the marks to prove it.

A gentle knock came at the door. Liz didn't wait before she walked into the room.

"I'm sorry, Cameron," she said, sitting on the closed toilet lid. "I shouldn't have gone off on you like that. I'd been waiting around for you to come home and had been looking forward to starting our first Christmas holidays together, and then when you didn't show up, I just thought… Well, I don't know what I thought. I didn't expect this though."

Cameron remained silent, still leaning against the now warm tiles.

"What did the police say?" Liz asked.

"They said to keep a log of it. That it's somebody trying to prank me. They weren't worried. But, Liz, the photograph is of me…"

"It does look like you," Liz agreed.

"But?" Cameron asked, always able to tell when there was something she wasn't saying.

"Well, you're pretty generic looking, if you don't mind me saying that. You're a tall dark-haired man, with a medium build. The guy in the photograph is swollen and bruised. How can you be certain it's you?"

Cameron felt a stab of rage at the question. She was questioning him, again, making him feel even more unstable than he was.

"It's me," Cameron said, definitively. "But, even if it wasn't, somebody is stalking me and sending me images of somebody being tortured. That can't be legal!"

"You're being stalked?" Liz said as the colour drained from Cameron's face.

"Yes."

"By whom?" Liz's question was loaded. She was annoyed that she'd been kept in the dark.

"I don't know who he is. But I see him a lot. He's always standing there, smiling at me. It's creepy as fuck, Liz."

“What does he look like?” Liz was excruciatingly calm. It riled Cameron more than it should have.

“He’s bald. Tall, stocky. Older than us, maybe in his late fifties or early sixties.” Cameron moved so that the water ran down his back.

“And you told the police this too?” Liz said. Cameron watched as her eyebrow raised. He couldn’t quite read the facial expression.

“Yes,” he said.

“And what did they say about that?” Liz continued her line of questioning.

“They said to keep a log of it and let them know if I feel unsafe or threatened.”

“And do you feel unsafe or threatened?”

“Of course I do! I told her that. She looked at me like I was stupid and practically ushered me out of the doors.”

From the living room, Cameron heard his phone ping, signifying a message.

The two of them looked at one another in silent, unspoken recognition. Liz stood up and walked out of the room to collect the phone.

Cameron finished washing his body and wrapped a towel around his waist.

“It’s another message,” Liz said when Cameron approached her. She was staring at the phone.

“What does it say?” Cameron asked, unable to bring himself to take the phone from Liz.

“It says, ‘You’ll finally feel the pain I do. I’m watching you, Cameron.’” Liz stared at Cameron, wide-eyed.

“What if we’re not safe? What if he’s watching us?” Cameron faltered.

“I don’t see how he could be. The curtains are closed, and it’s impossible to see in without standing right outside the window. I think he means metaphorically. Like, he knows you went to the police.”

Cameron pushed his damp hair back from his face and looked at Liz.

“This is insane, I need to call the police again,” Cameron said. He moved to take the phone but couldn’t make his arm cooperate. Instead, he just looked at the object in her hand. Who would have thought that something so small could cause so much pain?

“If you think you should, but you don’t want to piss the police off. Don’t you think you should log it like they said?” Liz asked

He wasn’t sure what to do. In the end, he headed back to the bedroom to put on his pyjamas. Every fibre of his being was telling him to phone the police, but Liz didn’t seem bothered by it. Perhaps he was too close to it. Over-reacting. He picked up a pencil and a sheet of notepaper and wrote down the details of the message, feeling like his response hadn’t been enough.

The rest of the night passed by in a cool detachedness. Cameron and Liz sat down to watch TV and neither mentioned the elephant in the room. Cameron placed his phone on silent before going to bed, and he managed to sleep somewhat soundly. When he awoke the next morning, his phone was flashing three new messages. He counted his blessings that he'd had the forethought to put it on silent.

He stared at the phone for a minute, before unlocking it and opening the messages. They were all from the same unknown number. The first two were text, and the final one was a photograph.

WE'RE REALLY GETTING TO YOU, AREN'T WE? WHAT DOES IT FEEL LIKE TO BE WATCHED LIKE AN ANIMAL IN A CAGE?

DID YOU EVER STOP TO WONDER WHO WE ARE?

The final photograph was of a knife thrust under a person's ribcage. The blade was buried, and the hilt angled downwards, showing how it had slipped beneath the bone and into the soft organs below.

The body was that of a man, there was no doubt about that. For a second, Cameron wished that he had tattoos or some distinguishing features so he would know whether it was him or not, for definite. Would it make him feel better to know that it was 100 percent, without a shadow of a doubt, him? Or would that send him spiralling at a rate he couldn't imagine?

Laying his head on the pillow, he studied the texts again. The word "we're" stood out like a sore thumb, jumping out from the rest of the words. More than one person was tormenting him. Multiple people were in on this game. But who? Why?

Lying there, as the sun began to rise lazily, forcing its way through the curtained window, Cameron tried to think back to everybody he'd ever known, people who he might have hurt badly enough for them to want to ruin his life in this way. Other than a few ex-girlfriends who Cameron treated badly, and some guys from school he might have teased a little too much, there was nobody. And he was sure he'd never hurt anybody severely enough for them to want to waste their time doing this to him.

Then the thought struck him. It wasn't a waste of their time. They were getting what they wanted out of him. A reaction, and a pretty damn good reaction at that. If he was being watched, from a distance he hoped, then he'd have to pretend that none of this was affecting him. He had to act normal and get on with his life, pushing all of this shit into a box and hiding it in the dark recesses of his mind. Cameron could do that. He'd had a lifetime of practise in hiding his feelings, just like every other man he'd ever known.

Resolving to portray an image of total calm and peace on the outside and hide the cutting pain that pierced into his stomach whenever he thought about the text, or being stalked, Cameron decided to get up and go for a jog, hoping that the brisk morning breeze would return his life to a semblance of normality.

He didn't hear his text tone as he walked out of the door.

Savannah

Now that her studies were back on track, Savannah felt freer than she had in forever, so much so that therapy was becoming a chore. She searched every single day to see whether any photographs had been uploaded of her, and every day she was relieved to find that there hadn't been. Life was peachy. Her father had stopped taking her to therapy some time ago, when she'd proven herself reliable again. When everything was going her way, the last thing she wanted to do was to go into the therapist's office for an hour and a half and talk about things that no longer mattered to her. Whenever she was holed up in the office, sunken into one of the sofas, she wanted to get home and get to work.

The first missed appointment had slipped by without any recognition. Neither the therapist phoned her, nor did El realise she hadn't attended. During the time she should have been there, Savannah managed to finish another assignment that had been niggling at her. It felt incredible to cross that off the list. Now she could get back to reading books she actually wanted to read, rather than ones she had to.

With the open window and the cool breeze on her skin, Savannah settled down to read the latest instalment in the *Vampire Academy* series. After reading heavy books for some time, it was nice to sit back and fall into a world of sexual tension and vampires. Her bedding was fresh, crisp, and clean. With new pyjamas on too, Savannah felt truly at peace. What more could a girl want?

The next missed therapy session went very much the same way, with Savannah spending the time lounging around and reading, something she'd come to consider being better than therapy. After leaving Amanda's office, Savannah had always felt heavy and exhausted. Now, she felt free and relaxed. Surely that was a good sign, a sign that she didn't need therapy anymore.

As though on cue, her phone rang, startling her.

"Savannah, I just got a call from the therapist's office. You've missed two sessions." There were no introductions, no niceties. She was in trouble, a concept she'd been very familiar with after many teenage years of disappointing her father.

"I can explain," Savannah said.

"I'm coming over now. You'd better be home when I get there."

The line went dead. Perfect. It wouldn't take long for her dad to arrive, and her being in pyjamas would not give a good impression. She wanted to show that she'd been productive. Stuffing herself into jeans and an oversized jumper, Savannah rushed downstairs to put the kettle on. Anything to appease him.

The door swung open without so much as a knock. Of course he had a key. Why didn't she think of that? He could come over whenever he wanted.

"Savannah," he called when he walked into the hallway.

“Kitchen,” she shouted back, holding her breath and trying to look composed. The argument was already formed in her head. All she had to do was convince him that she was right.

When he walked into the room, his face was reddened. He shook his head and pursed his lips, a tell-tale sign that she had properly disappointed him.

“Here.” She handed him a cup of tea and gestured for him to sit at the kitchen table. Her father did so but grudgingly. “I can explain…”

“I’m sure you’re going to try,” he said, looking at her in a way that turned her insides to jelly.

“I’m feeling loads better, Dad. I’m on top of everything. I’m getting firsts in everything. I have a social life again. I have a boyfriend, and El. Things are good. Therapy has worked, and I don’t need to go anymore.”

“It worries me that you think that’s true.” His eyes pierced into her. It took all of her resolve to hold his stare.

“That I think what’s true?” Savannah sat across the table from her father, feeling better about there being a little distance between them. He’d never laid a hand on her, but her dad was an intimidating man when he wanted to be.

“That you think you’re fixed.” He shook his head, pursing his lips.

“I am fixed.” Savannah furrowed her brows, becoming annoyed that her father would think she was still broken. Had she not proved to him that she was more than capable of being normal again?

“Therapy isn’t a thing you do for a few months, and then everything is okay. You have to stick with it, Sav. I know you. I know how easily led you are. If you meet a person who’s not good for you, you’ll be straight back to your old ways if you’re not strong enough to stick up for yourself. That’s what I’m worried about. There’s only so much I can do to protect you. Therapy is part of that, and it is really bloody expensive. You need to go. That’s the end of it.”

“And what if I don’t want to go?” Savannah gritted her teeth as she spoke.

“What you want has nothing to do with it. You will continue to go because I tell you to. It’s not up for discussion.” His chair screeched back from the table, and he stood before her, staring down at her with an icy coldness, until he started pacing the room.

“I won’t go anymore. I’m better. I really am. You don’t need to worry about me.”

“Are you kidding? Do you hear yourself? I don’t need to worry about you? You nearly killed yourself. God only knows what would have happened if you hadn’t ended up in the hospital that night. Never mind what happened afterwards. What you went through with those cows you used to call friends. You will go to therapy and that’s the end of it.”

“I don’t need to, Dad. I’m fine!” Savannah said, trying to keep her voice stable.

“You’re fine? You’ve been cooped up in your bedroom all the time. You don’t have a boyfriend. You lied, Sav. You’re not fine at all.” Her dad turned to look at her, a vein at his temple popping uncontrollably.

“What?” Savannah tried to wrap her head around what her father had just said.

“You’re lying to me. You’re not fine. You made up a boyfriend. You spend all your time in your room.”

“But how?” Savannah said. Her father’s words didn’t make sense. How could he know? “El?”

“Of course! Why do you think I let you live here? She tells me everything, Sav. It’s the only way I can keep you safe.”

“You’re spying on me?” Savannah’s face broke out into an angry smile. El wasn’t her friend. Her father was using El to keep tabs on her. But why would she do that? “Why would she?”

Her father knew he’d said something he shouldn’t have. He rubbed his hands over his face and sighed.

“You’re paying her,” Savannah said. It wasn’t a question. Why else would another student turn into a spy?

“I had to. To keep you safe.”

“What kind of person are you? That’s sick. Does she report to you every night or something?” Savannah was reaching boiling point.

“It’s not like that at all.”

“That’s what it sounds like to me. You have her on the payroll for God’s sake. Get out of my house,” Savannah said, heading towards the door. “Do you know what? I felt bad until now. You’re a sick, sick man. I don’t want to speak to you ever again.”

Savannah left the room and headed upstairs. She needed to be alone, to plan what she’d do next. The prospect of facing El made her face ache. Slamming the bedroom door behind her, Savannah’s chest heaved. She felt tears pricking at the corners of her eyes, but they just wouldn’t come.

“Fuck,” she said, throwing her fist into her pillow over and over again.

Savannah awoke to a knocking on the door. She had no recollection of falling asleep but the scene out of the window showed her that it was no longer daytime. The sky was an inky purple, turning to black.

“I need to talk to you,” El’s voice came through the door, muffled and hesitant.

“I don’t want to talk to you,” Savannah said, aware that her voice made her sound like a bitch.

“I’m sorry, okay?” El said. Savannah heard her slide down the other side of the door, she could picture El crossed legged and resting against the frame.

When Savannah didn’t respond, El continued, “Look, when I agreed to do it, I didn’t know you. I needed money and a housemate, and it seemed like fate. I just had to keep an eye on you and check you were okay, that's it. I felt bad for you, with what happened with your old roommates. I really thought I was helping. Honestly."

"That's not it at all. You have to give feedback to my dad, reporting on my behaviour. That's low." Savannah pressed her eyes shut and prayed for El to go away. She just wanted to be alone.

"I'm your friend, Sav. I am. I'm sorry, I should have stopped it sooner, but I thought that maybe I was doing something good. When you first moved in, you were so fragile, and you were getting better. I didn't think…"

The words washed over Savannah. They were painful to consider, and so she didn't. Instead, she reached under the bed, into the hidden drawers, and pulled out a mini bottle of vodka. It held barely more than a shot, but it would be enough to take the edge off. Just one would do, and then she'd be able to confront El and tell her exactly how she really felt.

The liquid burned her throat as she swallowed deeply. The familiar sensation erased any regret she was feeling deep within her. Her father had driven her to this. If he hadn't spied on her, invaded her privacy, then she wouldn't have needed a drink.

Cameron

The messages had been incessant for the last few days. Cameron had done his best to ignore them, pushing them out of his memory and trying to enjoy the holidays. He'd eventually stopped opening them, after the images had become more and more graphic, and the words had become more threatening. The last straw had been what looked like a long-handled knife sticking out of the poor sod's neck. It took everything within him to not think of it as *his* neck, because it couldn't be his neck. If it was, he'd be dead. It was just that simple.

It didn't help matters that he'd barely seen Liz. She'd been invited out by Rose, Wendy, and Helen. They were having a girl's night. As such, Liz had spent all of her free time planning her outfit and buying new shoes.

"They won't care what you wear, they're not like that." Cameron had tried to assure her, but she wouldn't have any of it.

"I really like them, and I want them to like me too. If we're going to be together, then this is important. I want them to like me as much as they like you, if not more." Liz winked and kissed Cameron on the lips.

When the evening finally came, Cameron felt uneasy. Something about Liz spending time with his friends, alone, didn't sit right. He'd known them since he was in university, and they knew far too many things about him. The girls he'd slept with. The stupid drunken things he'd done. He supposed Liz would find out most of those things eventually, but it would have been nice to be there to supervise how they were revealed.

As Liz left, trailing behind Rose and into the taxi, Cameron tried to calm himself. "Have fun. Don't do anything I wouldn't do," Cameron called after them.

"Well, that doesn't leave a lot." Rose laughed. He laughed too, as he felt prickles of worry pierce his skin. Perhaps he should have told Rose, Wendy, and Helen to go easy on the incriminating stories, but surely that would only have egged them on. He should have organized a guy's night for the same night, but that took too much planning. They were babysitting their own kids tonight, after all, so the mums could go out.

Cameron passed the time by watching Netflix and going to bed early. By the time 3 o'clock had rolled around, and Liz still hadn't come home, he'd begun to worry. Three am nights out didn't happen to him anymore. They hadn't for a few years. And there he was, waiting for his girlfriend to come home.

When the door opened, and he heard Liz creep inside, he felt like he could finally relax. She'd come home to him, at least, so the stories his friends had told couldn't have been too bad.

"Hi," Cameron said as Liz stumbled into the bedroom. Her makeup had smudged slightly, like he was looking at her through dirty glasses, but she still looked incredible. The figure-hugging dress she'd chosen would have definitely put everyone else to shame.

"Hi there," Liz said. She caught her foot under the rug as she walked over to the bed. "I missed you tonight."

"I missed you too," Cameron said. "You a little tipsy?"

"Just a smidge." Liz laughed, holding her finger and thumb together to indicate how drunk she was.

"You deserve a night to let loose. You work hard," Cameron said. He wanted to be supportive but, in all honesty, he was a little annoyed that she'd come home in such a state, having not messaged him all night either.

"How are the girls?" Cameron asked.

"They were all good. Wendy was crying though. I told you things weren't right between her and Reese." Cameron sat up like he'd been shocked.

"Wait a minute. You asked her about that? Why would you do that?"

"Girls look out for each other, Cameron. I had to." Liz swayed slightly as she spoke.

"And what did she say?"

Liz shook her head. "I'm not supposed to say." She held her finger to her lips like a child would when keeping a secret.

“You have to tell me. They’re my friends, Liz. If something is wrong, I should know.” He tried to keep the exasperated tone out of his voice. He was so unbelievably annoyed at her for putting him in this position, but he needed to know.

“I shouldn’t,” Liz said. He could already tell from the tone of her voice that she was going to tell him.

“Okay, but you can’t tell her I told you.”

“I promise,” Cameron said. His skin felt simultaneously warm and cold as he waited for her to speak. He knew Reese was a good person, that he wouldn’t hurt Wendy. He’d loved her since university. Of course, around that time, they’d both cheated on one another. It was the way most university relationships went. There were too many tempting options to stay faithful to one person. From the sounds of it, both Wendy and Reese had been fine with the set-up at the time.

“Wendy caught him taking pictures of her when she was sleeping.” Liz’s eyes went wide when she spoke, like she was telling the most torrid piece of gossip she’d ever heard.

“So?” Cameron said. If Wendy was curled up looking cute and Reese wanted to snap a photo, then what harm did that cause?

“She was naked, and he’d pose her.”

“Oh,” Cameron said. That was different. And, admittedly, it did sound more like the Reese he knew than taking cute photographs did. If their university days had been anything to go by, Reese had always been a bit of a weirdo in the sex department. But taking posed, nude photos, well, that was creepier than anything he'd ever done before, to Cameron's knowledge.

"I know. Can you imagine doing that to a person? It's sick, isn't it?"

"Are you sure that's what Wendy said? You are a little drunk and I'll bet she was too." Cameron searched his mind, grasping at straws to make what he'd heard okay. To justify it in some way.

"I know what I heard. I told her to go to the police, but she wouldn't. I said that I'd ask you to speak to him and she made me promise that I wouldn't do that either. I don't know what to do. I mean, he hasn't raped her. Is it technically abuse if he hasn't touched her?"

Cameron didn't know what to say. It was abuse in his eyes. There were no two ways about it. But they were married and had been for a long time. Did that change things? It was too much to sift through at four o'clock in the morning.

"Let's talk about this tomorrow," Cameron suggested. He needed time to get his thoughts straight.

"Okay," Liz nodded gratefully. "I'm going to get some water and I'll come to bed."

When Liz returned to the room, Cameron pretended to be asleep. He didn't want to risk the conversation picking up again.

Savannah

Savannah stumbled through the doors of the club. Alone and in her day clothes, a pair of jeans and a checked shirt that she wouldn't usually be seen dead in on a night out. But this wasn't an ordinary night out. If she hadn't uncovered the conspiracy theory between her dad and El, then she would be safe and sound at home, drinking a cup of tea and watching a soap on TV. Instead, she was well on her way to drunk and in a bar that she couldn't quite remember the name of. The name tugged at her consciousness, and she thought it might be some kind of fruit, but she couldn't be certain. It didn't matter. The music was loud, and her purse was full of notes she'd collected from the cash machine. She scanned the crowd for a familiar face. If she saw Gemma or Penny, then she'd have to leave and go somewhere else. She couldn't handle being around them, not after the day she'd had.

It was the argument with El that had triggered the whole thing. She'd only had one mini bottle of vodka before it started. But then El had continued to talk at her through the door about how she was only trying to do her best for Savannah and that she really was her friend, she promised. Friends didn't spy on friends. Friends didn't take payment from friends' dads as reparations for the aforementioned spying.

Betrayal had made her blood run hot in her veins and she needed to let off steam. By the third mini bottle, she'd been brave enough to climb out of the window and down the trellis attached to the side of the house. The descent had been terrifying, and she'd ripped her jeans in a couple of places, but none of that mattered. She was out of the house and El still thought she was in her bedroom. Finally, she was safe from the watchful gaze of big brother.

At the bar, Savannah took advantage of the offer. Five Jager bombs for the price of three. Lining them up in a row, and tipping one back after another, Savannah allowed the velvet liquid to slide down her throat. She revelled in the taste, having gone so long without it. The warm feeling in her stomach made her feel ready for anything.

It was after the final gulp that she saw him. The guy from the coffee shop. Mark, who was probably not called Mark. The guy she'd spent the last few weeks daydreaming about. Creating scenarios in her head that made her fall in love with him. His group of friends were standing on the other side of the dance floor. They were all dressed in polo shirts and jeans, and they all looked almost identical. Except for Mark.

Savannah breathed out, trying to think for a moment. It seemed that fate had brought her here, tonight. Why else would this happen on a day when Mark and his friends were out? It was too much of a coincidence to be an actual coincidence. The dancefloor seemed like her best bet to bridge the gap between them. She might even get him to notice her that way. And maybe, then, he'd approach her. Mark had smiled at her in the café that day, after all.

The song was a familiar one, Avicii maybe, she wasn't entirely sure, but it was one she'd danced to before. An anthem that made every person want to throw their arms up in the air and forget themselves. But not Mark and his friends. They stayed where they were, watching the dancefloor like hawks, trying to see if somebody took their fancy. Mark's friends looked lecherous, like they were trying to choose a slab of meat to devour. But not Mark. He was looking directly at Savannah, smiling, and biting his lip.

In response, Savannah turned around so that her back was to him. She wasn't like the other girls in the club that night. They were all dressed like sluts, but she gave off the impression that she didn't care what she looked like. She wasn't on the pull. She was just there to have fun. If experience had taught her anything, it was that guys liked girls who were different.

Throwing her hair back and letting the lyrics fall from her mouth, the strobe lighting bounced off her skin. Savannah knew that he was still watching her. Waiting to make his move. All it would take was for her to smile back, once, and he'd be over there, proving that he liked her too. That he'd been dreaming about her since the day they'd met, just as she had been thinking of him.

Turning, Savannah caught his eye once more, breaking into a smile and raising her eyebrows. That was it. All it had taken, and he was beside her. She felt like she was dreaming. It was all coming together. The smell of his aftershave was overwhelmingly manly, mixed with a gentler scent of washing powder. His hand pressed into hers, his fingers sliding between her own.

They were facing each other, their eyes fixed, smiles plastered onto their faces. When he pulled her closer, Savannah could have screamed with glee. Instead, she pushed her body against him, allowing his hands to explore what was hidden beneath the modest clothes. He must have liked what he felt, as Savannah felt him harden against her, even through his jeans.

"Can I get you a drink?" he whispered into her ear between songs.

"Sure," Savannah said, allowing herself to be pulled from the dancefloor and over to the bar.

"What do you want?" he asked. His smile almost made her melt into her tatty old converse.

"Whatever you're having," she said, having to look away as she spoke. The way he looked at her sent shivers down her spine, and she wasn't sure she could behave like an actual human being if she continued to look into his eyes.

"I'm having a Tiger, will that do?" He tilted his head when he spoke to her, standing much taller than she did. Definitely over six foot. His long fringe fell forward when he did. it was so cute that she had to hold herself back from pushing it out of his eyes.

"Perfect," she said, although she had no idea what a Tiger was.

As it would turn out, it was a brand of beer. And it was also on offer.

"Two and a half each?" he laughed, gesturing to the five beers that had been placed on the bar.

"Are you sure? I can…" Savannah started rummaging through her bag trying to find her purse. One drink was fine, but buying her two and a half, she had to offer him something.

"No, my treat. Come on, let's go and find a booth and we can talk for a bit." Savannah held onto two beers, while Mark took three. Weaving her way behind him, Savannah couldn't help but notice how the girls in the club looked at him when he walked by. She wasn't the only one whose eye he had caught.

Only one booth was free, the farthest from the bar. A darkened corner where the revolving strobe lights never quite reached. The sticky leather benches would have stuck to her bare skin, if she'd had any on show. It was the kind of material you'd always avoid sitting on if you were wearing a dress, although that hadn't prevented many of the girls from laying themselves out in other booths like Kate Winslet from the Titanic. "Paint me like one of your French girls, Jack!"

"I'm Zack," Mark said.

"Oh," Savannah replied. The shock of Mark's name not actually being Mark had taken her by surprise. "I'm Savannah."

"Whoa, that's a beautiful name. Does it mean something?"

"It means 'open plain.' You know, like the desert," Savannah answered quickly. This was a question she was asked a lot and so the answer was prepared and ready to go.

"Wow, that's sweet! So, what do you do?" His voice was raised over the sound of the music. They had to lean close to hear one another. Savannah could feel his hot breath against her neck.

"I'm a student. Creative writing. What about you?" She'd imagined that he was doing something like law or engineering when she'd been dreaming about him.

"English language, so I guess that's something we have in common. Similar fields."

"Yeah," Savannah agreed. She didn't know what to say next. In her dreams, the conversation had always flowed easily, although, she had to admit, there wasn't much talking in her dreams

"So," Savannah said, when she'd got fed up with smiling at him sheepishly and waiting for him to say something.

His lips were against hers so suddenly that she almost jumped backwards. He tasted of beer, as she'd expected. His lips were soft, as she'd hoped. She kissed him back deeply, opening her lips and allowing him to explore her mouth with his tongue.

The vague sound of his friends' wolf-whistling in the background couldn't tear them apart. But her need to breathe did.

"Whoa," Savannah breathed heavily, reaching for a beer from the middle of the table.

Zack laughed shyly. "Fucking hell." He was panting too. The fact that she'd made him breathless made her want to be close to him again, as soon as possible. Downing her beer, and then reaching for another (only half of which was technically hers) she downed that too, slamming the empty bottle back onto the table and leaning closer to Mark. Zack.

"You're something else," he admired, pulling her against him once more.

Time seemed to, all at once, move both too quickly and not at all.

"Let's go back to my place," he said. "Let me tell my roommates we're leaving. They might want to share the taxi home."

Savannah's heart leapt as she smiled and nodded, contorting her face into something that she hoped didn't portray just how eager she was to follow him home.

She waited patiently as Zack went to find his roommates. She hoped that they wouldn't want to come back at the same time as them. Sharing a taxi with his mates wouldn't be quite so romantic.

When he walked over, a friend standing on either side of him, Savannah tried not to show how disappointed she was.

"Ready?" Zack said. His friends were practically salivating over her. It made her feel sick to her stomach. How could Zack live with these people? It didn't make sense. He was so lovely, and they were, well, gross. The last thing she wanted to do was alienate his friends, and so she reached over, shaking their hands in a way that made sense to a drunk person.

"Savannah," she said.

"Mitchell," the taller of the two said.

"Reese," the other said. He looked older than Zack and Mitchell, by quite a considerable amount.

They walked out together to the taxi, Savannah's hand in Zack's. It was nice that he wanted to hold her hand, especially in front of his friends.

The taxi seemed to be waiting outside of the door to the club, which was perfect, because the heavens had suddenly opened, or at least they'd opened some time after Savannah had arrived at the club. Either way, the fact that the taxi was waiting outside was beyond perfect.

She and Zack crawled into the backseat, along with Mitchell. Reese got in the front next to the taxi driver. He immediately struck up a conversation about something Savannah had no intention of listening to. She turned away from Mitchell and sidled closer to Zack.

Pushed up against one another in the backseat, so that her body fit in the crux of Zack's side, Savannah breathed in the scent of him. The clean scent from earlier had now been mixed with something else, tangy and sweet. The smell of his sweat mixed with aftershave. The arm that wasn't wrapped around her, caressed Savannah's leg, painfully slowly, stopping just before her apex. When she turned her head to look at him, he was smiling down at her.

Leaving the taxi was a blur, as was walking through the door to his flat and to his bedroom. His roommates vanished, which suited Savannah perfectly. A hurried experience that made her ache for him. He evidently wanted her as much as she wanted him.

Mark closed the door behind him and locked it swiftly. From her position on his bed, Savannah watched as he walked deliberately over to her, opening her knees with his hands and sliding his body over the top of her. The full weight of his body against her should have hurt, but it didn't. It felt right. His hands found her hair, and hers found his shirt, pulling it over his head and landing on the lean body below. Mark was on his elbows, leaning so he could pull her shirt off, and then her bra. He adjusted himself so he could tear down her jeans, and then his own. When they were completely naked, he placed himself back on top of her. She could feel his erection pressed against her, and she arched her back to show how much she wanted him.

He was inside her, his lips pressed against her neck as his breathing quickened. It felt incredible, like it had never felt before. Savannah almost expected to see butterflies and fireworks.

Mark's moan was loud and made her stomach knot. He stopped moving, lying on top of her once more.

"Wow," he breathed, rolling off to the side and smiling at her. "That was… Just, wow."

"Yeah," Savannah said, not sure what else to say. Disappointment curled in the pit of her stomach. That wasn't how she'd imagined it would be, and she'd imagined loads of different scenarios.

Zack, *not Mark*, placed his arm over the top of her and pulled her against him, so that her back was against his stomach. It felt nice to have the heat of him behind her, so nice that she managed to write the sex off as beginner's nerves. Next time would be better.

As his gentle snores became regular, and his breathing became slower, Savannah too found herself tugged into sleep, unable to remember the last time she'd slept, like actually slept, with a guy she liked and wanted to be around. Her dreams were of Mark, and what would happen in the morning when they woke up together.

Cameron

Christmas day had rolled around far too quickly, and Cameron found himself sitting in his mother's living room, with Liz at his side, and the whole family bustling around him. Never before had he felt like an outsider in his childhood home. This time was different. As he sat there, detached from the conversations around him, the happy and cheerful buzz, he found it harder to push the messages out of his mind. In his pocket, his phone kept vibrating, signalling another unwanted message. Possibly. There was always a chance that it was one of his friends or colleagues wishing him a merry Christmas, but he didn't want to take the risk and open his phone, just in case it confirmed what he dreaded the most. His plan of acting nonchalant and ignoring the stalker had only seemed to infuriate him more.

His mother's voice broke him from his thoughts. "Cammy, what's wrong? Why the long face?" She was bouncing one of his nephews on her lap and drinking a glass of sherry.

"Nothing, Mum, sorry. What were you saying?" Cameron tried to paint a smile on his face, one which might convince his mum that he was telling the truth, although she'd always had an uncanny ability to figure out when he was lying.

"You were away with the fairies for a while there, Cammy. Something is wrong. I'll figure it out. Wait, do you have news for us? Is that why you're being weird. Are you and Liz pregnant? Is that why you moved in together so soon?"

"No, Mum!" Cameron half-laughed, half-shouted. He looked to Liz, who was currently holding a jug-sized glass of red wine and shook his head.

"You don't have to sound so offended." Liz elbowed him in the ribs, playfully. Neither of them had mentioned Wendy and Reese since her night out. It was an unspoken agreement between the two of them. He had caught Liz furiously texting a few times, to Wendy he'd assumed. But other than that, it was like the conversation had never happened. That suited him just fine. Things were far easier before he'd found out about Reese. Besides, Wendy was a big girl; she could take care of herself.

"So you're not pregnant, Liz? Are you sure? You're looking a little bloated." Cameron's mum laughed, almost sloshing the sherry onto the child.

"No, but thank you, Mrs Nicholson. I appreciate that." Liz laughed kindly, and Cameron wanted to crawl into a hole and die.

"Mum, you can't say things like that to people. And Liz, you look incredible, as always. Ignore her." At that moment, it should have been easy to forget everything that was happening behind the scenes. The messages, the torture, the stalker, but it still niggled in the back of his mind.

"I'm an old lady, Cammy. I can say whatever I bloody well want," she said indignantly.

"First of all, you're not old at all. You're sixty-three, Mum. And secondly, you can't be asking women if they're pregnant, full stop. It's like the first rule of being a properly functioning human being."

"Who's pregnant?" Cameron's sister, Jessica, peeped her head around the door.

"Nobody, apparently," his mum said, rolling her eyes like Cameron was the one at fault. A regular old Christmas in the Nicholson household.

"Dinner's ready, if that's the case," Jessica said, beckoning the group into the dining room. Cameron's mother hadn't cooked a Christmas dinner since the year she gave everybody food poisoning, and so the baton had been passed onto Jessica, who didn't mind too much, and simply drank twice as much wine to accommodate for her new job.

The Christmas dinner was laid out buffet style, along the kitchen worktops, and Cameron waited patiently for the rest of the family to fill their plates before he filled his own. Liz went first, as it was her first Christmas with the family. Then his mother and sister, followed by his sister's partner, Jeremy, and their teenage son Troy. Their smallest child, the one who had taken up residence on his grandma's knee, was Walter, who had been placed in a highchair at the side of Jessica.

The table was filled with laughter and conversation, as it always was at Christmas. Liz fitted into the dynamics perfectly, taking all of the gentle teasing she was subjected to on the chin. Cameron noticed Jeremy's eyes flickering to Liz's low neckline every so often, which should have annoyed him, but instead filled him with a strange sense of pride. Yes, he'd managed to catch this incredibly beautiful, intelligent, and witty woman.

Grabbing hold of Liz's hand under the table, and giving it a squeeze, Cameron felt a rush of love for her. She really was perfect, and had stuck by his side, even though he was very clearly going a little crazy at the moment.

Liz looked to him, quizzically, before smiling and squeezing his hand back. Troy was regaling his grandma with the story of his latest skateboarding accident, in which he bruised his tailbone, and his ego, and managed to make himself sound heroic in the process. The video of the event, which Jessica had sent to Cameron, proved to be extremely different from the story Troy was weaving.

"What are you thinking about?" Liz asked him. It's always a dangerous question, particularly from a partner or somebody you're dating.

"How lucky I am," Cameron said, which wasn't strictly true, but from the smile growing on Liz's face, he knew it was the right thing to say.

"Do you ever think about having kids?" Liz asked, nodding across the table to where Troy was still recounting his heroic tale, and where Walter was smashing mashed potato into the tray of his highchair.

Cameron's body flushed in response to the question. Liz had a special talent for asking loaded questions at exactly the wrong time. There was always a response that the other party wanted, and if you answered incorrectly, that was the end of the relationship right there and then. The truth was that he did want children. But Liz didn't necessarily seem like the child-rearing type, with her expensive (and incredibly well-tailored) clothes and important job.

"Honestly," Cameron started, steeling himself for the rejection that would inevitably occur. "I do. I love children, and I'm in a place in my life where I'm ready to start properly thinking about it."

The conversation was whispered in hushed tones between the two of them, protecting their words from the rest of the room.

"Me too," Liz said. "I always wanted children. And, you know, at our age when *accidents* happen, they tend to be happy ones, right?"

"Sure. I mean, when you're comfortable and have the means to take care of a child, then I suppose accidents are happy ones."

Cameron knew he was being auditioned for the role of baby-daddy and he wasn't entirely sure how he felt about that.

"Don't you think it's strange that when you're younger, having a baby feels like the worst thing in the world that could possibly happen to you, and at some point in our lives, people actually decide to start making them? It's like a switch gets flicked, and it goes from being the worst thing ever, to the best thing ever." Liz shook her head like she was amazed by how strange humans, and their desire (or not) for children, were.

"Very strange," Cameron agreed, gulping down the rest of his wine and wondering where Liz was going with the conversation. Yes, having a baby was something he'd like in the future, but if the aim of this conversation was to start trying for a baby now, especially in the midst of everything going on, well, that would be out of the question completely.

Thankfully, the conversation was dropped as Jeremy had finally worked up the nerve to ask Liz about her job.

Cameron was sucked back into a conversation about nothing whatsoever with his mum and Jessica, and the children headed back to the front room to play with their toys (or their phones in Troy's case) and watch TV.

"Uncle Cam!" Troy shouted from the front room.

"Yes," Cameron called back.

"Your phone is vibrating. You have a text or something." His voice was tinged with annoyance about the fact he'd had to act as secretary for his uncle.

"It's okay, I'll get it later," Cameron said, the familiar rush of panic blooming inside his chest.

"But it looks urgent, it's gone off like six times!"

"Fine, I'm coming." Cameron all but stomped off into the front room and retrieved the phone from his nephew's sweaty palm.

If he returned to the kitchen, he'd be asked who the messages were from and have to make up something plausible. He should look at the messages. Ignoring them for much longer wouldn't do any good. He'd managed to pretend they didn't exist (somewhat unsuccessfully) until now, and with a bottle of wine coursing through his system, he felt relatively confident he could cope with whatever had been sent, he could handle it.

Cameron threw himself down onto the sofa, beside Walter, who was staring at the TV, wide-eyed and tired. He unlocked the phone and clicked on the message icon.

Troy wasn't kidding when he said there had been loads of messages. A few from work, which he answered quickly, building himself up to the one conversation he didn't want to click on.

WHERE HAVE YOU BEEN?

WE MISS YOU.

WE LOVE HOW YOU DECORATED THE PLACE.

MERRY CHRISTMAS, HERE'S A SPECIAL PHOTOGRAPH JUST FOR YOU.

That message was followed by a photograph of the man on the chair. Only, this time, it was very clearly Cameron. There was no mistaking it at all. Not that he hadn't been certain the last photograph was also him, but this time, it confirmed it. The head slumped backwards so that the face could be seen by the camera. There were black eyes still, and the face was matted with blood. But it was, without any doubt, him. The picture was so clear, that you could see the day-old stubble on his cheeks.

The room filled with suffocating heat, and his head began to swim around him. The tortured man was Cameron. There was no plausible doubt left in his mind that this was the case. But he still didn't have an explanation on how that was possible. How could he have been tortured, stabbed, and beaten, and be here to tell the tale? And not have any memory or scars from the process?

With the phone in his hand, Cameron felt it buzz once more. Closing his eyes, he scrolled back to the most recent message. It was a picture of Cameron without any trousers on, still tied to the chair in the hideous room. The bottom half of his body was completely naked, his penis shrivelled and contorted against his thighs. His face was in the picture, which left no room for any questions regarding who the picture was of. Even if his face hadn't been visible, he'd have recognised himself. What man wouldn't?

His eyes found the knife that was pressed into the scrotum, so hard that it was denting the skin. A tiny droplet of blood circled the tip of the knife.

The message tone vibrated once more.

NO BABIES FOR YOU.

Savannah

When she awoke, she was alone. The soft, warm bedsheets cocooned around her, but Zack was nowhere to be seen. Instinctually, Savannah presumed that he'd simply gone to the bathroom and waited for him to either return, or to hear the shower turn on. When neither happened, she decided to venture out and look for him. The house was eerily quiet, and the alarm clock on his bedside table blinked that it was 11 am. Hopefully, that would mean that Zack's housemates were in lectures, and she could sneak out of the house without seeing anybody, except for Zack, who might be making breakfast for her, the prospect of which made her smile. It was definitely the kind of thing he would do.

Pulling on her clothes, Savannah saw that there was a note on the sideboard. Her heart plummeted as she picked it up and read it, knowing that Zack had gone without saying goodbye.

Thanks for last night.

Had an early lecture this morning and didn't want to wake you up.

Below the words was Zack's phone number, which, Savannah supposed, was a good sign. It must mean that he wanted to see her again. Knowing that she wasn't going to find Zack anywhere in the house, Savannah headed out of the door and walked the hour-long walk home.

She wasn't at all looking forward to seeing El after last night's arguments. However, over the course of the previous night, Savannah had come to terms with some things. Firstly, she loved living in that house and didn't want to leave. Secondly, El wasn't entirely the one at fault. The blame lay, very clearly, with her father. Thirdly, El was her only friend and, with a bit of compassion, they might be able to work it out, but only if El stopped spying on her and telling her dad of her every move.

When she opened the door, El ran down the hallway and flung herself at Savannah.

"Oh my God, you're okay. Where have you been? I was so worried!"

"You mean my dad was worried?" Savannah said, unable to let the bitterness drop from her voice just yet.

"No, I mean me. I didn't tell your dad anything, I promise. I feel so bad about what happened. I really was just trying to do the right thing. You're my best friend, Sav, I shouldn't have done what I did." El was standing a few feet away, her arms draped by her side. The very picture of sorrow.

"No, you shouldn't have. But…" Savannah took a deep breath. "I understand why you did it. You didn't know me, and it got out of hand. Do you promise that it's over?"

"Yes, I promise. I'll tell your dad I won't do it anymore. That it isn't right." El closed the gap between the two of them and placed her arms around Savannah once more.

"Well, maybe don't be so rash. It might come in handy…" Savannah said, pulling away.

"What do you mean?" El asked, raising her eyebrow.

"If you tell my dad that I'm doing well, and that I'm better, maybe he'll back off. I won't have to see the therapist anymore, and he'll let me just get on with things."

"I don't know," El said, tentatively. The look on her face showed that she was thinking about the proposition.

"You owe me, El. This could make my life so much easier! So much better. Please?"

After a pause, El said, "Sure, okay. Let's do it. But only if you promise to tell me what you got up to last night."

"It would be my pleasure." Savannah smiled as the pair of them walked into the kitchen arm in arm.

"I met a guy last night," Savannah confessed.

"I presumed as much when you didn't come home. Tell me about him." El stuck the kettle on and pulled mugs out of the cupboard. It was her go-to response to anything that happened in life, good or bad.

"Well, I've seen him around campus before. He's incredibly hot, like next-level hot." Savannah hesitated, trying to decide how much of the story to tell. She definitely couldn't tell El that she'd dreamed about this guy for the longest time before they got together. And that she'd fantasised about everything from their first date, to having kids. That this guy, alone, had got her through her exams. It made her sound crazy, and she wasn't crazy.

"What does he look like?" El asked, placing the coffees on the table and leaning over.

"Kind of like a young Keanu Reeves, or Christian Slater. Dark hair, tall, mysterious. You know, exactly my type!" Savannah laughed as memories of their intimate conversations, and their bodies intertwined, came rushing back to her.

"That is exactly your type! So, sort of like a dark-haired Edward Cullen?" El said, poking fun at Savannah's minor crush on the vampire from *Twilight*.

"Yes, pretty much exactly that!"

"So, what did you do?" El pushed further, drinking in the gossip.

"We met at a club, I know I shouldn't be drinking, but I didn't drink loads. Just a little, which proves I'm better, don't you think?" A white lie, but a necessary one. "Anyway, we danced, talked, and really got to know each other. He's just perfect, and did I mention how hot he is? Like, every other girl in the club had their eyes fixed onto him, and he left with me!"

"Why wouldn't he leave with you? You're gorgeous, Sav. You don't give yourself enough credit." El tapped her hand onto Savannah's in a comforting gesture, waiting for the rest of the story.

"We went back to his house, and in the taxi, we couldn't keep our hands off each other. It was like something you read about in books or see in movies. And then we went to bed. He was so tender and loving. It was incredible. I didn't know that sex could be like that." Savannah felt her skin flush as she spoke. It was usually El telling her stories of her sexcapades, not the other way around.

"It sounds amazing! I'm happy for you. When are you seeing him again?"

"He had to go to a lecture this morning, so he wasn't there when I woke up. He let me lie in! But he left me this sweet note and his phone number, so I'll text him later."

Savannah's cheeks were starting to hurt but the smile on her face just wouldn't go away.

"I'm happy for you," El said.

"Yeah, me too."

Savannah got up the nerve to message Zack at around 7 pm that evening. She didn't want to appear to be clingy or annoying, and thought that leaving it until later on was her best bet.

She spent a solid half an hour deciding what to write, wanting it to sound casual but also let him know she was interested. It was a fine balance between the two. She finally settled on.

Hi Zack,

Had a lovely time last night.

Fancy meeting up for coffee or something?

Savannah x

She held her breath as she pressed the send button, hoping the reply would come quickly. When it didn't, Savannah decided to busy herself by changing her bed and having a bath. By the time she got out, surely he'd have responded.

Nothing.

There was likely a good explanation though. He might be at the gym, or somewhere he couldn't have his phone on, like the cinema.

For the rest of that evening, every fifteen minutes, Savannah found herself checking her phone for a message. Each time she was disappointed, and the feeling of embarrassment and upset ballooned in the pit of her stomach.

She went to sleep that night having not heard from him. And awoke the next morning to the exact same thing. As much as she tried to deny it, maybe Zack wasn't like she'd dreamed he would be.

Cameron

There was no better way to describe how Cameron was feeling than an overwhelming sense of dread. The photograph was already scorched into his mind. He closed the screen off instantly. The phone turned into a mirror. His face looked back at him. His eyes were puffed out, wrinkles deepening across his forehead like scratches peeling their way across his skin. Burning with humiliation, his breathing came in ragged jumps. There was talking around him, children arguing, his family talking, Liz laughing. None of it penetrated his senses. He was lost to the world. Numb.

Staring back at his reflection in the phone's black surface, Cameron tried desperately to keep a hold of himself. To figure out what the hell he was going to do next. That photo. It caused his throat to burn, his legs to weaken. He hadn't thought it could get any worse. And then the photograph. The words.

NO BABIES FOR YOU.

The knife against his naked crotch. Glinting surface against mottled skin.

Pulling himself upright, Cameron stumbled to the bathroom, vaguely aware of a voice asking him what was wrong. He couldn't answer. No words would come to him. The questions were distant, as though he was underwater. He wasn't sure why this time should be any different. His body had shown no other signs of any other forms of torture. Why should this be any different?

Climbing the stairs felt like climbing Everest. Cameron could barely draw in a breath, never mind stand upright. By the time he'd slammed the bathroom door closed behind him, and jammed the lock into place, Cameron felt like he'd lost himself entirely. Sinking into a puddle on the floor, he stripped off his trousers awkwardly, throwing them into a crumpled mess in the corner of the room. An abandoned dog shying away from an abusive owner. His underwear followed. He didn't have the energy to heave them towards his trousers.

His back compressed against the icy tiles. Unable to look down, Cameron allowed his head to loll backwards, crunching uncomfortably against the wall.

"This isn't right. This can't be happening to me," Cameron muttered over and over again. Bangs shook the room. Somebody was at the other side of the door trying to get in. Thank God he'd locked it.

"Cameron!" It could be anybody. The voice meant nothing to him.

As his pulse pounded against his eardrums, he looked down. His penis rested there against his legs. Using his fingers, he pulled at his scrotum, trying to find a mark from the knife. A small scar, a considerable scar, anything to prove whether the photograph was real. It was impossible to prove a negative. If he'd been drugged and had blacked out, then it wasn't something he would remember. And so he needed to check. It was the only logical thing to do in that situation.

There were no marks. No scars. Nothing out of the ordinary. The photo couldn't be real. The photo wasn't real.

But it was definitely you... The voice inside his head reasoned with him. *There should be a mark. How else would they have that photograph?*

"It doesn't make sense!" Cameron snarled, slamming his hand against the wall so hard his fist crunched, and he yelped in pain. Noises of frustration left his mouth. He sounded like a wounded animal, spit leaving his lips as he tried to hold it back.

What the fuck is happening to me?

Cameron didn't know whether the words were spoken aloud or in his mind. Not that it mattered. His family already thought he was insane, after the stunt he'd just pulled.

"Shit," he said, aloud this time. The words left his mouth in a foamy mess. He stood and walked slowly over to pick up his trousers. Catching a glimpse of himself in the bathroom mirror, he was a sorry sight. No trousers. Shirt untucked. No underwear. This shouldn't happen to him. He was a put-together person. He'd always stayed abreast of things and never let anything get on top of him. Hell, he'd never even touched an anti-depressant or anti-anxiety medication. Which was saying something these days.

He dressed himself and left the room, ready to make pretend that everything was okay.

It was almost like his mother wanted to gloss over his little breakdown because when he left the bathroom she accepted the excuse of an upset stomach with a sickening ease. Liz, on the other hand, not so much. She glared at him from across the living room, her eyes boring holes into his brain. He knew that she'd ask him more when she got the chance. But he couldn't tell her about the last message. It was all too much. She'd want to see it and that couldn't happen. There was no way you could go on loving a person, or at least being attracted to them, after having seen them in such an embarrassingly awful state.

The way he looked in that photograph, Cameron was certain, would haunt him forever. The lack of power, the helplessness of it, made his skin crawl with fear. If that photo got out and people saw him so feeble, so sad, it would kill him. It wasn't the prospect of people seeing his nude body that petrified him. Hell, he'd been seen nude by plenty of people over the years. What hurt the most was people seeing him so broken and pathetic.

Trying his utmost to continue with the conversation around him, Cameron said the odd sentence, trying to appear as normal as possible. He even made excuses to visit the bathroom a couple of times to back up his story. Whenever he stood, he placed his aching hand into his pocket for fear that his family might notice the growing bruise.

On his third trip to the toilet, he made up his mind to delete the image. He wouldn't message back. That would surely just cause them more joy. The thought of the bald man laughing over his naked body while he pressed a knife into him was already too much. There was no way he was about to chance Liz seeing it too.

The photograph vanished from the chat. Cameron was still unable to breathe easily, but it came easier. The photograph no longer lived on in his phone. But did it live on elsewhere? Was it saved on somebody's computer? Or posted to their social media? God only knew where that image had circulated. The question still remained of when, and where, and how, the photograph was taken. It couldn't have already happened. The explanation that he hadn't ever been tortured seemed to withdraw that from the running.

What if it is yet to happen? What if this is somebody from the future sending me these images?

For a second, the thought seemed reasonable. Like it was the only logical explanation. Only a few moments later, he realised that this thought was beyond ridiculous. That the very fact that he was contemplating somebody from the future sending him these images proved that he'd finally reached a point of insanity in which he should seek professional help.

The phone vibrated in his dry hands.

YOU SHOULDN'T HAVE DONE THAT.

Savannah

Savannah forced herself to carry on as normal, even in lieu of a text from Zack. She hadn't expected him to answer immediately, but this was just cruel. What kind of a person waited two days to text back? There was not wanting to look desperate and then there was this. She'd have to say something when he finally answered. Make a joke about it but let him know that it wasn't acceptable.

She had assignments to do and deadlines coming up once more. Now wasn't the time to be distracted by boys. It could be worse, she supposed. She could be having her stomach pumped, another nervous breakdown, or have found more photographs of herself online. None of those things had happened, and so she should count herself lucky, she decided.

The library was the perfect place to work on her next paper. *What do modern writers tell us about the world that historians don't?* In all honesty, it was the perfect question. Something she could really get her teeth stuck into. It was sad, but she loved her degree, and this question was the equivalent to drawing the best hand in poker, she presumed, although she wasn't sure how to play poker.

Choosing a computer that overlooked the huge windows, which showcased the quad, Savannah logged in and got down to business.

She was only a few hundred words in when she heard a laugh that she was all too familiar with.

Gemma was alone, walking through the library with a stack of books in her hand. It was strange, Savannah had never actually seen her study before. The library was the last place she'd expected to bump into her. Savannah turned and looked at her computer, praying that Gemma hadn't seen her.

"Fancy seeing you here." The words caused Savannah's teeth to clench. She looked up at her ex-roommate. She hadn't changed at all. Her hair was slicked back in a bun at the base of her neck. She wore a tight jumper over loose jeans. She was every single lecturer's wet dream, until they realised she didn't actually live up to her appearance and put exactly no effort into her work.

"Please just leave me alone Gemma," Savannah said, turning back to face the computer.

"It's a public space, Savannah. I have just as much of a right to be here as you. Or is it because you're famous now? Those photos made the rounds, didn't they? I bet everyone has you signing autographs. I'm jealous." The sarcasm dripped from Gemma's voice.

"Look, Gemma, I'm over it. I know it was you and Penny. And it says more about the two of you than it does about me. I would have never done that. Ever. So just leave me alone."

"But I have work to do," Gemma said sweetly. She dumped her books on the table so that they were overlapping Savannah's workstation. *The Basics of Graphic Design. Thinking With Type. Adobe Photoshop Classroom in a Book.*

"Please," Savannah said, a final last-ditch attempt to not have to give up her space.

"I'm staying put. I'm a student, using the student library. I'm doing nothing wrong."

"Fine, whatever." Savannah gathered her stuff up while Gemma smiled at her. She wasn't sure whether she wanted to cry, scream, or lash out. Instead, she just walked away. She decided not to mention it to El. She would just get angry and want to say something and that would just make the situation worse.

When she got home, she checked the internet again, using all of her saved searches, just to make sure there were no more photographs of her online. There were none. Seeing Gemma did have a benefit, at least. It stopped her from thinking about how Zack hadn't texted back. Every cloud had a silver lining.

Still nothing. No response from Zack and it had been days, coming up to a week. She'd texted another few times, unable to prevent herself from picking up the phone and tapping the message back to him. Each time, she held her breath until she couldn't anymore. Each time: nothing. Self-loathing had begun to build up inside of her, a pressure cooker ready to explode. She still went to classes and did assignments, but her brain was fogged over with thoughts of Zack and how he'd lied to her.

"Maybe he wrote his number down wrong by accident? You could go round to his house, seeing as you spent the night there?" El suggested when Savannah told her of Zack's failure to live up to her expectations.

"Yeah, like I could just show up at his house. That doesn't suggest I'm a crazy stalker or anything, does it?" Savannah laughed, hoping it hid her true feelings. "I hope he gave me the wrong number by accident, but I'm not sure. Why hasn't he tried to find me? That night was special, or at least I thought it was. Why didn't he search for me?" Savannah sighed and threw herself back onto the living room sofa.

"Have you tried to look for him? Not at his house, of course. Like you said, that might be a bit OTT, but like, out and about?" El said, reasonably.

"Of course. I've been to the coffee shop where I first saw him every day since then and he hasn't been there. I even asked around campus to see if people know somebody named Zack who studies English language and nobody knows him. I'm starting to think he lied, and he studies something else. But why would he do that?"

“He might have wanted to impress you and try to find something you have in common. You love English, words, and books, so maybe he panicked and said he studied English language.”

El was grasping at straws but Savannah appreciated it. The disappointment was the worst. It left her feeling sluggish and heavy, like she moved more slowly than she used to. If only she could find Zack and ask him what had happened. She just needed answers, even if they weren’t exactly the answers she wanted.

“What if he gave me a fake name and number on purpose?” Savannah said, airing her thoughts aloud in the hope that it would make her feel better. It didn’t.

“Why on earth would he do that? Have you seen you?” El shook her head, answering in the way that friends do. Of course, El would think that, but boys were a different species entirely. She’d behaved in a way she thought Zack would like. Girly, pliant, and appreciative, and perhaps he’d wanted the opposite. What if he’d wanted somebody who would argue with him, be fun and ballsy? That just wasn’t Savannah.

“Why don’t we ask the admin staff at uni?” El said. The words appeared to have broken her thoughts, coming out of nowhere.

“Ask the admin staff what?” Savannah said.

“For Zack’s information. You know his address, right? You slept there. Maybe you say you found something of his and would like to return it to him, and ask for his class schedule. A letter? You found a letter addressed to him."

"But wouldn't they say to just shove it back in a letterbox?"

"Maybe. But maybe not. What else could we say we've found?" El lost herself in thought.

"What about a set of keys? It has the name Zack on it, and a key fob for the English Department. We want his phone number so we can return it to him?" Savannah suggested. There were loopholes in the plan, obviously. The fact that she could just hand the keys in, for one. The second, that anybody would be stupid enough to have their name on a key ring. But it was their only option, other than just showing up at his house, and there was no way Savannah could face the mortification of doing that.

"Perfect, let's go!" El was already out of her seat and heading for her shoes and jacket before Savannah had even registered the fact that they were going to the admin building right that second.

"What, now?" Savannah asked.

"Why not? I want to know what the hell this guy is thinking. I'll tell you something, it had better be an accident because if he's written the number down wrong on purpose, I'm not going to be a happy lady," El said, putting her fist into the air like a suffragette.

"Sure, okay." Savannah scuttled around, pulling on her boots and plaid jacket. "Ready?"

The woman at the admin office, Pam, was helpful. Her chirpy little voice and can-do attitude made Savannah want to smile from ear to ear. Unfortunately, the information received was not what Savannah and El were hoping for.

"I'm very sorry but we don't have anybody registered for the English language courses with the name Zack." She smiled sadly, as though sensing that there was more to the story than Savannah was offering.

"What about Zachary, or Zachariah?" El asked, stepping in when Savannah found herself unable to speak.

"No, I'm sorry. There's nobody by any variation of that name on the course. Are you sure it's an English language key fob? Maybe I could take a look at the keys?" Pam stretched out her hand, ready to receive the set of imaginary keys.

"We don't have them with us at the moment," Savannah said, feeling her skin burning at the lie.

"Can I offer you some advice?" Pam said. "If he's given you the wrong information, he's not worth your time."

"Excuse me?" Savannah said, taken aback by the comment so much so that she found herself stepping away from the desk.

"It doesn't take a genius to figure out what's happening. I get this a lot, believe me. People wanting to find long lost lovers from wild nights out. I give the information when I can; it makes me feel like cupid, but you've been lied to, sweetie. Either he gave you the wrong name and number, or he's ignoring your calls, or all of the above. He's not worth it, I can assure you of that." Pam's sad smile made Savannah's gut clench inside of her.

"Thank you, Pam," El said on Savannah's behalf. She slipped her arm through Savannah's and guided her away from the admin desk.

The next couple of weeks passed in a blur. Savannah felt like she was on autopilot. She still visited the coffee shop every day, just on the off chance she'd bump into Zack so that she could ask him to explain himself. She felt dirty and used like an old, crumpled tissue cast onto the causeway. How could she have been so naïve?

El was constantly checking in with her, avoiding the topic of Zack at all costs but, instead, talking about everything else. Savannah felt simultaneously numb and on edge. More than once she'd considered going to Zack's house and demanding answers. But she couldn't bring herself to do that. It felt like crossing a line. Scorned lover turned stalker, and that wasn't her. She wouldn't, couldn't, give him the satisfaction. Not that she didn't want to storm over there and rip him a new one.

She hated him with every fibre of her being. It was a waste of time and energy to do that, she knew. She wasn't stupid. Especially given the fact that he wouldn't be thinking about her at all, other than the fact that he'd been able to use her body for his sick sexual satisfaction. It said a lot about a person who spends all that time pretending to be sweet and tender and charming, and then falls off the face of the earth and feigns that you don't exist.

Savannah worked every day to try and think about the bastard less than the day before. Each day became a little easier. She felt less used. Less dirty. Less embarrassed. It wasn't until El mentioned that she was nipping to the corner shop to buy sanitary pads, as she'd been caught off guard by her *monthly gift from hell,* as she called it, that Savannah realised she was late. At least two weeks late.

The blood rushed from her head, ironically, and she felt her body go faint. Pulling the calendar off the wall she checked the dates. She'd always been meticulous about tracking her cycle. It meant that she was never caught off guard like El was every month. Savannah had been as regular as clockwork since the third year of secondary school.

There, in black and white, on the Women Reading Books calendar, were the dates she should have started her period. Sixteen days ago.

"Fuck," she muttered under her breath, throwing the calendar across the room.

Cameron

"I have to go to work," Cameron said to Liz, his voice gruff with sleep, or a lack thereof.

"Don't be stupid. You're not well, you need to stay at home today. See how you feel tomorrow." Liz was sitting beside him with a coffee in hand, the bedsheets wrapped tightly around Cameron's body. He longed to stay in the bed but couldn't. He had to go to work. That's what happened when you're an adult with responsibilities, even if the world was going to shit around you.

There had been no more messages since Christmas day at his mother's house, thankfully, but their presence loomed over him. A rain cloud ready to burst. Every second of every day he was expecting the text tone to sound. It was exhausting, and yet he couldn't sleep. His insides felt constantly chilled with dread, like somebody had forced him to drink a gallon of ice-cold water.

"They won't be able to find cover for my classes at such short notice," Cameron said, pulling himself out of bed. He knew it was unreasonable, especially given his apathy towards his job as of late, but he couldn't shake the feeling that his students needed him. The cold air hit him like a brick, and he almost fell back into the soft recesses of his king-sized bed. But he didn't. Instead, he went to the bathroom to splash water on his face, hoping it would make him feel just a little more human. It didn't. Yet, he pulled on his trousers, shirt, and tie and headed to make a coffee for the commute.

"I really think you should stay at home. You don't look well at all." Liz's voice cut into him. Her nagging tone made him want to lash out, to tell her to stop treating him like a child, but he didn't have the energy to argue. It was the first day back of the new year. He was exhausted and the children would be high as kites thanks to two weeks of junk food and presents. There would be arguments about new phones, about who had the best Christmas holiday or whose parents spent the most money. Once the day was over, Cameron planned to throw himself into bed and get some sleep before following the same rituals the next day. A prospect that he found less than thrilling.

"I'm going. The children need me. End of story," Cameron said as he looped his bag over his shoulder and made for the door.

"Fine, at least take some paracetamol. You look like you're feverish. Your forehead is sweating." Liz passed him the paracetamol, and he dry swallowed them giving her a small smile of thanks. She didn't know the real reason he was unwell. He hadn't mentioned the texts since, and neither had she. Living in denial appeared to suit her, almost as much as it suited him.

"I'll see you later," Cameron said, shutting the door tightly behind him and walking slowly to the car. There was no energy left in his body and so when Mr Mallins, the headteacher, reminded all of the staff to tell the children about parents' evening the following week, Cameron fought back the urge to scream and cry, and paddy like a two-year-old. Parents' evening was exactly the opposite of what he needed.

The week passed by quickly, in a haze of pre-planned lessons from the online syllabus. He'd usually write his own plans, try to make the subject matter a little less dry than it was, but he genuinely couldn't be bothered to do so. The children were learning, he was doing his job, so what did it matter if the lessons weren't all singing and dancing? They should be thankful that he was even there at all, given that he was sleeping a maximum of three hours each night, constantly turning over to check his phone for messages, the blue light waking him up further, and Liz failing to notice it at all.

By the time parents' evening rolled around, Cameron was well and truly spent. There was nothing left within him to give. With each parent, he outlined the facts and figures. The predicted grades and how well the child behaved in class. There was no conversation or smiles; a robot going through a series of commands. If the parents noticed, they didn't say anything, and that worked just fine for Cameron.

As the evening drew to a close and the final dribs and drabs of parents walked by the open door of his classroom, a familiar figure caught his eye.

"No," Cameron breathed, the air escaping his lungs with force.

The man from before. He'd almost managed to convince himself that he'd dreamt of the bald, smiling man. Almost. It had been so long since he'd seen him.

Rising slowly from his desk, Cameron walked out of the room, his heels clipping on the linoleum floor. The old school building was complete with wooden cladding on the bottoms of the walls that lined the never-ending corridor. He looked both ways, as though crossing a street. Blood thrummed in his ears.

The man stood at the end of the corridor, just as it was about to make a right-angle. He was smiling that macabre smile that sent splinters of unease through Cameron's body. Even from twenty feet away, Cameron could see the too-white teeth stretching against his lips. He was wearing an expensive-looking suit that fit him like a glove, hugging his body as he stood motionless.

"Who are you?" Cameron asked, unable to move from where his feet were glued to his classroom floor. His voice bounced from the walls of the empty corridor.

The man didn't move. Didn't flinch. Didn't answer.

Cameron couldn't make himself step forwards to face the man. It felt like his body was on the verge of collapse, only held up by scaffolding.

“Why are you following me?” Cameron didn’t like the way his voice sounded. It was shaky and raw, like a child on the verge of puberty.

At these words, the man tilted his head, smile widening impossibly. His stare was fixed onto Cameron’s.

“Is it you who’s sending the texts?” Cameron pushed for answers, knowing that no response would be given. He was being toyed with, and what made matters worse, was that it was working.

Without a word, the man turned on his heel and vanished out of sight down the corridor. It was as though a spell was broken, for when the man moved out of sight, Cameron felt his body surge forward in pursuit.

“Wait!” Cameron ran down the corridor, heart hammering in his chest. Swinging around the corridor, Cameron searched for the man. He was nowhere to be seen. The corridor was empty, save for a piece of paper floating delicately to the ground like a feather.

Catching his breath, Cameron picked up the paper. The colour drained from the world around him as he fell to his knees, panic setting in. His face flushed, his mind fogged, tears threatened to burst through his eyelids.

“This can’t be,” he whispered to himself.

Alone in the empty corridor, Cameron studied the sheet of paper in his hand. Ordinary printer paper. Nothing special about it other than the photograph filling the centre portion of it. And the writing scrawled in biro diagonally across the photograph.

The photograph was of Cameron. Completely naked from the waist down. Tied to a chair. Blood and bruises bloomed over every visible part of his body. He was facing the camera this time. Eyes wide and pleading, sweat dripping from his brow and spit stringing from his chin. His lips formed a word he could make out. Stop? Please? Don't? He didn't know. But it was desperate, ripping from within him.

Too consumed with the photograph, Cameron didn't read what the scribbled words said, at first. The blue pen had been pressed so hard into the paper that it had almost broken through the other side. The ink bled and bloomed. Cameron balled up the paper in his fist, closing his hands tightly and trying to retain some level of composure. His nails dug into the flesh of his hands.

HAPPY NEW YEAR.

Savannah

The pregnancy test felt heavy in her hands as she walked to the till. Who knew there were so many different types you could buy? Budget ones, ones that promised to tell you whether you were pregnant before you'd even missed a period, ones with little electronic screens. In the end, Savannah picked up a Clearblue one, which was on offer, as well as two of the budget ones. She had to make sure of the result.

"Will that be all?" the woman in the white Boots outfit asked. Savannah never looked at her face, had no idea what she looked like.

"Yes, thank you," Savannah said, rifling through her purse for the correct change.

"Do you have a points card?"

She did. But she wasn't going to stand there and dig it out of the recesses of her purse.

"No."

"Well, here you go then." The woman put the tests into the, thankfully, opaque carrier bag. "Have a lovely day."

Have a lovely day. That wasn't particularly likely, but Savannah thanked her anyway before walking home. El was in lectures all day and so Savannah could do this alone. She couldn't bear the mothering looks El would give her while they waited for the tests to do their thing. She was better doing it alone.

The bathroom was on the same floor as El's bedroom. The sink was cluttered with all kinds of lotions and potions, things to fight acne, prevent aging, and make your hair iron straight. All of that seemed stupid, frivolous, as Savannah unpacked her bag. She took out the Clearblue one first. If any test was going to be accurate, then it would be that one, surely.

The instructions were long-winded, despite the pictures on the box showing "three easy steps." It stressed that you had to only pee on the edge of the stick and that if your urine got on the patch where the results showed, the test would be voided. It would have been so much easier for a man to do that. Alternatively, you could wee in a bowl and dunk the test in there. That seemed like an easier option.

The glass measuring jug from the kitchen seemed like her best bet and once she'd collected everything she needed, and drank a pint of water, she pulled her pants down, squatting over the jug. Just when it felt like peeing on command would be impossible, she heard the tell-tale tinkle filling the jug.

Looking at her own waste was disconcerting. Pulling the blue cap off the pregnancy test, and hearing the little click as it came free, Savannah sighed. This was actually happening. She submerged the tip, fighting back tears.

Once done, the pregnancy test stared at her from the countertop. And then to wait. Unable to leave the bathroom, Savannah sunk to the floor. The bathmat, still slightly damp, warmed her skin. After an eternity, she stood up, drew a shaking breath, and allowed her eyes to fall to the test. In the main window was a little cross. She knew what that meant, having made herself memorise what a positive result would look like.

"Shit," she murmured into the empty room.

She had to take another test. Just to be sure. There was still a chance, however small, that it was a false positive. Perhaps the jug had been contaminated. She'd have to try peeing onto the stick this time. Unwrapping the budget brand, and reading the instructions again, just to be sure, Savannah sat on the toilet, holding the test between her legs with a trembling hand.

Nothing would come. Water. She needed more water. Re-filling the pint glass, she gulped the water down hungrily. She wanted to do the test now. Waiting wasn't an option. She sat back down and waited for the floodgates to open.

With the tests stuck firmly into the outside bin, underneath at least two black bin bags, Savannah went back inside, sat in front of her computer and Googled something she hoped never to have to. *Abortion.*

The NHS website was *nice*, informative, and made it sound like an easy procedure that would only take a few minutes and she would be back to normal, minus a baby, in no time at all. It was the forums that threw her. Horror stories of blood clots, of “babies” surviving after the abortion had taken place, sometimes for hours. It made her feel sick to her stomach. Until that moment, she’d always thought that if she’d got pregnant, the decision to have an abortion would be an easy one. She was an advocate of the whole process. What woman in their right mind wasn’t? But having it happen to you, well that was a different story.

Her friend had one in high school and said it was the easiest thing ever. Over in seconds. She’d bled for a couple of days and then that was it, back to normal. A girl in the year above told a different story, of blood clots the size of her fist, or the worst pain imaginable. Although Savannah knew that, more than likely, both girls were exaggerating their stories, as high school kids do, she never actually thought she’d become part of the same group as them.

What surprised Savannah the most, was that she didn’t want to cry. She didn’t want to scream or break down. In fact, she didn’t really want to deal with it at all. Abortions could take place up to twenty-four weeks, so there was no rush, not really. She just had to figure out how she felt. Placing her hands on her stomach, Savannah held them there. Inside of her was something that might eventually turn into a real-life human being if she allowed it to do so. Otherwise, it would end up being her period. It was not yet a baby, in her eyes at least, just a cluster of cells, much like a tumour, floating inside of her.

She had work to do. Things to be getting on with. She would deal with it later. Later. Crossing off the NHS treatment page, Savannah opened up her latest assignment, took a cleansing inhale, just like the therapist had taught her, and started typing.

Savannah

It was fairly easy to hide being pregnant. This had come as a shock to Savannah. Having toyed with the idea of what the hell to do with the baby, and a great many sleepless nights as a result of that, Savannah had decided to keep it (almost certainly). It wasn't that she wanted a baby. On the contrary, that was exactly what she didn't want. It was the fact that the idea of having an abortion scared her more than having the baby. Throughout school, she'd heard horror stories of the pain of an abortion. Of the judgemental nurses and the bath that evening filled with huge chunks of blood. She just couldn't do that. After only a few weeks of knowing she was pregnant, Savannah had taken that option off the table. Which was how she'd come to be almost six months pregnant.

El hadn't noticed anything and so Savannah was able to go along happily, burying her head in the sand, along with all of her thoughts about Zack. As far as she was concerned, her baby had no father. It was neat and simple. An immaculate conception of sorts. With summer fast approaching, it was becoming more difficult to hide her growing bump. Genetics had been kind to her, thus far, but there were only so many times you could wear hoodies and oversized checked shirts without people questioning whether you were boiling. Which she was. Most of the time she had a sheen across her forehead, upon which she dabbed face powder like it was going out of fashion.

Most evenings, when Savannah stripped off her clothes for bed, she stood in front of the mirror and stared at the growing bump. She couldn't quite believe what the human body was capable of. She was growing an actual person inside of her, with barely any effort. In fact, if the bump hadn't started getting in the way, it would be really easy to forget she was pregnant.

As Savannah had anticipated, it was El who'd asked the difficult questions. It had started one evening, around five and a half months into the pregnancy. The bump was noticeable, but looked more like bloating, Savannah hoped, or at the very least she'd convinced herself.

"Why are you wearing a sweatshirt with your PJs? Aren't you warm?"

They'd been sitting together watching the soaps on TV, both grasping hold of a too-hot cup of tea.

"No, I'm fine," Savannah lied.

"You look warm. Aren't you well? Do you have a temperature?"

Before Savannah could stop her, El reached over and placed the back of her hand against Savannah's wet forehead.

"Jesus, you're burning up! We have to get you some ibuprofen. You should go to bed. Come to think of it, you don't look very well."

"Thanks!" Savannah joked, trying to laugh off the questions.

"I'm being serious. Go to bed, and I'll bring you up some tablets and some water."

"Okay," Savannah agreed. Arguing would only lead to more questions that she couldn't answer.

El looked at her quizzically and paused a moment too long before she went to the kitchen cabinet to get the medicine.

Upstairs, Savannah put herself to bed. She pulled off the sweater and revealed the t-shirt below it, then dragged the quilt up to her chest, hoping that would be sufficient to hide the bump.

El knocked gently before she entered. Savannah felt a pang of guilt that she was hiding something so huge from her best friend. Since their falling out, and subsequent making up, El had doted on Savannah, becoming almost more of a mother figure than a sister, despite the fact they were the same age. It was a kick in the gut to not feel like she was able to tell her friend about the person growing inside of her.

"Come in," Savannah called, propped against the headboard, a book already in her hand.

"Here." El entered the room and placed the glass of water on the bedside table and the white chalky pills into Savannah's open hand. She tilted her head and looked down Savannah's body.

"What?" Savannah smiled, narrowing her eyes.

"Nothing," El said, beginning to back out of the room.

“No, seriously, what is it? Do I have something on my face?” Savannah laughed and threw in a cough for good measure.

“No, it’s just, well, from this angle your boobs look huge!” El giggled, shaking her head at the absurdity of what she’d just said.

A sliver of ice made its way slowly down Savannah’s spine. El was figuring it out.

“Oh, it must be all those extra biscuits you’ve been shoving down my neck.” She prayed that her face didn’t betray her worry.

“Sure.” El smiled, kindly. “Well, whatever it is, it suits you.”

As El left the room, Savannah replayed the conversation over and over again. Did El know? Would it matter if she did?

Savannah knew deep down the reason she wasn’t telling anybody that she was pregnant. It wasn’t that she was embarrassed to have gotten pregnant from a one-night stand. It wasn’t the fact that she was still in university. It was the fact that she didn’t know for sure she wanted to keep the baby. She felt so unbelievably ashamed of herself for feeling that way. She was a woman and should want a baby more than anything. That was the way women’s brains were programmed.

The prospect of raising a child, by herself, filled her with dread. If she dwelt on it too much, she felt herself becoming resentful of the being inside of her. It wasn’t the baby’s fault, of course. She should have been more careful. But, irrationally or not, Savannah blamed the baby for having ruined her life.

After that night, El's questions hadn't stopped. In fact, they grew in intensity. The stress of this, plus the fact that Savannah had to make up excuses not to see her dad, was making her truly ill. Not just ill like she pretended to be. The stress of it all had caused her hair to begin to fall out. Huge chunks sloughed off her head every time she brushed it. It was vain, she knew, to want to cry about that. She was growing a baby inside of her and she was worried more about the fact she was losing her hair. If anything, this solidified the fact that she didn't want to be a mother.

When El came into Savannah's bedroom one evening and said two little words, relief flooded over Savannah, so much that she burst into tears.

"I know," El said, smiling sadly in the doorway. "Oh, sweetie!"

As Savannah had collapsed onto the bed, shoulders wracking with great heaving sobs, El ran over and wrapped her in her arms.

"It'll all be okay, Savannah. I promise you. You'll be okay."

Savannah couldn't speak. The words wouldn't form. Her thoughts wouldn't untangle. El continued to whisper into her ear that everything would be okay. That Savannah wouldn't have to be alone, no matter what happened.

"I'll be there for you, Sav. I promise. I promise."

El's hand stroked down Savannah's long hair, pulling with it strings of blonde. If El noticed at that moment, she didn't say anything.

"How far along are you?" El asked, eventually pulling away from Savannah. She held her at arm's length, the way you would if you were trying to have a serious conversation with a child.

"Six and a half months," Savannah said, dry sobs shaking her body as she tried to speak.

"Okay, and do you know who the dad is?" El's eyes bored into Savannah's, they were wide and serious, in a way Savannah had never seen before.

"Yes," Savannah breathed.

"That Zack guy?" El asked, pursing her lips as though holding back tears herself.

"Yes," Savannah said. "He's the only person I've been with since I moved in here."

"And you still haven't been able to get in touch with him?" El's fingertips gripped tightly into Savannah's skin.

"I haven't tried," she confessed.

"Okay. Look, we'll figure this out together. Okay. You and me. We've got this. What did the doctor say, is everything okay with the baby?"

Savannah released a weep, wanting to cower, to hide her face. Not only was she not sure she wanted the baby, but she hadn't even been to the doctor. The prospect of telling El just how much she'd failed sent her into a frenzy.

Savannah's breath came quickly. Her head swam. Her heart beat out of her chest. She felt like she was going to die. A panic attack. She'd had them before, but none like this and never while pregnant.

She closed her eyes and tried to count her breaths. Breathe in for five. Hold it for three. Out for seven. Over and over again. Faintly, El's voice broke into her consciousness. Words that were not words. Desperate, forceful. Savannah pushed them away and concentrated on getting herself back under control. Five. Three. Seven. Five. Three. Seven.

Eventually, she was able to breathe without her breath hitching erratically.

"Savannah, it's okay. It's not too late. You've got me now. We'll talk and figure out what to do next. No pressure at all." El's voice was soothing, motherly. it made tears build in Savannah's eyes.

"But I'll be in trouble," Savannah said in a barely audible voice.

"Nobody will be in trouble. People have babies all of the time and don't know they're pregnant. Remember that story about somebody having a baby in the toilet? It happens, Savannah. Nobody's going to tell you off. I'm just really sorry you couldn't tell me. I would have helped you with everything."

"But you know now," Savannah said, nodding and trying to prevent her chest from rattling and panting.

"Yes, and we're going to book your doctor's appointment and go from there. First thing tomorrow. From here on out, things will be better, Savannah. Okay?"

"Okay." Savannah smiled a genuine smile.

"You know we'll have to tell your dad though, don't you?" El said apologetically.

"I know. He's going to be so mad at me."

"You let me worry about that." El smiled. "Now, come on, let's get you back into bed. We have a busy day tomorrow."

El tucked the blanket around Savannah. She turned on the lamp in the corner and shut off the light.

"No matter what happens, it will all be okay. Goodnight Sav," El's voice trailed away as she closed the door.

"Goodnight," Savannah said. Placing her hands upon her baby bump, Savannah rolled to the side and fell into her first dreamless sleep in months.

Cameron

"There have been complaints about you, Cameron."

The words cut into him like a knife. He was in the headteacher's office, feeling exactly the same as a child would in his situation. He was in trouble. Being reprimanded by his boss. Not the way he wanted this day to go.

Parents' evening had led to a sleepless night and copious amounts of whisky. His head was banging, a deep pulsating rhythm hitting his temple like a metronome. He now had proof that his stalker, the photographs, and messages, were linked explicitly; no doubt remained that the bald, smiling man was at the root of everything happening to him. Except for the bollocking he was currently receiving from Mr Mallins. Although, if you looked at it objectively, even those two things were intrinsically linked.

"What complaints were those?" Cameron asked. He tried to keep his face calm, a demeanour of quizzical absurdity about the whole situation. But he knew that he was abrupt with the parents. Perhaps stand-offish. This was the kind of school where parents complained about whatever they could, so he should have anticipated this reprimand.

"That you were rude. You wouldn't answer questions. That it was clear you'd rather be somewhere else. One parent even said that they were surprised you were a teacher, as you clearly didn't like anything about children or English." Mr Mallins, Rob to the teaching staff, placed his chin atop his folded hands. "Look, I wasn't going to say anything just yet, but it's not the first complaint we've had. You've changed, Cameron. Your lessons are dull. The subject matter is boring. The children don't like coming to your lessons. Is something happening at home? I'm worried about you. I had hoped that you would come to me, but that time has passed, I'm afraid."

"Oh," was all Cameron could say. It was difficult to get your head around so many different criticisms at once. He'd always loved his job, and he'd been good at it. To have your boss rip apart your entire teaching persona was tough to face.

"I want to help you. Tell me what's wrong with you. Is something happening at home? Don't you like working here anymore?"

Cameron waited a moment before answering the question. He needed to think carefully about how to phrase his response. He needed to be cut some slack, to be allowed to work but under less strenuous circumstances, but he couldn't tell Mr Mallins about the photographs and the stalker. It would make him a laughingstock.

"I, well, I have been a bit down recently. I think I might be depressed. I don't know. I'll sort it out, I promise. Just give me a chance to make things right."

"The thing is, Cameron, I don't think you're in a fit position to be here. I can smell whisky on you…"

"I had a drink last night. Not today for god's sake!" The words flung at Mr Mallins with force, taking him by surprise, evident upon his pinched face.

"I just think that you need a bit of time to get better. I think, perhaps, you need to take some time off. Go to the doctors and see what they can do for you."

"I don't need to go to the doctors," Cameron said. "I'm fine to work. You have to believe me. I'll step my game back up."

"I'm afraid, at this point, it's not really a choice. I'm sorry, Cameron. You have to go home. We'll talk about when you can come back to work once you've had a couple of weeks of rest, okay? Don't worry, we'll get you back and raring to go soon enough."

Cameron's jaw fell open comically like a ventriloquist dummy.

"You're sending me home," Cameron said, confirming what he already knew to be true. He simply had to say the words aloud.

"Yes. I'll come with you to get your things from your classroom and then walk you to your car." Mr Mallins's voice was apologetic.

"You're escorting me off the premises." Cameron shook his head, wanting to laugh aloud at the sheer ridiculousness of the situation.

"Yes," Mr Mallins breathed.

"Fine."

After Cameron had collected his things, he headed back to the car and sat there for a while in silence. His classroom had been, mercifully, empty. He couldn't quite believe what had just happened to him. He'd never once been reprimanded at work, never mind for multiple things at once. The prospect of breaking the news to Liz, that he'd essentially been suspended from work, gnawed at his insides. She already thought he was on the verge of insanity. To add this to the mix might well push her over the edge. She'd probably leave him. Any sane person would.

He slammed his fist into the steering wheel so hard that a red splotch instantly began to bloom on the flesh of his hand. He cradled it against himself, willing the tears to stay inside of him. As with everything else in his life, he failed to be able to control them and they fell in floods down his cheeks. He wanted, more than anything, to scream, but couldn't draw any more attention to himself. Already a few staff members had walked past his car, looking inside with questioning glances.

After dabbing at his eyes with the cuff of his sleeve, Cameron slammed the car into gear and set off home, ready to face Liz. It was sod's law that she didn't start back at work until the following week, which meant she'd be at home when he arrived. He wouldn't have any time to compose himself or come up with a convincing story, or even grab a whisky to steady his nerves. Instead, he'd have to face her head-on.

The front door creaked as Cameron opened it. He held his breath and prayed she was out shopping or at the gym. She wasn't, of course. Her voice called out to him.

"Cameron, what are you doing back?" She stuck her head around the doorframe and into the hallway. "Oh my god, what's wrong?"

She ran to him and wrapped her arms around his neck, sensing that something was very wrong.

"I've been told to come home," Cameron stuttered into Liz's neck. Her soft perfume lulled him closer. He wrapped his arms tightly around her and prayed, once more, that what he was about to tell her wouldn't lead to her leaving him.

"Do you feel sick? I told you that you weren't well enough to work. Come on, get in bed, I'll get you a cup of tea and you can tell me what happened."

Cameron did as he was told without arguing. He stripped off his clothes and got into bed in his boxers and a white undershirt. When Liz walked back into the bedroom, she was carrying two cups of tea and sat down beside him.

"Tell me what happened," she said kindly.

"Some parents have complained. Apparently, my work hasn't been great recently and then some parents weren't happy with me on parents' evening. Rob has decided it would be better if I have some time off to recuperate, and maybe see a doctor. He thinks I'm sick. Maybe I am, I don't know."

Liz studied him. Her unwavering eye contact made him uneasy. She was going to leave him.

"Okay, then we'll get you into the doctors and we'll sort you out ready to go back. We all have lapses sometimes, Cameron. Plus, those weird texts did a number on you. I know that you've not mentioned them in a while, but I can see that they upset you. You haven't had any recently, have you? That's not what this is about, is it?"

"No, it's not that. I haven't had a text for a while. I think they got bored," Cameron lied with ease. Somehow, it would be easier for Liz to think he was depressed rather than stalked and tormented. It was the lesser of two evils.

"Right. I'll book you a doctor's appointment and we'll get this whole thing sorted out. Don't worry, I'll look after you. It's what I'm here for."

"Thank you," Cameron said, pulling the sheets up to his neck. He laid his head on the pillow and prayed for sleep. It did not come.

Savannah

Savannah gripped El's hand while they sat across from the midwife. They were being interrogated about why they didn't come sooner. What happened that it took Savannah so long to realise she was pregnant? In all fairness, it was not so much an interrogation as a gentle questioning, but Savannah was on the defensive from the beginning. The plump nurse asked her to sit in a squeaky vinyl chair and had begun to fire questions at her before she'd even sat down.

It started with the usual. Name, age, date of birth, address. Then the conversation took a turn.

"And who is the father?" the nurse, Jamie, asked.

"Oh, I don't know," Savannah said truthfully. She knew the father in essence, but had no further details about him, which was the same as not knowing who he was, she decided.

"Could it be more than one person? There are ways we can narrow that down once the baby is born. You wouldn't be the first to not know the father." The nurse smiled kindly, thinking that Savannah was a slut, of course.

"I've only been with one person but don't know his name or how to contact him. It's fine. I'm doing this alone." Her voice was harsh, brash.

Jamie looked taken aback by Savannah's outburst but drew a smile across her face anyway.

"That's totally your choice. Now, let me ask you a few more questions. Okay, we ask these to everybody, just to get an idea of your situation and home life and to see if there are any places we can help support you more."

"Okay." Savannah smiled apologetically for her overreaction. She was a university student who was pregnant and didn't know who the father of her baby was. Of course, she could hardly blame the woman for thinking that she was a bit of a slut.

"Great. So, you're at university right now?"

The questions trailed off and Savannah answered them robotically. The meeting ended with Savannah being told that she needed to have a blood test and urine test for certain STDs, seeing as she didn't know the sexual history of the father of the baby. And, that a scan would be set up to check everything was okay with the baby.

The baby. Those two words whirled around and around in her head, way after the appointment was finished. *A baby.* She was having a baby.

"Let's go and get lunch," El said, as they walked out of the GP surgery.

They settled on a café next door. A little, cosy, hole in the wall kind of place, with mismatched chairs and mixed wildflowers in milk bottles on each table. It was what they called quaint in movies. Charming.

Savannah sat on a chair in the corner while El went and ordered. Decaf coffee for Savannah and a full-caffeine latte for El.

"You hide the bump well, you know," El said as she sat down opposite Savannah.

"Thank you. It's taken some trial and error!"

"I swear that if I didn't know you, I would never guess you were pregnant."

"It'll only last a little longer, I would have thought. Soon I'll not be able to hide it. People will know. That's the part I'm dreading." Savannah gripped the coffee in her hand, allowing the steam to blow past her face.

"Why are you dreading that?" El asked, leaning forwards as though sharing a secret.

"Because I don't know what I'm going to do once the baby comes. If I give it away, then people will know. But also if I keep it, I'll forever be known as the girl who got pregnant at uni from a one-night stand." Savannah sighed, and as she often did, she wished for a get-out clause. If she could go back in time and take that night back, to just live like a normal teenager again, she'd do it in a heartbeat.

"You really care that much about what other people think of you?" El asked, brows furrowing. She didn't understand, would never understand. She was beautiful, friendly, smart, she didn't have to worry about what other people thought. If she'd have got knocked up, she would have owned it, no matter what she decided to do with the baby. Savannah wasn't like that. She worked hard to be comfortable in her skin. And now under her skin was a baby that she didn't want, or at the very least, hadn't wanted beforehand.

"Of course, I care about what other people think," Savannah shook her head and tried to hide her grimace.

"You really shouldn't. So what if people judge you? If they're judging you, they're clearly not happy with their own lives. Your life has nothing to do with anybody else but you. Those that love you won't judge you for this. Plus, you've done nothing wrong. You've done nothing that every single other student hasn't done." El's voice was only a notch above a whisper and filled with exasperation.

"Other students don't panic and hide their pregnancy for months," Savannah said, knowing it was better to own up to her strange, possibly psychotic, behaviour. She sometimes wondered whether she should have continued to see the shrink after all.

"Some do. Look, you can't change what you've done in the past. But you can change what you do with your future. No matter what you decide, whether you keep the baby or give it to some couple who desperately want a baby of their own, you've done something you should be proud of. I am proud of you. Okay? You've been through a hell of a lot, and you're coping remarkably well. You don't give yourself enough credit. Look, we'll figure this out together. I got some leaflets from the lobby about adoption, so you can research it properly and decide what you want to do. From here on out, you'll make the difficult decisions, and you won't hide, because I'll be by your side the entire time."

"Thank you," Savannah whispered. "I don't know what I'd do without you."

"You'd be just fine. However, I'm going to say something you don't like. Seeing as you won't be able to hide your bump for much longer, you need to tell your dad."

"Shit, I know."

"I think we should do it now, okay? Get it out of the way. The longer you wait, the worse it's going to be," El reasoned. Savannah knew she was right but the prospect of telling her father that she was very pregnant and didn't know who the father was, and that she might not even keep the baby, well that left her feeling overwhelmed, exhausted to her bones.

"I'll message him now and tell him to come to our house," Savannah said, pulling her phone from her pocket and trying to ignore the rapid beating of her heart.

"I think that's the right thing to do." El smiled, patting Savannah on the shoulder.

As they walked back to their house, Savannah tried to push down the panic attack that was slowly building within her. Her dad had always been strict and relatively emotionally distant, even when her mother had died. But this would be different. This would push him over the edge. She wasn't sure she'd be able to handle the consequences.

Savannah

Savannah's dad sat across the table from her, staring at his hands. He hadn't spoken since she'd said those two fateful words; words that changed everything. *I'm pregnant.*

The expectation to be bombarded with questions had floated away in the atmosphere of the room. He hadn't asked anything. Not whether she planned to keep the baby. Who the father was. How on earth she planned to support the child. Nothing.

They were alone in the kitchen, sitting at the table. Two mugs of tea sat before them, made by El before she'd vacated the room, feigning to have university work to do. Her father had been convinced, Savannah knew better. El was giving them both the space to celebrate the pregnancy or grieve the life Savannah had been expected to live. Time passed slowly. The ticking of the clock made everything seem all the more painful. Each second that went by and her father didn't speak, Savannah felt worse. The guilt for making him feel that way tore at her insides. She wanted him to be okay with it, whatever *it* might be.

"Dad?" Savannah said, when she was unable to take the guilt any longer.

"I…" he began. His voice wavered in a way that tugged at her heart. She stood up and walked to the other side of the table, wrapping her arms around his neck.

"I'm sorry, Dad," she said into his neck. The smell of his aftershave reminded her of home.

"You don't have to be sorry, Savannah. It's not your fault. You need to tell me who did this to you."

Peeling herself away, Savannah studied his face.

"It is my fault, Dad. As much as it was his fault, anyway. As much as I wish it wasn't, it is."

"Who is he?" Her father's voice was strict, an edge to it that set alarm bells ringing.

"It was a one-night stand. A stupid mistake. I don't know his name."

"Oh, Savannah." He shook his head as he spoke, refusing to meet her eye.

"I thought he liked me, but he didn't. I can't change that. I haven't spoken to him since."

"How far along are you?"

"Close to seven months." There was no nice way to say those words. To admit that she'd lied to her dad for so long.

"Jesus, Sav, why didn't you tell me?" He turned on his chair.

"I didn't want it to be true. When I told people, it became real. Only El knows, and I told her a couple of days ago."

“Wow, okay. That’s a lot to take in. Are you healthy? Is the baby healthy?”

“Yes. I’m having a scan in a couple of days, but the midwife said everything was good earlier. I have to have some of the tests that I missed by not going to the doctor earlier, but everything should be fine.” It was difficult to admit that she’d not even gone to the doctor until that morning. She hoped she’d properly skimmed over this fact with her father, and he didn’t pick up on her failure to follow the proper pregnancy protocol, so all was well in that regard.

“Okay. Well, I know now. I’ll go with you to all of your appointments. We’ll switch to private, of course, make sure you have the best treatment around. We need to keep you and the baby safe.”

“Thank you.” Savannah couldn’t begin to recognise just how relieved she felt at her father’s words. It wasn’t for a few seconds that she realised he thought she would definitely keep the baby. Another obstacle she didn’t want to have to jump over, but that she knew she had to. Eventually. For now, her father was onboard, and that was all that mattered.

“Anything, sweetheart. You’re not going through this alone. I’ll help you through it all. You can move back in with me, and we’ll make sure you can carry on with university. We can hire a nanny or something once the baby is born. That way it doesn’t have to ruin your life.”

Ruin your life.

She took the bait. "Why would it ruin my life?"

"It's a baby, Savannah. You're still a child, practically. You've only just got over your breakdown, and you're pregnant. This isn't going to be easy. You'll need help."

"And your answer to that is to buy me a nanny?" Savannah couldn't hold in her anger. It boiled over. "You don't think I can do this?"

"I don't think you can do it alone. Nobody can, Sav. Come on! Everybody needs help when they have a baby. Your mum..."

"Don't talk about her. She left us, Dad. She couldn't hack it. You had help, and she still left."

His words had touched a nerve frayed raw over the years. Her mother had left of her own accord when Savannah was barely old enough to talk. It was something she actively tried not to think about and had been successful until she'd become pregnant herself. At that point, her mum's face had filled her mind whenever it was blank. The picture she formed in her head was one she only knew from photo albums. Sun-faded and still.

He didn't answer. Instead, he raked his hands through his thinning hair, pulling it away from his face.

"Savannah," he finally broke the silence. "I'm sorry. I'm not suggesting... I'm just shocked, I suppose. We'll figure this out. You'll be a great mother." Turning to face her, her father held out his arms and pulled her close to him, kissing her on the forehead. "My baby is having a baby. I'm going to be a grandad. Oh god!"

Once her father had finally left, Savannah went upstairs and threw herself down onto El's bed. The soft blinding white sheets enveloped her as she exhaled in relief. She'd done it. She'd told her dad she was pregnant, and from a one-night stand, no less. She might have missed the minor detail of the fact that she might not keep the baby but that wasn't the end of the world. The worst bit was done.

"I'm so proud of you!" El said, pulling Savannah close to her. They laid together on the bed, El's arm around Savannah's shoulders, her head on El's chest.

"Thanks. It's hardly something to be proud of, though. I did what I should have done ages ago." Savannah tried to laugh. She'd always had an issue taking praise, especially if it was for something everybody else wouldn't have a problem with doing.

"Don't do that! Your dad is pretty intimidating. You did well. Onwards and upwards from here on, babe. We've got this." Savannah couldn't look at El. Instead, she focused on the minimal bedroom, scanning the white gloss walls and surfaces.

"Yeah, I suppose. It's done now. He said he'd pay for anything I need for the baby, so that's good. I don't have to worry about being able to afford the right things. He even said he'd pay for a nanny."

At this, El threw her head back and laughed. "Oh my God, that's so your dad. Only our Micky Windsor would do that!"

"He hates it when you call him Micky," Savannah pretended to chide.

"Yeah, but what's he going to do? He has to put up with it because we're friends. And I love you. He won't say anything to me because you love me too." El giggled again, Savannah's own laugh melding with it perfectly.

"You're not wrong there. My dad thinks you're a good influence, so he won't say anything. You did, however, allow me to get pregnant. That was a dramatic oversight on your part, don't you think? He might have something to say about that." Savannah smiled as she spoke, knowing that El would be smiling too.

"What you do with your bits and pieces is no business of mine." El stuck out her tongue like a child having a tantrum. "Do you know what? I think we should celebrate. Let's go out for tea."

"Celebrate what? Me using my bits and pieces to make a baby?" Savannah laughed, genuinely and fully. She loved the way El could make light of any situation when needed. The phrase *bits and pieces* she could have done without, but beggars couldn't be choosers when it comes to friends, especially when you were the kind of person who gets pregnant and doesn't tell anybody.

"No, you putting on your big girl pants and telling your dad you're pregnant. That took a lot of guts, Sav, all jokes aside. I'm taking you out for tea. My treat. You can choose anywhere you want to go."

"Anywhere?" Savannah teased. There were some expensive restaurants nearby. Ones which she would never choose in a million years. But it felt nice to be able to tease El, just a little.

"Within reason. I'm not made of money. You're the one whose dad is rich, might I remind you." El gave Savannah a gentle punch on the arm.

"Okay. How about Pinocchio's? The food is always beautiful there, and it's not super expensive." Pinocchio's was Savannah's favourite restaurant in the whole world. One of those cheap yet fantastic places that was such a rarity. Whenever she walked into the somewhat dated restaurant, she felt like she was going home.

"Good choice. I'll ring and book. We'll go this evening, yes?"

"Sounds good to me. Thank you, El."

Savannah gave her friend a squeeze before jumping off the bed and heading to her own room. Once there, she opened up her laptop and typed something into Google that she'd not yet had the guts to do.

MUST HAVES FOR A NEW BABY.

Scrolling through the articles listing various "top ten" items all new mothers should have for their baby, Savannah began to compile a list of all the things she would need, should she decide to keep the baby.

"Just in case," she whispered to herself as she began to write down a list of all the things she would have to buy. She thanked her lucky stars that her dad was on board with the idea. Only the very basics would come in at around £1000. If she wanted a *nice* pram, that figure would almost double. That didn't even begin to factor in clothing, nappies, and baby formula. Babies were expensive.

Somehow, Savannah found herself looking at babygrows. The website she was on had ones in every colour and pattern imaginable. Peter Rabbit, Winnie the Pooh, flowers, dinosaurs, the whole nine yards. It was mesmerising to think that soon enough the little thing growing inside of her would be out in the world and big enough to fit into one of those outfits. It wrenched at her heart. A little boy in blue. Or a little girl in pink. She had a feeling it was a boy, something deep within her bones told her that. On some level, she just knew.

Unable to stop herself, Savannah added three babygrows to her basket. Neutral colours. For good measure, she added in a handful of matching bibs. Feeling her heart in her throat, she pressed buy, knowing that as she clicked on that button, she'd sealed her fate. She would keep the baby.

The restaurant was fairly quiet, given that it was a weekday evening. That suited Savannah just fine. It meant that she and El could have a proper conversation without competing with other voices. They sat at their favourite table, in the window overlooking the street. The night was light, still illuminated by the sun. People walked by, many of them in groups, lost in chatter. Some had smiles. Some had frowns. Whenever Savannah had the chance to sit and people watch, she would often find herself wondering what was going on in other people's lives. Were they happy, sad, grieving, celebrating? Were they loved or hated? The realisation that other people out there led lives as full and complicated as her own felt more powerful than ever. Chalking it up to pregnancy hormones, Savannah turned her attention back to El.

The meal was beautiful, as it always was there. Sitting back, Savannah placed her hand on her stomach, revelling in how full she felt. She allowed her gaze to float out of the window, watching people saunter by. The sky had darkened while they'd been eating. Many of the people were in couples now, rather than groups.

That was how she saw him. Hand in hand with a girl Savannah couldn't quite see.

Her face flushed.

Zack.

Unaware of what he'd done to her. All of the shit he'd put her through. Just living his life without a care in the world.

Without stopping to think, Savannah scraped her chair out from under the table, rushing out of the door.

“Zack!” she shouted, almost forgetting that wasn’t really his name.

The couple turned around to look at Savannah. His face fell when he saw her. Fumbling for words, his face contorted from confusion to calm. The girl followed his gaze too, her eyes landing on Savannah.

“Me?” he said, feigning innocence.

“Yes. You gave me a false name. You never called me. Never looked for me. You used me. Had sex with me and threw me away.”

Anger built within Savannah until it felt white hot.

“I don’t know who you are. Are you okay? Do you need help?” To an outsider, Zack would look thoroughly affronted by the situation. A stranger shouting at him in the street. But Savannah knew better. She knew what he’d done. What he was capable of.

“I’m pregnant. The baby is yours. I gave up looking for you. But you have a right to know. Even if you did treat me like shit. Even if you hid away from me once you’d got what you wanted.” Savannah took a step closer to him and watched as Zack and the girl stepped back.

“Who is she?” the girl whispered to him.

“Who am I?” Savannah laughed aloud, aware that she probably looked entirely insane. “I’m the girl who fell for his lies. I let him use me. And now I’m alone and pregnant.”

“Do you know her?” the girl said again, turning to Zack and pretending that Savannah didn’t exist. This irritated her more than anything else.

“Yes, he knows me,” Savannah said at the same time as Zack spoke.

“I’ve never seen her before in my life.”

“You picked me up at a bar. Took me back to your house. Shagged me, and then left before I woke up, leaving a note saying to call you but you gave a fake name and number.” Savannah’s voice grew high pitched. She sounded manic, crazy.

It was at this point that El walked out of the restaurant.

“What’s happening?” she asked, looking from Savannah to Zack and the girl he was with.

“This is the guy who got me pregnant,” Savannah explained.

“Oh shit,” El said.

“Can you stop saying that?” Zack said. “I don’t know who you are. I’m sorry, you're clearly going through something, maybe you’re off your meds, but I have never had sex with you.”

“If Savannah said you did, then you did. What has she got to gain from lying? We tried to find you, *Zack,* but you don’t exist. You gave a fake name. That’s not cool. What’s your real name?”

“His name is—” the girl began to speak.

She was cut off by Zack. “Don’t tell them my name! They’re clearly mental! Come on. We’re leaving.”

Zack grabbed hold of the girl's arm and went to pull her away. From the look on her face, Savannah could see that she was torn. Women usually had a good radar for when other women were telling the truth. Hopefully what Savannah had said would set some alarm bells off in the girl's head and she would leave Zack before he had the chance to mess up her life too. Hopefully.

"He's not what you think," Savannah said to the girl. "He knows me. He did this to me." She cupped her stomach to show the curve of the baby bump. For a split second, she saw Zack's eyes flit to her stomach. His face warped into an emotion she couldn't quite place.

"You're fucking crazy, bitch. Go get help for fuck's sake." Zack's words were bitter, like poison. Savannah froze where she stood. There was such malice and hatred in the way he'd spoken to her. She knew then and there that she'd dodged a bullet by him not wanting to be a part of her life.

"Do you know what? Go, I'm better off without somebody like you stuck to me for the rest of my life. The baby will be better for never knowing you. But you…" Savannah turned to the girl. "You need to leave him. He's not a good guy, you can see that now, can't you? You heard how he spoke to me."

The message had landed. The girl would leave him the second she could. Savannah allowed herself to feel happy with the result. At least that was one girl saved from Zack's charms.

"You had better stay away from us," he snarled. "Fucking stalkers. Get fucked."

"Have a nice life." El smiled, pushing her arm through Savannah's. "You'll be better off without him too." She addressed the last part to the girl.

"Go fuck yourself," Zack shouted over his shoulder as he walked off. The girl trailed behind him, glancing once more over her shoulder at Savannah and El.

"What a nasty bastard," El said, eyes wide.

"He wasn't like that when he was with me," Savannah said, her voice filled with sadness. She'd trusted him. Believed in him. But she'd been wrong. Her radar was off. It was difficult to face the fact that you couldn't read people. Who else did she trust that, perhaps, she shouldn't?

Looking to El, Savannah smiled and shook her head. "Well, that went well!"

"You're better off without that twat," El said, her voice pregnant with anger.

"Yeah, I know," Savannah agreed. It was disappointing to realise that the man she'd allowed to be intimate with her was such an arsehole, but she supposed she wasn't the only person in the world to come to the same conclusion.

"You've got me," El said, squeezing Savannah. "Come on, let's go home."

"I decided to keep the baby," Savannah said, unsure of where the words had come from. She'd blame it on the adrenaline from the argument with Zack.

"I knew you would. Now, shall we do some online shopping? I'm sure there're loads of stuff you need to buy."

As they walked back to their house, Savannah felt relief flood through her body, as though it was coursing smoothly through her bloodstream. The prospect of bumping into Zack had weighed on her mind, and now it was out of the way. Her life was no different for having seen him that evening. This baby was hers and hers alone. He'd made that perfectly clear, and she intended to do right by it.

Cameron

The days passed in a fog. Cameron refused to get out of bed. He refused to do anything except sleep and use the bathroom. His room stank of stale sweat, despite Liz having changed the bedsheets twice. Both times, the fresh smell lasted hours until it returned to the usual sick odour. It was so thick in the room that at times, Cameron felt that he could taste it.

He had no dreams and barely any thoughts. His phone must have run out of battery some time ago because he hadn't heard it vibrate once. Other members of staff would have messaged him, he was sure, messages of support and condolences for fucking up his life. Liz tried to pull him out of bed every single day, and every day he refused.

He had no idea whether she left for work each day, or whether she was home, caring for her invalid boyfriend of only a few months. The idea of both made him feel sick to his stomach. She slept beside him, but she was a stranger, unable to pull him out of his fugue state.

That's why, when she slapped him with the words, "That's enough! What the fuck are you doing with your life, Cameron? You're letting everything go to shit because you messed up at work. Come on! That's not the Cameron I met. My Cameron would have told them to fuck off and found somewhere better. Not done this."

Until that point, they'd been kind and supportive. The day of the week, the hour of the day, were lost on him, but something about Liz's words made him listen.

He didn't move, nor did he speak, not right away. Instead, he opened his eyes and looked at her.

"This isn't you, Cameron. This is embarrassing." Liz shook her head as she peered down at him in the cocoon of his bedsheets. "I can't live like this. Pull yourself together or I'm leaving."

The words felt like they'd slapped him. If he placed his fingers on his cheeks, he almost expected to feel a heat there.

"You'd leave me?" Cameron mumbled.

"Yes. This is no life, Cameron. I can't live like this. You have one more day. One more day to mope, and then I expect this to be over. I'm going to work now. When I get back, I expect you dressed and out of bed."

"Or you'll leave?" His words were small, childlike.

"Yes, I'll leave." He noticed the tears leaking from the corner of her eyes before she turned to walk away, shutting the door closed behind her.

"Fuck," he muttered to himself. He pulled the pillow from Liz's side of the bed and pressed it tightly across his face. After a few moments, he found it hard to breathe. A few more moments and he felt on the verge of passing out.

“Fuck, fuck, fuck!” He threw the pillow against the wall and caught his breath. Liz was right, of course. Eventually, he managed to peel himself out of bed and headed for the shower.

When Liz arrived home from work, Cameron was sitting on the sofa watching TV. Some sitcom about dirty cops. He was not strictly following it, but he wanted to give the impression to Liz that he was.

“Hi,” Liz said, sitting down beside him. There was a huge smile on her face. Her delicate warm-beige skin beckoned to him. He placed his hand on hers, pulling her towards him.

“I’m sorry,” Cameron said.

“You smell clean.” Liz laughed into his neck, and he knew he was forgiven.

“I showered.” He chuckled, releasing her from the hug.

“Thank God!”

“I also changed the bed.” Cameron shook his head, knowing that Liz would find his attempts at being human once more to be endearing.

“My hero! Wait, do I also smell cooking?” Liz pulled away, a puzzled look on her face.

Cameron caught a glimpse of something he couldn’t quite place his finger on. Annoyance? Surely not.

“Don’t get too excited. It’s only something from the freezer.” Cameron stood and went to check on his cooking. Sausage and chips. Not the most gourmet meal, but the first one he'd cooked in a while.

"That's amazing, well done you." Liz remained on the sofa. She pulled out her phone and began tapping away, allowing Cameron to continue preparing the meal. It irritated him, that she'd not offered to help. That she'd come in and sat straight down on the sofa, but he pushed those feelings aside. Liz had put up with a lot, over the last few days. He wouldn't say anything this time around.

A phone vibrated. A low tone. Long, drawn out stretches. Cameron gripped the worktop to stop himself from collapsing.

"Hello, Sally!" Liz said into the phone. "Yes, the photos are retouched and ready to go. They're on the shared drive. The file named New Models. Great, thanks. Have a lovely evening."

When Liz hung up the phone, Cameron was still gripping the countertop, knuckles white with the strain of keeping his body upright. That noise, the vibration, it sent him spiralling. He hadn't expected that.

When did you become so fucking weak?

The words jarred him, flashing across his mind so clearly that he could see them. He never used to be like this. He was strong. Together. Back in university, he was the kind of man women fell in love with the second they spoke to him. And now, he was having a fucking nervous breakdown over a phone vibrating.

“What’s wrong?” Liz asked. She walked over to him and placed her hand on his arm, worried eyes focusing on his own.

“Nothing, I’m fine. Just went dizzy, that’s all.” The lie came easier than it should have.

“Probably all that time you spent in bed!” Liz laughed.

“Yeah, maybe.” Cameron tried to smile.

The beeping of the oven pulled him out of the moment.

“Hungry?” he said, grabbing plates from the cupboard.

They sat at the kitchen table as they always did before Cameron became a bedbound recluse that was. Usually, the room was filled with conversation about their days at work, or about something a friend of theirs had done. Instead, today’s meal was completely silent. They ate their food, glancing at one another occasionally.

“Oh, I charged your phone for you. I plugged it in just before we ate, so you should be able to turn it on now. It was dead, dead.” Liz smiled and Cameron fought the urge to leap across the table and punch her in the jaw.

“Why would you do that?” He couldn’t keep the acid out of his voice.

“Because you haven’t checked it for days. What if there are emails from work, or messages from your friends? Just because you’re on sick doesn’t mean you can stop living, Cam.” Liz said the words like she would to a child, and once more the rage filled up within him.

“You shouldn’t have done that without asking me.” The words sliced through the air like a knife through butter.

“What? I shouldn’t have charged your phone? Seriously, what are you talking about? Why the hell are you angry about that?” Liz needled him.

“Maybe I don’t want to deal with people right now.” Cameron slammed his knife and fork onto the table. His face reddened, and he could feel the heat building within him.

“Well, maybe you should be an adult and answer your damn messages! Christ, Cameron. I thought you were feeling better. I was happy to let it slide while you were hidden in your dirty little hovel, but now you’re up. Be a fucking adult!” Liz pushed her chair out from under the table so abruptly that it tipped over.

“What are you doing?” Cameron looked at her. For a split second, he felt that he hated her so intensely he could hurt her.

“I’m going to bed. Some of us have to work tomorrow.”

Cameron remained in his chair, reeling for some time after that. *Some of us have to work tomorrow.* He couldn’t quite believe the bitch would say that to him after all he’d been through.

He didn’t expect it when Liz walked out of the bedroom and into the living room. She picked up his phone, unplugging it from the snaking white cable. She pressed the power button as he stared at her, unable to speak.

“Be a fucking man,” she said as she slammed the phone down onto the table, leaving again.

The phone stared at Cameron as it went through its reboot cycle. When it was finally finished, and his background glared back at him, it was a matter of seconds before it began to vibrate.

Message after message. Email after email. Missed call after missed call. With each one he felt the tell-tale stab of anxiety behind his ribcage. The vibration went on forever, hammering into his skull.

Stop. Stop. Stop, Cameron begged of the phone. It eventually listened. The room filled with silence now. The absence of the phone’s incessant noise made it feel more alive than ever. He almost found himself wishing that the phone would buzz again.

The lock screen showed the messages, the missed calls, the emails. Seven messages. Four missed calls. Thirty-two emails. The calls and emails felt relatively safe. They would be work, family, friends.

It was the messages that filled him with dread.

Steeling his nerves, Cameron picked up the phone and typed in his password, fingertips slick with sweat. Clicking the messages bubble, his eyes widened as his eyes skimmed the names. Work. Liz. Mitchell. Dan.

He could feel the relief fill his veins like a drug. Nothing sinister. Nothing that would throw him off-kilter, that he’d need to run away from.

He placed the phone back down, raking his hands through his hair. A smile broke across his face as he revelled in the feeling of respite. Nervous laughter escaped from his mouth. He could only imagine what he'd look like to somebody else. Sitting at the table, alone, shaking with laughter. It wasn't right. He wasn't well.

The vibration shook the table, the phone moving across the smooth surface.

Cameron stopped and stared at it.

Fuck.

Unknown number.

Three words that completely fucked everything up. Thoroughly and completely.

GLAD YOU'RE BACK.

After a beat, the phone vibrated again.

WE'VE MISSED YOU.

"No, no, no." Cameron exhaled. Eyes widened. Jaw tensed.

For a second, just the briefest of seconds, he'd allowed himself to believe it was over. Stupid.

Another message broke through. A photograph. It took too long to load. Fear burned in Cameron's cheeks. His neck. It burned through him. Eating him alive. The picture was blurred. A close up. It took him a second to realise what it was. A foot. His foot. In the shot was a hand clasping a pair of hedge trimmers. They were slick with red. Blood. Beside his foot was his little toe.

It sat there. Entirely separate.

Bile tore his throat as he surged forwards and out of his chair. He ran into the bathroom, the photo scorched into his mind's eye. When there was nothing left inside of him, Cameron slid down to sit on the cold tile floor. He rested his head against his knees. They pushed into his eye sockets sending coloured whirls across his view.

He could not slow his thoughts. He could not slow down. The walls closed in on him. He had to get out. Leave his house for a while. Staggering to the front door, Cameron threw it open, the cool evening air hitting his face. It was too much. It was all too much.

He slammed the door behind himself and walked down the street. No thoughts of Liz being left alone at home, without an explanation of his quick departure, crossed his mind.

It wasn't until he got to the end of the road that he noticed he was not wearing shoes. His socks were damp, clinging to his feet.

His feet.

Sitting down on the curb, Cameron pulled the sock from his left foot. The toe was still there. Of course it was. He couldn't justify why he'd needed to look. To check. It didn't make sense, and he knew it. None of this made any sense.

The streetlight loomed over him, illuminating his hunched form. It cast the world in an eerie glow.

A rustling noise brought Cameron back to the present.

Just off to his right. The sound of somebody brushing past a bush or hedgerow.

His eyes flitted up towards the direction of the sound.

Nothing.

You're going crazy, he reprimanded himself. *You need to stop this.*

The same noise startled him again.

This time it came from his left.

At the end of the narrow lane, spotlighted beneath the streetlight, was the man. His stalker. The blood ran from Cameron's face. He couldn't move. Frozen with fear. He was out there alone. No phone. No shoes, even. Just him and the man intent on ruining his life.

Savannah

Savannah stood in the nursery, never having felt quite so alone before. Whenever she'd thought of having a baby, she'd always imagined that she would be in her own home, stable financially, and with a doting partner. She knew she was lucky in some ways, but in others, she felt that her life was lacking. That she'd taken a wrong turn at a fork in a road. She should have gone right, but instead veered left. She'd spent the last day trawling through Facebook posts on university forums, trying to find a photograph of Zack, or the girl he'd been with. That night had passed a month ago, and this was the first time Savannah had gotten up the nerve to do some digging.

Zack had given her a fake name. That much was obvious. What was also glaringly obvious was that he was still definitely a student at the university. She'd steered clear of Facebook until this point for two reasons. One, finding him wouldn't be an easy task. It would be infuriating and take forever, just for him to block her upon the first message as he didn't want to be found. Two, as much as she didn't want to admit it, she blamed him for what he'd done to her. He'd taken her life away with shit sex that had only lasted a minute. That one minute had ruined everything. She hated him, especially after their chance meeting, and would do anything to not have him in her baby's life. As far as she was now concerned, the baby was hers and hers alone.

That didn't mean she wasn't lonely. She wanted Mark. The idea she'd conjured up in her head had thrust her into this predicament anyway. That was what she wanted. But he didn't exist and now she was alone. Perhaps she'd just caught him off guard the other day. She had kind of ambushed him. For all Savannah knew, he might be trying to find her too, and he had no means to do so either.

Sitting beside the cot her dad had bought for her, a beautiful white antique looking monstrosity, Savannah scrolled through photographs uploaded to various nightclubs' Facebook pages. Photo after photo of drunken people having the best time, smiles plastered across their faces and drinks in their hands. That life was so far removed from the one she was now living. It was strange, but she no longer felt that pull. She'd simply progressed a few steps ahead of her fellow students. She'd passed Go and collected £200, while they were still stuck in jail.

With her spare hand, she rubbed at her stomach, thinking of the baby boy held within its warm cocoon. Travis. She'd settled on the name as soon as she'd seen the sonogram photograph. It was the name of the drummer from her favourite band. Plus, the name just seemed sweet. Little baby Travis Michael Windsor. She couldn't help but beam when she thought of the little baby inside of her, swimming around in there, being born and becoming an actual physical being who she would love and who would love her in return.

The photograph slapped her in the face. There he was. In the photo, he had his arm slung around two other guys. Upon their faces were dopey grins. She hated herself for the twinge she felt in her stomach. God, he was gorgeous. *He's also a world-class dickhead,* she had to remind herself

Taking a deep breath, Savannah hovered the mouse over not-Mark's face. A name popped up with a link to his Facebook page.

Cameron Nicholson.

Cameron. Cameron. The name rolled around inside of Savannah's head. At first, he'd been Mark. Then Zack. Now Cameron. It was hard to wrap her head around. The person she'd been thinking of by another name was actually somebody else. He was out there, living his life, while she sat there alone except for the tiny human being growing inside of her.

Before she could stop herself, she clicked on his name. It brought her to a public profile. Nothing was hidden. Cameron Nicholson's life was there for all to see. Photograph after photograph of him having a good time with friends. Drinking, paddle boarding, lounging beside a pool. None of this matched with the image she'd created in her head. She hovered her mouse over his friends' faces and their names popped up beside them. Mitchell Smith and Dan Lowery. She stared at their faces for a moment before she allowed her eyes to draw back to Cameron. They looked familiar. Maybe they were part of the group at the club that night? Or his roommates? She'd definitely seen them before. The next few photographs in the sequence showed him and his friends in various poses, showing off for the camera. A few other people were tagged in them too. Reese Jameson, Rose Matlock. She looked to be going out with one of Cameron's friends. She was in quite a few photos snaked up next to Mitchell. In one, a group of girls had sidled up to them and the boys had wrapped themselves around them, pulling them close. The girls' heads were thrown back in laughter, languishing in the attention from the boys. Savannah's heart sank. Penny and Gemma, and some other girls she didn't recognise, there, with their hands all over Cameron and his mates. Bile built up inside her stomach. How was it possible that they knew each other? Not only that, but they knew each other pretty well. They were in a few photos together.

Savannah clicked on Gemma's page, "Page not found." Then Penny's, "Page not found." They'd blocked her. It didn't seem fair that Cameron was linked to the two people who'd nearly ruined her life. She was certain they'd run the smear campaign, the hideous photographs online. How was it fair that they got to know the one person Savannah had thought she'd be able to fall in love with, who just happened to be the father of her baby?

Closing her eyes, she tried to gather her thoughts together. She had to see if there were more photos of Penny and Gemma with

Cameron. It wouldn't make a difference to her situation, but she was better knowing the true extent of their friendship, right?

Scrolling back through Cameron's photos, only photos from the last few months showed Gemma and Penny. They were sparsely scattered through the many photos he'd been tagged in from nights out. He'd never actually uploaded a photo with them in it. Which, strangely enough, made her feel a little better. What didn't make her feel better, were the photographs of Cameron, which he was tagged in, kissing what looked to be random girls. His friends had clearly made a habit of uploading photographs of each girl they'd caught him with. Except, there weren't any of her. It was like that night failed to exist.

Hatred boiled within her. She was better off without him, she knew that. But what if he wanted to be a part of her life, the baby's life? Maybe he was scared when she'd told him she was pregnant. It had been out of the blue. And in front of the girl he'd been, presumably, dating. Why should he believe a random woman who said she was pregnant with his child?

Placing her head in her hands, Savannah tried to clear her mind and think about what to do. Maybe she should give him another chance? Yes, he'd given her the wrong name, and he'd been an arse to her when she'd approached him on the street. But other than that? He'd done nothing wrong. Plus, it would be nice to have her baby grow up with a father.

Savannah bit her lip and pulled the laptop closer to her. She clicked on the little button that could change her life indefinitely.

ADD FRIEND.

She also clicked on the message button by his name. She wanted to give herself the best chance of Cameron listening to her, of hearing her out. He'd want a paternity test, of course, but that could be arranged easily enough. Looking at the blinking cursor, Savannah typed out a message that she hoped would win over Cameron, explaining herself and giving him a chance to do the decent thing.

HELLO CAMERON,

YOU MIGHT RECOGNISE ME FROM LAST MONTH OUTSIDE OF PINOCCHIO'S. I'M SORRY IF I SCARED YOU. I DIDN'T MEAN TO. WE SLEPT TOGETHER A FEW MONTHS AGO, EIGHT AND A HALF MONTHS TO BE PRECISE, AFTER WE MET AT A CLUB AND YOU TOOK ME HOME. YOU LEFT ME A NOTE AND GAVE ME A FAKE NAME. DON'T WORRY, I'M NOT ANNOYED ABOUT THAT. I WANTED TO GIVE YOU A CHANCE TO DO THE RIGHT THING. I'M PREGNANT. YOU'RE THE FATHER. YOU'RE THE ONLY PERSON I'VE SLEPT WITH IN OVER A YEAR, SO THERE'S NO CHANCE IT'S ANYBODY ELSE'S BABY.

I'M SORRY IF THIS COMES AS A SURPRISE, OR IF YOU'RE SCARED BUT I WANTED TO LET YOU KNOW

THAT I'M WILLING TO TALK IF YOU ARE. I'D LIKE FOR US TO GET TO KNOW ONE ANOTHER. IT DOESN'T HAVE TO BE IN A ROMANTIC WAY, OR ANYTHING, BUT A BABY DESERVES TO KNOW WHO THEIR FATHER IS.

MESSAGE ME IF YOU'D LIKE TO CHAT MORE OR MEET UP. I THINK WE SHOULD GIVE EACH OTHER A CHANCE TO WORK THIS THING OUT.

OH, AND THE BABY IS A BOY, BY THE WAY. HIS NAME WILL BE TRAVIS MICHAEL WINDSOR, UNLESS YOU'D LIKE TO BE INVOLVED TOO AND THEN WE'LL DOUBLE BARREL THE SURNAMES, OF COURSE.

SORRY IF THIS IS OUT OF THE BLUE.

SAVANNAH XXX

Savannah waited for a reply for the rest of the day. And the rest of the day after that. And the day after that. On the fourth day, she could see that the message had been read. That tell-tale little blue tick felt like a kick in the gut. Would it have hurt him just to answer? Even a simple, *I'm not interested in getting to know you or the baby,* would have been better than nothing, right?

Even though she knew it was the worst possible thing she could do, Savannah clicked on Cameron's profile again, wanting to scan through his photographs or see if there had been any new updates. There was a tiny part of her mind that thought there might be a reasonable explanation as to why he hadn't answered her. She couldn't think of what that might be, but there was always a chance.

Then she noticed it.

There, by the side of Cameron's photograph and name, was a little blue button. ADD FRIEND. He'd deleted her friend request.

The twinge in her stomach came as soon as the realisation set in. He'd read her message, seen her friend request, and deleted her like she meant nothing to him. Like the baby meant nothing to him.

Her email notification snapped her back to the present. In the corner of her laptop screen, it said NEW EMAIL: shegotwhatshedeserved@hitmail.com. Strange. The email contained only a link to a random webpage. On that webpage was only one photograph.

Savannah stood there, naked, and very pregnant. The photograph was portrait style, like she'd posed for it, standing and cupping her baby bump. It wasn't her. She'd never posed for the photograph.

Scrawled across the photograph in red letters were the words: BEING A SLUT PAID OFF.

Her throat closed. She couldn't breathe. Zooming in on the photograph, it looked so much like her, but it had to be her head on somebody else's body. But it looked so real. Everything about it looked scarily accurate, and everything about it was on display. The most intimate parts of her, there, for the whole world to see. But it couldn't be real. There was no way it was real.

A cramping sensation clawed at her insides. She screamed out in pain. She'd read about Braxton Hicks contractions, but her instincts told her that this was the real deal. This baby was coming, and it was coming now. She crossed off the page and tried to push it to the back of her mind. She'd deal with it later. Closing her laptop, Savannah walked to the top of the stairs, trying her damndest to remain calm.

"El! I think the baby is coming."

Cameron

"STOP!" The word came out with a force that Cameron didn't know was possible. It burst out of his mouth like a shot. It took a moment for him to bring himself to his feet. He stumbled and corrected himself, suddenly aware of how cold his feet had become. They were verging on entirely numb, prickling with thousands of tiny needles.

"Stop, please, I want to talk to you. Just tell me who you are. I'm sorry for whatever I've done to you. Please just stop this. I can't take it anymore."

The man remained in place. Standing smiling. Once again, Cameron thought that the smile was too wide. Too many teeth. It was a mockery of a real smile. Something there to distract rather than communicate happiness.

Cameron stepped forward. The man didn't move. His body flickered beneath the glow of the streetlight; he managed to look like a phantom. A ghost. Something not born of this world. It made Cameron's skin itch to think about.

"Please," Cameron begged. The word was full of emotion. More than anything, he wanted this man to go away and leave him alone. To go back to the life he had before. Where he was normal, and happy.

The man didn't react.

"What did I do?" Cameron staggered ahead. It was reasonable to think that he'd done something in the past to hurt this man. He had no recollection of what. The man was familiar, yes. But he couldn't place where he'd seen him before, or at what point in his life he'd come across his tormentor.

The man slowly shook his head. Left. Right. It was a warning. *Stay put. Don't move.*

Cameron needed answers. Gathering what strength he had left, he broke into a run. The man released a laugh before turning and walking slowly away.

By the time Cameron reached the corner, the man had vanished. The laugh, something about that laugh. He'd heard it before. But where? He wanted to tear at his mind with his fingers and pull the memory from within. But it was just outside of his grasp, unbearably so.

He fell to the floor and placed his head between his legs. His breath came too fast. His thoughts were intangible. The world swam around him, ebbing and flowing. Pulsating. Flash after flash. He was saying words but didn't understand them. His skin itched. Nothing felt right.

"Cameron?"

The word felt disassociated, too far away to grasp.

His world continued to spin. Like he used to feel on the waltzes at the fair as a child. A swirl of light and sound.

"Cameron."

"Sir, hello! You are Cameron Nicholson, right? Your missus is looking for you. What are you doing out here?"

The words took too long to sink in. They sounded strange, foreign.

"Cameron?"

Cameron looked up from his position on the kerb. Two men were standing over him. Their clothes were dark, and they almost blended into the black sky.

"Who are you?" Cameron mumbled.

"Sorry?" one of the men asked.

"Who are you?" Cameron repeated.

Their blank stares showed that they still had no understanding of what he was saying.

"We need to get him home."

"No!" Cameron forced himself to stand up. He backed away from the men.

"We're the police, Cameron. We're here to help you. We're going to take you home."

The prospect of returning home triggered something within him. His phone was at home. Yes, his stalker was somewhere outside. Yet, the phone was the thing he wanted to avoid more than anything. He couldn't be in the same room as it. It disgusted him.

"No," Cameron repeated. The men looked from one another and turned to look at him, their eyebrows furrowed in confusion.

"Sir, have you been drinking or taking controlled substances?"

"No, I'm fine. I don't want to go home. I'm perfectly within my rights to walk around the streets," Cameron said, indignantly.

"Look, Liz, your girlfriend, rang the police to say that you'd gone missing, and you were a risk to yourself. She said you'd been feeling depressed recently, after losing your job, and she was scared you'd hurt yourself. We just want to take you home, safe and sound, that's all." The policeman spoke as though he was talking to somebody stupid, who couldn't comprehend basic English. The words he was saying didn't make sense, though. Yes, he'd been depressed, but he had bloody good reason to be. Why on earth would Liz have told them he was a risk to himself? He'd just needed to clear his head when the bald fucker who was stalking him had shown up.

"I'm not a danger to myself, or anybody," Cameron said, trying to sound confident but failing at that hurdle.

When the policemen gave him a questioning look, he continued, "Look. I'm going through a lot right now. I'm being stalked. Somebody is sending me fucked up texts. I've probably lost my fucking job. I just needed to walk for a while, you understand that?"

"You're being stalked?" the policeman said, his face composed into a melody of sympathy and confusion.

"Yes. I reported it a while back, but nothing happened. I haven't reported it since because you guys didn't believe me in the first place. For fuck's sake, this is ridiculous! He was just here. The man was just here. I can tell you don't believe me, so what's the point?" Cameron felt his voice rising and couldn't do anything to temper it.

"Let's go and talk about this back at your house. You can make a report about it, and we can look into it. If you're being stalked and tormented, then we need to look into that properly." The way the policeman formed his words was too careful, too precise, talking to a mental patient. Cameron.

"*If, if,* you don't believe me. Just leave me alone. I'm not going anywhere with you." The police had their chance to help him and had all but laughed in his face. He had no intention of listening to them now.

"Sir, we can't leave you here. You're clearly not well."

Not well. A euphemism. Not well, meant fucking mental.

The policeman reached out for him, attempting to grab his arm.

"Don't touch me. Don't fucking touch me!" Cameron batted out with his arm, attempting to keep the policeman from connecting with his body. Misjudging the move, Cameron swiped at the policeman's face, and he jumped back as though he'd been shot.

"Cuff him. The bastard punched me."

Before Cameron could begin to protest, he felt the handcuffs tighten behind his back, so tight they cut into his wrist. He was bundled into the back of the police car.

"Mind your head," the policeman said, pushing Cameron's head to his knees. The door slammed closed behind him, hitting his shoulder, and tipping him over. He scrambled upright and turned to look out of the window. The street was empty. The streetlights illuminated funnels of light across the now slick pavement.

When did it start raining? Cameron thought. How could he have not noticed he was wet? Shivers racked through his body.

Then the man stepped into view.

"He's there!" Cameron cried at the two policemen in the front seats. Neither of them turned to look in the direction Cameron was wildly gesturing. Their heads remained forward, eyes fixed on the road.

"He's there! Fucking hell. Listen to me. He's there, my stalker!" Cameron's voice felt raw, like his throat was bleeding.

His eyes flitted between the policemen and the bald man. The smile on his lips twisted into something toxic, a mask of pure enjoyment at Cameron's agony.

"Please, please listen to me!" Cameron felt the tears streak down his cheeks. Hot and salty against his skin.

"Please," Cameron pushed the word from his mouth like a prayer.

As the police car drove away, Cameron watched as the man held up a hand and waved.

Savannah

Before she knew it, Savannah was laid in a hospital bed with legs in stirrups, a nurse elbow deep inside of her. The hospital was a private one. Her father wouldn't have it any other way, obviously. At that moment, with her legs akimbo, she was thankful for his insistence. She'd been told that you forget all about your dignity when you're trying to expel a human being from your body, but Savannah hadn't reached that point just yet. With her nightdress around her stomach and her privates hanging out for all to see, she was feeling very much self-conscious.

"You're progressing very quickly, for a first-timer." The nurse smiled, peeking up from between Savannah's legs.

"Is that a good thing?" Savannah asked. She'd only had a month or two to throw herself into the pregnancy and birthing research, seeing as she'd buried her head in the sand for the first few months of the pregnancy.

"It's a very good thing. It means this will be over and done with sooner rather than later. Which, believe me, is a good thing!" The nurse patted Savannah on the knee, a signal that she could remove her limbs from the stirrups, close her legs again and pull down her nighty.

El smiled from the seat beside her. She was on the phone with Savannah's dad.

"Yes, Mick. She's fine. Don't worry about it. Just get here when you can. The nurse said everything was fine, and that things were progressing quickly." El rolled her eyes to Savannah.

She heard her father say, "Is that a good thing?"

She couldn't help but smile at that. She and her father were more similar than she could ever imagine.

The tightness started in her stomach. A small pinch at first. Then it began to radiate deep within her, down her abdomen, and then her legs. Nothing could have prepared her for the pain of contractions. Nothing. In films, they looked bad. But the reality was so much worse.

Pushing the gas and air into her mouth, she tried to breathe through the agony. It came from a place deep within her, that shouldn't have been possible, she was sure. It was hard to pinpoint exactly. Her sensibilities told her that it was her cervix widening and her uterus contracting. But her mind told her it came from an unfathomable place akin to the fiery pits of hell.

Eventually, it passed, and Savannah collapsed back into the bed, closing her eyes. Praying that there was a sizeable gap between that one and the next one.

"Is he coming?" she managed to say.

El bent over and dabbed at the sweat on Savannah's head with a damp cloth.

"He's on his way. It might take a few hours, though. He was in Coventry, working, when I phoned. I heard him jump into the car while we were still talking."

"I wanted my dad to be here," Savannah confessed, feeling childlike in the way you do when you're feeling ill or vulnerable.

"I know you did, sweetie. But he might get here in time. You never know." El's voice was soft and serene.

"I hope the baby is out in less than three hours though! Jesus, three more hours of contractions might kill me."

"You won't be alone. I'll be here. Plus, you can handle anything. Three minutes, or three hours, you'll do it, Sav. And, at the end of it, you'll have this gorgeous baby boy."

"I can't actually believe that. Can you? That soon, I'll be holding a person that I made. It seems like something out of a sci-fi book."

"As long as the baby doesn't come bursting out of your stomach like that scene from Alien, then all will be well."

Savannah laughed and took a small sip of water. Her mouth was as dry as the desert. Her tongue scraped against the top of her mouth. She looked at her phone on the bedside table. There had been no Facebook notifications. She hadn't told El about messaging Cameron/Mark/Zack, or whatever his name was. She also hadn't mentioned the fact that he knew Penny and Gemma, and that her world was subsequently falling apart at the seams. The webpage and the photograph too, she couldn't bring herself to mention that. Not right now. It wasn't real, at least, even if people would think it was. El would go absolutely sick if Savannah told her about that, and right now, she needed El to be calm and 100 percent present on what was happening in the hospital room, not plotting to kill (or at the very least report to the police) Savannah's ex-friends.

Even at that moment, in unimaginable pain from the baby currently ripping its way out of her, and from what she'd discovered online, she still wanted Cameron to be there. There was still a chance that he would come around. That he'd decide that he wanted to be a part of her life, of her baby's life, and she would let him. Every child deserved the chance to grow up with two parents who loved them more than anything.

"El," Savannah said. "Would you do me a favour?"

"Anything," El said, and Savannah smiled because she knew her friend meant it.

"Would you go and get me a magazine from the shop downstairs? I have a feeling it's not going to be as quick as I'd like." She gestured down to her stomach to illustrate her point. She had no intention at all of reading a magazine. She could barely keep her eyes open. She wanted El gone so that she could check her phone and let Cameron know that she'd gone into labour.

In her mind, she justified that it might be the push he needed. Pregnancy is an abstract thing. Labour and the delivery of the baby, well, that's a hell of a lot more concrete. Maybe he'd show up. It would be perfect. He could be there from the start.

"Of course, any preference?" El stood up.

"Something with shitty stories like *I hid my pregnancy for seven months.* You know, the usual unbelievable crap they write." Savannah half-laughed.

"Sure, you can't believe anything those magazines write. It's all a load of nonsense. I mean, who would be able to hide their pregnancy for seven months and nobody noticed!" El winked and walked out of the room, shutting the door behind her.

Quickly picking up her phone, Savannah opened Facebook. Still no notifications or messages. Annoying, but expected. She clicked on the messages button and then on Cameron's face. Her message was there, stark and unanswered. She felt white hot tears burning at her eyes when she saw that the message had been read and the bastard hadn't bothered to answer. She couldn't bring herself to open her emails and look at the photograph again. All she wanted right now was for Cameron to do the right thing.

Perhaps her labour would push him to respond.

HELLO CAMERON,

JUST TO LET YOU KNOW. I'M IN LABOUR. YOUR SON WILL BE HERE ANY MINUTE. I'M IN ROOM 4 AT MEADSTEAD HOUSE MATERNITY SUITE. YOU ARE WELCOME TO COME AND JOIN ME AND MEET YOUR SON. I DOUBT YOU WILL BUT I WANTED TO GIVE YOU THE OPTION. YOU'LL PROBABLY REGRET IT LATER IF YOU DON'T.

LOVE, SAVANNAH.

The magazine remained untouched as Savannah's labour progressed. Two hours after El had returned with the magazine, Savannah was told that she was ten centimetres dilated and that it was time to start pushing. A shiver of fear coursed through her body as reality sunk in. In a few minutes, she would have a baby. A real live baby.

Gas and air weren't enough, but it was too late for anything more substantial. She had nothing left to do but push.

"Ready?" the nurse asked, a gentle smile on her face.

"Yeah, it's coming," Savannah answered. She could feel the contraction building inside of her. When it reached its peak, she pushed down into her arse, just as the nurse had told her to. The pain was like nothing else she could ever imagine experiencing. The contractions had been tickles compared to the ripping sensation she felt at that moment.

When the contraction ended, Savannah panted, trying to regain her breath.

"You're doing so well," El said.

"It hurts." Savannah sighed, exhausted already.

The next contraction built, and Savannah wanted to throw her head back and pray for it to stop. She couldn't do it again.

"Please," she heard herself muttering.

"You can do this," El said. Her eyes were determined, focused on Savannah's own.

Once more she grunted, animalistic, and pushed her chin to her chest, and her weight into the bed. The burning, tearing, searing sensation heightened and Savannah tried to fight the urge to scream and cry.

"I can see the head," the nurse said. "Do you want to feel it?"

Savannah felt herself nod, and the nurse guided her hand between her legs. Where it was usually soft, she felt a hard, round dome shape pushing against her opening. A baby. Travis was there. He was almost out.

"With the next one we might get his head all the way out." The nurse's positive attitude compensated for how ill Savannah felt. She hadn't realised that labour could make a person feel like they could simultaneously vomit and faint.

"Is it coming?" El asked.

Savannah nodded as the next contraction wracked through her drained body. She pushed again, feeling herself rip and then a moment of relief.

"Is that it?" Savannah asked.

"That's his head. The next one he'll be out. Come on, one more." The nurse beamed at her, crinkles forming at the corners of her eyes.

"Okay," Savannah breathed.

The next contraction started almost instantly. She pushed. There was a moment of blinding pain and then of complete relief.

"He's here!" El shouted, touching Savannah's face with her soft hand. "You did it!"

Savannah wasn't listening. "Why isn't he crying?"

"Give me a second. Let me get him cleaned off. He looks very healthy. Very pink."

Savannah tried to watch what the nurse was doing, but she had her back to her. She shot a worried look at El who shook her head in a way that said, *stop panicking*.

The cry was the most beautiful sound she'd ever heard. It shook the earth upon which she lay.

"Here he is." The nurse pulled Savannah's neckline to the side and slipped the baby inside against her skin. The warmth of his frail little body against hers, sent tears cascading from her eyes.

How was it possible to love someone so intensely so quickly?

The nurse went back to the bottom of the bed and sat on the stool she'd placed there for herself. Savannah paid her no attention. Instead, she gazed into her baby's face, touching his pink cheek with her ring finger. He was so delicate, so new, and he relied entirely upon her. The love she felt from him, not to him, but from him was instantaneous. Even though the baby in her arms was barely able to think other than in needs, she could feel in her bones that he loved her.

There was movement at the bottom of the bed.

She heard El ask what was wrong, her voice shaking.

"There's some bleeding that we hadn't anticipated, nothing to worry about. I'm just getting the doctor to look."

Savannah had already begun to swim in and out of consciousness. She was barely able to worry that she might drop her baby if she fell asleep. Her brain was an impenetrable fog, but it was okay. Because she knew that she was so loved and would love in return. She caught the odd word and phrase.

El's voice rose to the point of hysteria. "What's happening?"

Heart rate.

Blood pressure.

Blood loss.

Haemorrhage.

Surgeon, ASAP!

At some point, but she couldn't remember when or how, the baby had been taken away from her. She needed him back. Why would they take him away from her? She loved him more than anything else in the world. She would die for him. They needed to give him back.

Her father's voice.

She couldn't make out his words.

His face in front of her own.

He swam in and out of contrast as her world faded to black.

Cameron

Spending the night in the cells wasn't exactly in Cameron's life plan. Other than what he'd seen on TV, the thought of ever even entering a police cell hadn't crossed his mind. He hadn't even been sure of what to expect. After arriving at the police station, he and the officers had stood at the front desk while they "booked" him. They said it was for his own safety, suspecting he was on drugs or too drunk to go home. His blood-alcohol level came back at zero. There were also no drugs in his system, much to the officers' surprise. Nobody had mentioned the fact that Cameron had punched an officer, and so he didn't either. He didn't fancy digging his own grave.

When they told him the news, he wanted to scream in their faces, "I told you so!" But he didn't have the energy to do it. Instead, he laid back on the thin rubber mattress and waited for morning to come.

As the sun rose in the sky, and the officers on shift changed, Cameron allowed himself to sit up on the bed, showing that he was awake and ready to go home. The officers initially ignored him, carrying on with their daily routine like he wasn't a priority. As frustration built within him, he did what he could to keep it under control. All he wanted to do was to go home and get in bed, whether his phone was there or not. His heightened emotions from the previous night had ebbed away.

The knock on the door finally came. "Mr Nicholson, I'm Officer Handley. Are you ready to get out of here?"

"Yes," Cameron said, running his hands over his tired face.

"Okay, we'll be releasing you now as we don't feel you're a danger to yourself anymore. However, we would strongly advise you to go and seek medical attention. Your tests all came back negative, I can see, and you're fairly calm now so we're not worried about drug abuse. We do note that you may potentially have mental health problems that might have contributed to last night's episode. You should see your GP as soon as possible, or if it's an emergency, go to A and E."

He wanted to scream and cry and tell the officer that he had a damn good reason for acting the way he did. Nobody had mentioned the stalker since he'd arrived in police custody, and it was clear that they all thought he'd imagined it. Cameron didn't have the energy to prove them wrong. He just wanted to go home.

"Okay." His non-committal answer seemed to do the trick, and the officer unlocked the door to the cell, escorting him out of the building and thrusting a clear plastic bag of his possessions into his hands.

"I assume you're able to make your way home?" Officer Handley said. For the first time, Cameron really looked at her. She was younger than he was. Early twenties perhaps. Long blonde hair wrapped up into a bun that leaned precariously at the back of her head. There was the tiniest hint of makeup on her face. She looked at him with sympathy, like an old man who was struggling to take care of himself.

"I'm perfectly capable of getting home." Cameron resisted the urge to roll his eyes.

"In which case, I hope you feel better soon." The smile didn't reach her eyes as the double glass doors shut in front of her. He could feel her eyes on his back as he walked away.

The walk home took less than twenty minutes. He did it as though on autopilot. As he walked through the door to his home, he realised that he couldn't actually remember the route he'd taken.

"Hello," Cameron called into the house, half-expecting an answer. Liz should be at work already, sitting behind her desk and editing photos of models so that they looked absolutely perfect and ready to be placed front and centre in the magazine.

He didn't expect Liz to walk out of the living room, glaring at him. The look on her face was new. He didn't recall ever having seen her so mad before.

"Jail, Cam, really?" she said. There was no ounce of sympathy or regret in her voice. It almost made him miss Officer Handley's overly concerned response.

"It was hardly my fault," he said, walking past her. He was not in the right frame of mind to deal with her mood swings and reprimands. He needed his bed. Needed proper sleep.

"Are you actually going to walk away from me after what you did? No apology? No explanation? Jesus, Cameron, what the fuck is wrong with you?"

"What is wrong with me? I have a fucking stalker, Liz. I'm being sent photographs of myself being tortured. The police think I'm mental. I'm lucky I wasn't sectioned. They think I'm imagining it. I'm pretty sure I'm going to be fired too, on top of all that. So, excuse me if I'm not chirpy all of the fucking time." Cameron continued to walk towards the bedroom, leaving Liz to trail along behind him if she wanted to continue with the argument.

She did. "We're back to the stalker again? Back to the photos? I thought all that had stopped. You can't have it both ways, Cameron. Either you're being tormented, or you're not. It can't change on a daily basis." The way she looked at him made him ball his fists. He'd never hit a woman before. Never even considered it, but at that moment, dear God, he wanted to.

"Did you ever think I didn't tell you because of the way you reacted before? Nobody believes me. You think it's a prank, a joke, and yet I'm seeing this bald man stalking me. He turned up at school, Liz. That's why I lost my fucking job. None of this is my fault."

"You really don't see that you're at fault, do you? You're a grown man, Cameron. You have to take responsibility for your actions. You chose to be a dickhead to the police officers. You chose to not do your job properly. You chose to not get help. At the end of the day, all of this is on you. You need to understand that. Now, if you do have a stalker, or whatever, why the hell aren't you doing something about it?"

Cameron's shoulders sagged at those words. *If.* She didn't believe him. "I tried to get help from the police. I've tried twice now. I don't know what else to do. They look at me like I'm crazy."

"Well, maybe you are? This isn't normal behaviour, Cameron. I'm sorry but it isn't." Her hands were on her hips like a mother telling off a naughty child.

Cameron blinked. He had no idea how to respond to that. For weeks he'd felt like he was going crazy. If Liz thought he was too, then maybe it was true. Her stare made him want to crumple to the ground, to dissolve through the carpet and never be seen again.

"Look, if you want to do this, then you need to get help. We're booking you in at the doctors' tomorrow and you're going to let them put you on any medication they want to. Something isn't right in your head. If we get that fixed, maybe everything else will fall back into place."

"You think I'm imagining the stalker? How could you think that? You saw the photographs and the texts." Cameron took one step towards her, waiting to gauge her reaction before he tried for another.

"I saw some photos a while back, Cameron. You've not mentioned it since. And, you have to see that your mental health has deteriorated since then. I'm wondering if it might be a figment of your imagination, or the result of some kind of medical condition. That's why we need to go to the doctor."

A laugh escaped his mouth. He didn't mean to. The whole situation was just too ridiculous. The woman he'd chosen to spend the foreseeable future with thought he was making up a stalker at best and, at worst, hallucinating one.

"I have the photos," Cameron said, trying not to push past her with too much force. Domestic abuse wasn't something he wanted to add to his list of offences. The phone was where he left it on the table. "Here." Cameron thrust it into Liz's hands after unlocking it.

"What am I supposed to be looking at?" Liz held the phone out to him, away from herself, as though it might burn her.

"Look at the texts. Everything is there. I can't prove that I've seen him in real life, but you can see for yourself the sick messages and photos he's been sending. I haven't figured out how he took the photos of me yet, or if they're even me, but they're there. And they're fucked up, Liz." He said the words so fast that they blurred together into one long breath.

Cameron watched as Liz navigated through his phone. Her manicured finger tapped away at the screen. Slowly her brow furrowed. Her lip twitched.

"Cameron, honey, there's nothing here." Her voice was as soft as silk, and her eyes filled with tears. "It's okay. Let's go to A and E. They might be able to help you there. There will be a psychiatrist there, I'm sure. Cameron, you're hallucinating things. I'm scared."

The words barely grazed his consciousness. He snatched the phone away from her to find the messages. His heart plummeted. The messages, the threats, the photographs, they'd all vanished.

"One minute, they're here somewhere." Cameron furiously scrolled through his messages. Trying to find a recycling file or something. The messages had been there. They were real. There was no doubt of that in his mind.

"Cameron?" Liz's voice begged from what felt like a million miles away.

"They were here. Google, how do you retrieve deleted messages?"

The robotic voice broke through the room. "If you use Android Messages, you can touch and hold a conversation to archive or delete it. For details, tap more info. If you use another app for text messages, check the app's online content."

The phone smashed into the wall before he'd even realised it had left his hand. Two sets of eyes stared down at the broken mass on the floor. Neither moved. The gravity of what had happened weighed down upon them.

"Cameron," Liz prompted, trying to edge closer to him now. When he met her eyes, he could see that she was scared of him. Approaching him like you would a person thinking of throwing themselves off the top of a building.

"There were messages," Cameron repeated.

"Cameron," was all Liz said in response. Her hands found him, fingertips featherlike against his arms.

"There were messages."

"Come on. Why don't you have a shower? You'll feel better after. We'll have a cup of tea and try and get an emergency appointment at the doctor."

"Liz. You're not listening to me. There *were* messages." Those three words already sounded strange on his tongue. They didn't quite make sense anymore. Lost meaning, washed away with overuse.

"I know, Cam. I know. I know."

Sinking into Liz's shoulder, Cameron allowed himself to be wrapped into a hug. Everything about it was familiar. Comforting. It didn't stop the embarrassment from welling up under his skin, trying to push its way out through his pores. He would not allow himself to question whether the messages were real. He wouldn't do that.

“Shower.” He caught the word as it floated by. Like a dog, he followed Liz into the bathroom and allowed himself to be undressed. For a split second, he thought that Liz would join him. A pang of excitement exploded in his stomach. Then Liz rolled up her sleeves and reached for a flannel, squirting shower gel onto it. As the water washed over his body, and Liz rubbed the flannel against his skin, Cameron’s mind fell into a pit of nothingness. Painfully blank. Mercifully blank.

Just out of reach, he could sense the thought that he should be ashamed by what was happening to him. His girlfriend was showering him. Washing his most intimate areas like she was bathing an elderly relative. The detachment she showed through the process made him feel sick.

At some point, Liz dressed him. He couldn’t remember it happening. He sat on the bed, vaguely aware that she was on the phone. He heard various words but couldn’t follow the whole thing.

Emergency appointment.

Cameron Nicholson.

Depressed.

Hallucinating.

Risk.

Hurt himself.

Please.

The word "please" hurt. The pitch of Liz's voice showed that she was not handling the whole thing with the detachment he'd thought. There was a hitch in her voice.

"Two pm, with Dr Wawrosz, thank you."

Liz hung up her phone and looked to Cameron. "Don't worry, Cam. We'll get you better. I promise."

He was too weak to argue that he didn't need any mental health help. He needed to be taken seriously.

Cameron

Cameron's eyes were glued to the packet in his hands. It contained a month's worth of little white pills that were supposed to solve all his problems. The doctor's appointment had gone exactly as he'd expected. Liz had talked all the way through it, telling the doctor of every single one of Cameron's failings since they'd been together. After a few minutes, he had switched off. When the doctor asked him questions, of which there were many, he answered simply.

"How are you feeling in yourself?"

"Exhausted."

"Tell me about the photographs."

"Somebody has been sending me photographs of me being tortured."

"Can I see the photos?"

"They're not there anymore."

"Why?"

"I don't know."

"Are you certain they were there to begin with?"

"Yes."

The doctor had scribbled something down here.

"And Liz mentioned that you have been seeing a man? Somebody who is following you? Tell me about that."

“There’s a bald man who follows me around. I think he’s the same one sending the messages. I saw him at school, but he ran away before I could catch him.”

“How often do you see him?”

“Every now and again.”

“Are you certain he’s real?”

“Yes.”

Again, the doctor scribbled something else down on his piece of paper.

This was how he’d ended up with the prescription for a second-generation antipsychotic, with a name he couldn’t pronounce. And also a small dose of anti-depressants too, just to be on the safe side. He’d also found himself on a waiting list for Cognitive Behaviour Therapy, which sounded like a barrel of laughs.

“Take your pills.”

He hadn’t seen Liz standing in the door until she spoke. She sounded like a schoolteacher. Despite the fact that she was trying to help him, Cameron was mad at her. Mad to the point where he wanted to scream at her for putting him through that fucking doctor’s appointment.

Instead of arguing, he dry swallowed one of the tablets. The doctor had told him that his symptoms would get worse before they got better. It was just how the tablets worked. Once they’d built up in his system, he'd be golden. Then they could start playing around with the combination, and doses, so that they could find the right fit.

There was a small piece of him that hoped he was a psychotic depressive. The doctor hadn't diagnosed that, no, that would take a psychiatrist to determine, but he had strongly hinted that he believed this to be the case. If the medication worked, and then the therapy, and the bald man and the messages had all been a part of his mental illness, then Cameron could get on with his life. It felt fucked up to think that way. But it was easier to deal with than this shit show being real.

"Good boy," Liz said, as she turned and walked out of the room, closing the door behind her, and leaving him to sit on the bed and wait for the tablets to kick in.

He was completely and utterly exhausted. After spending a night in the cells, and barely sleeping a wink, he knew that he should try and sleep. There was a part of him that didn't want to. Sleep would be too easy after the pain he was causing Liz, and himself.

"I'm going out," Cameron heard Liz call. There was no further explanation as she closed the door behind her, leaving him fully alone.

The doctor had warned that his symptoms would get worse, so why would Liz leave him on his own right now? There had been talk of suicide, of hospitalization, of self-harm, and she'd gone and left him to his own devices. The thought of her leaving him alone burned within him. What kind of a girlfriend would do that?

Feeling annoyed, so much so that jolts of electricity coursed through his body, Cameron pushed himself off the bed and walked into the front room. Perhaps he should show her that he shouldn't be alone. He should do something stupid that would make her regret leaving him.

He looked around the living room for inspiration. He could set a fire. He could cut himself. He could break something.

Slumping down on the sofa he knew that he wouldn't do any of those things, as much as he would love to see Liz's reaction. He grabbed the TV remote and went to turn it on when a thought came to him. His phone. After he smashed it against the wall, he hadn't seen it again. Liz must have tidied it up. Perhaps, thrown it away. Once more the irrational flood of anger built within him. How dare she touch his stuff? He allowed her to live there, and she messed everything up. Invading his space and touching his things.

He only had to walk into the kitchen to find his phone. It sat there on the worktop, a gigantic crack down the screen, slicing it across the diagonal. He wondered if it still worked. Reaching out to touch it, his fingers stopped millimetres away. He couldn't cross that barrier. He couldn't bring himself to touch the phone.

His hand shook vigorously as he pulled it back to himself. He felt like he'd been electrocuted.

“Fuck,” he cursed to the empty kitchen.

The phone stared back at him, daring him to pick it up. Cameron stared back, unable to move, barely able to think. The only thing that crossed his mind, over and over again, like a stuck record, was the word “coward.” Eventually, his eyes began to blur and water. He hadn’t blinked. His mouth filled with saliva. He hadn’t swallowed. The clock on the wall said 5.30 pm. He didn’t know what time Liz went out, but it felt like hours ago. And all he’d done since she’d left was have a staring match with a fucking phone.

“Damn it!” Cameron smashed his fist into the marble worktop. He felt something crack in the base of his hand but didn’t register the pain immediately. It wasn’t until the phone gave three sharp vibrations, sliding across the counter with each, that he noticed the crumbling sensation in his hand.

He knew what the message would be before he looked at it. The cracked screen was difficult to navigate but the second he unlocked the phone, the message filled the screen obnoxiously.

A photo attachment.

It was a close-up of Cameron’s head and neck. Only above his shoulders. The red slit under his chin was the focus of the photograph. The ragged wound dribbled blood down his chest. Using his finger and thumb, Cameron zoomed in. There was no doubt in his mind that it was real. Through the deep red blood, he could see bright white. His spine? Cartilage? Something else? He wasn't certain. The head was rolled backwards, over the back of the chair, opening the gash so that it looked like a smiling mouth, twisted, telling a sick joke.

His own breath cloyed and clogged in his throat. He couldn't force air into his lungs, or out of them.

Police.

The thought brought him back to the present as a rushing of air filled his lungs. If they saw this, they'd have to do something. They'd have to believe him. He almost didn't want to shut off the photograph, scared that it would vanish and never return with the rest of them.

"Nine nine nine, what's your emergency?"

He stumbled over his words. They tumbled out of him. Nonsensical. But he thought he got his point across. "My name is Cameron Nicholson. I reported that I'd been stalked and sent threats a while back. It's been happening ever since. I need somebody to come. Now. Please. They sent me a photo of my throat being slit. I think I'm dead. Please."

"Sir, are you a threat to yourself or to others?"

"What, no. Please, can you send somebody to look at this? It's bad. Really, bad."

"What's your address, sir, I'm sending somebody right now."

Cameron opened the photograph back up on his phone as soon as he'd hung up. Still there. He breathed a sigh of relief knowing that they would have to believe him. It was irrefutable evidence.

When the door opened, he took his phone and sprinted down the hall, panting, sweat dripping off his brow. He was finally going to be able to prove them wrong.

"What's wrong?" Liz stood there in the doorway.

"Look at this." Cameron pushed the phone into her hand before she could even step through the threshold.

"What am I looking at?" Liz stared at the photograph, eyebrows dipping close to her eyes in concentration.

"Somebody just sent this to me. It's me, Liz. Look, somebody has slit my throat. They've killed me."

"Honey, come and sit down." Liz placed a hand on his shoulder to try and guide him into the living room. He resisted. Her reaction wasn't right.

"Why aren't you upset about this, Liz? Somebody has sent me a photo of them killing me." His face flushed and despite trying to hold them back, tears spilt out of his eyes.

"This is just some kind of sick joke, Cameron. This isn't you. You can't even see the person's face. It's clearly a fake. Look at the wound, it doesn't even look realistic."

"What the fuck are you saying? Of course it's me! Of course it's fucking real!" His fist slammed into the wall, shattering the plaster, and hitting the brick beneath it. The crunching sensation further heightened.

"Is everything okay?" The police officer approached behind Liz. It was a woman, young, perhaps mid-twenties. The cop who stepped behind her was an older gentleman. It was him Cameron wanted to talk to. Not the child playing dress-up.

"No," both Liz and Cameron chorused at the same time.

"Shall we go in and talk about it, sir?" the younger officer said, and Cameron wanted to roll his eyes. He didn't because he needed them to listen to him.

All four of them walked into the front room and he and Liz started talking at the same time.

"I'm sorry, but my partner is suffering from some mental health issues. The doctor has given him new medication and…"

"I've been sent photographs of myself being killed. And tortured. The most recent one has just arrived. Show them Liz. I'm being stalked too."

Liz reluctantly passed over the phone as suspicion washed over Cameron. Why was she trying to make out that he was crazy, and all of this is in his head?

The officer looked at the photograph for a moment before she passed it to the elder male policeman.

"This could be anybody," the child playing dress-up said.

"It's me," Cameron said at the same time as Liz said, "Exactly."

"You mentioned other photographs and messages on the phone? You also mentioned a stalker?" Relief overcame Cameron as the male officer started talking. He would take it seriously.

"Yes. I've had loads of messages, both words and photographs, making threats and showing different methods of torture against me."

"Can we see them?" Cameron's throat plummeted into his stomach at those words.

"Well, the messages vanished. I can't find them."

The policeman turned to Liz and raised his eyebrows, a silent question.

In response, she shrugged. "I saw a couple of messages a few months ago. They were blurry and could have been anybody. He's a teacher, so I thought it might have been a student in his class playing a joke on him."

If looks could have killed, Liz would have been dead where she sat. He'd never felt pure hatred like that before.

"Okay. Mr Nicholson, what about this stalker?" He wasn't sure which officer had spoken as he was too busy directing his revulsion at Liz.

"I see him everywhere. He's tall. Bald. Stocky. I feel like I know him but don't know where from. I see him everywhere. He smiles at me. This terrifying smile. He doesn't really speak. And then he vanishes into thin air, and I can't find him. He's watching me all of the time though. Some of the messages proved that, but they're not there anymore."

"What kind of clothes does he wear?" the female officer asked. Cameron decided that he actually quite liked her.

"Just normal clothing. Trousers and a shirt. Sometimes a suit. Usually dark, I think. His face is what catches my attention. It's maniacal."

"Wow, big word," the policeman said. Cameron shot him the same look as he gave Liz, hoping he would drop dead as a result.

"I'm an English teacher."

"Was an English teacher?" the policeman corrected. "Our records showed that you wound up in the cells last night, Mr Nicholson. You told the officers you'd been fired from your job. That's bound to have an impact on your mental health. In all fairness, they did say that you were talking about having seen your *stalker* just before they picked you up."

"I did see my stalker last night. I am still an English teacher. I'm on sick leave at the minute."

"Because of your deteriorating mental health?"

"No. Because a parent complained about me, and this is just an easier route for the school to take."

"What did the parent complain about?" The policeman was becoming argumentative now. Trying to get a rise out of Cameron. He wouldn't give him the satisfaction. Despite how things looked, he wasn't mental. He had a stalker. Somebody was sending him torture porn, featuring himself in the role of leading man.

"That's not relevant."

"Well, perhaps it is, but I can see that's a contentious subject right now. So, let's get back to the task at hand. Somebody has sent you a photograph you didn't like. And you see a man fairly often, and you think he's stalking you. So we need to figure out what to do."

Cameron found himself turning away from the policeman and looking at the young girl for support. His eyes pleaded with her, begging her to take him seriously. Normal Cameron, the Cameron of a few months ago, would be mortified to look this way, to act this way, in front of anybody. Now, he didn't care. He just wanted this whole thing to be over. To go back to normal.

"Please look into it. I have a stalker. I promise. I might be on medication, but I'm not hallucinating. I promise you."

"I'm going to suggest that what we do is to send out routine patrols, every day or so, just to check in on you. I can see how scared you are, Mr Nicholson. It's our job to keep the public safe, and this will allow us to do that. In the meantime, you call if you see the man and we'll try to have a word with him."

Liz and the policeman looked at the young officer with shock, as though they couldn't believe she caved so easily. Perhaps it was his puppy dog eyes and terrified expression that convinced her to help him. Maybe she was simply placating him to make her job easier. Either way, Cameron was grateful.

"And the messages?" Cameron asked her, not caring about the tiny broken voice.

"I suggest you block the number. Maybe screenshot everything you receive and save it to the cloud. That way they can't vanish."

"I'll do that! Thank you."

"I'll organise the patrols when I get back to the station. You'll see them occasionally. Flag them down if you need anything."

"I appreciate that. I really do. Thank you so much."

"I'll show you out," Liz said. Her words were tight. Her face scrunched in a way that made her unattractive, something he'd never noticed before.

When she returned, she sat down across from him and looked dead in his eyes.

"Cameron, I can't do this anymore. Calling the police because of a text message isn't normal. I've had enough. I don't want to live like this anymore. This isn't what I signed up for." The words melted together in one long string.

"Somebody sent me a photograph of my throat being cut, Liz. It's a normal response to phone the police." Cameron didn't remove his eyes from hers. He would not let her convince him that he was being crazy. Calling the police was the sanest thing he'd done in a long time, and he knew that.

"No, Cameron. It's not. Phoning the police because someone texts you a photograph is not a normal response."

"I'm being stalked, Liz. For fuck's sake! Why don't you understand that?" He could feel the tendons in his neck forcing against his skin, trying to break free.

"No, Cameron. You're not. You're not well. I can't handle this. I'm not going to be your carer while you don't even try to get better. I can't do that. I'm sorry. I just can't."

"You don't look sorry at all. You look like you're happy to leave me. And do you know what, if you're going to try and gaslight me then I'm happy for you to leave too. Send somebody to get your things. I don't want to see you again. You make me sick."

"Really? That's how we're going to do this? I thought we might be civil, but fine, I'll go. But I will come back for my things, Cameron. They're *my* things. You can't prevent me from doing that." She was already on her feet, handbag in hand, walking out of the living room. The front door slammed behind her.

Everything had happened so fast that he couldn't even replay the conversation in his mind to see where he'd gone wrong. What had been the tipping point? The straw that had broken the camel's back? He had no clue. All he knew was that he'd be better off without her. He needed people who trusted him by his side right now, not people who pulled him apart.

He picked up his phone and began to scroll through his contact list. There must be somebody he could ring for him to talk to. He sent texts to people he thought could take his mind off things. Not his mum, and certainly not his sister. Reese, Mitchell, Dan, and Joe.

FANCY A CATCH-UP? DRINKS ON ME.

He waited for a response. None came immediately, and so he decided to go and pack up some of Liz's things into boxes. It would make life easier when she came to collect her things. The argument still didn't seem real, but it had been. She'd walked out of there and was ready to never come back.

In the bedroom, he emptied the wardrobes of her clothes and piled them into bin bags, hangers and all. He began to feel relief, like he was doing something worthwhile. He moved on to the medicine cabinet in the bathroom, throwing all of her products into another bin bag. A smirk grew on his face as he thought of her response to all of her expensive perfumes and body butters thrown into a shitty bin bag. It would infuriate her. Exactly the response he wanted.

When his phone buzzed, for the first time in weeks, he opened it readily, eager to see which friend would come to his rescue. Blood ran cold in his veins when he saw the unknown number. Another photograph. Mentally preparing himself to see his dead body lying in a ditch somewhere, or chopped up into little pieces, Cameron clicked on it. The photo loaded and instantly he wished it hadn't.

He wasn't the subject of the photograph.

Strapped into a chair still slick with Cameron's blood was Liz. A dirty rag cut through her face, holding her mouth into a perpetual grimace. Her wide eyes were pleading, bloodshot. There was a slight concave to her forehead where it looked like she'd been hit hard with something.

Her wrists and ankles were bound to the chair arms and legs. The red wire looked too tight. He could see where her skin bulged and curled around it.

Cameron scanned the rest of her body for signs of torture but there was nothing visible. Thank God. Overwhelmed with regret for their argument and his subsequent actions, Cameron stared at the image, ready to phone the police, when another message crept onto the screen.

NOW WE WILL MAKE YOU PAY FOR WHAT YOU DID.

YOU TOOK HER FROM US.

NOW WE WILL TAKE HER FROM YOU.

184 HOPWOOD ROAD.

SEE YOU SOON.

Shoving his feet into his shoes, and his phone into his pocket, Cameron barrelled out of the door, leaving it yawning open behind him.

Mick

The baby was thrust into his arms as his child was wheeled out of the room. He couldn't remember much after that. It was a blur of movement, of air electric with tension. Of not understanding what the hell was happening. His daughter had died in surgery. They couldn't stop the bleeding no matter how hard they'd tried. A postpartum haemorrhage the doctor said. The uterus didn't contract when the placenta was birthed. There was no way they could have foreseen it happening, and they'd done all they could to save her. It didn't make it easier to deal with.

El looked at him with questions etched upon her tired face. Mick couldn't bring himself to answer. There were no words to explain what had happened. To justify it. A life snuffed out without any warning. The baby wriggled in his arms as he was shown his daughter's body. They'd cleaned her up after surgery. Wrapped her in a crisp white cloth. She looked like she was sleeping. Peaceful. Her stomach protruded from the table, mountainous. She had grown the baby in his arms inside of her for nine months, and now she no longer existed.

Mick wanted to hate the baby. To be filled with disgust and to be able to ship it off to some other family. But he couldn't do it. He couldn't bring himself to get rid of the only tie he had left to his daughter. Two emotions fought tooth and nail within him. The agony for the loss of his daughter, and the love for his grandson.

Before he left the morgue, he kissed Savannah on the forehead.

"I love you. I will keep him safe, no matter what."

As soon as the baby was given the okay—he was perfectly healthy, not a single thing to concern the medical staff, which felt like a sick joke—Mick and El walked out of the hospital together. She carried a bag of Savannah's things. Mick carried the baby. It shouldn't have been that way. To leave the hospital without the mother of the child. His daughter. Together, they figured out how to put the car seat into the back of Mick's car. It was thanks to El that they managed to get the baby strapped in quickly. Left to his own devices, he was sure he'd still have been in the car park hours later.

They sank into the front seats of the car. Neither of them reached for their seatbelts.

"What are we going to do?" Mick said, not tearing his eyes from the windscreen and the view of the cinderblock building.

"The only thing we can." El's voice was hoarse, strained with hours of crying. Mick hadn't shed a tear yet. He wouldn't allow them to fall. Not until this was over, and he was alone.

"What is that?" Mick shook his head. How did you live a life without your child? How could you look to the future knowing they wouldn't be there?

"We raise Travis the best we can. Savannah would want that." El's voice broke and throbbed.

"We?" Mick turned his head towards El. The practical stranger in the seat beside him. His child's friend. Savannah's best, and possibly only, friend.

"There's no way you can raise a baby alone, Mick. Let me help you. I need to be near him. I loved her too." El looked at her knees. It was obvious that she was willing the tears not to fall.

"But you're in university? You have your whole life ahead of you. Savannah made the mistake, not you. You can walk away from this guilt-free."

"You know there's no way I can do that. Let me help you."

"Okay." Mick wasn't sure why he'd agreed. The word had escaped from him before he could think on it further. El was right. He couldn't raise a baby alone. He'd never been the most hands-on dad with Savannah. Hell, after her mum left, he hired people to do the child-rearing for him. He wouldn't do that this time around. In the back seat of the car was his second chance, and he wasn't going to let that slip through his fingers.

The funeral was quiet, except for the raking sounds of Travis's screeching cries. Mick wondered if some part of him knew that they were burying his mother. The woman who nurtured him for nine months and died bringing him into the world.

El organised the whole thing, while Mick shamefully isolated himself with Travis. So far, he'd only managed to put Travis down for two reasons: for El to hold the baby, or for the baby to sleep. Anything else felt like a betrayal. Savannah had given him the chance to raise a child, and that was something he couldn't help but be thankful for, as much as he wished to be Travis's grandfather, rather than father. Savannah's mother had taken away all possibility of Mick having another child of his own during their painfully short marriage. Her last act of manipulation was to convince him to get a vasectomy. Whenever he thought of that cow, his blood would boil. Pulling himself back to the moment, he looked at the baby in his arms, and allowed it to centre him.

When it was Mick's turn to stand at the front of the crematorium and make his speech, he took Travis with him, holding him against his chest tightly like a security blanket. The faces below him were all familiar, but in his grief, he didn't want to see any of them. Co-workers. Employees. Some of Savannah's lecturers and classmates. Nobody that truly loved Savannah as he did, other than perhaps El, and the baby who would never know her.

"Thank you all for being here to celebrate the life of my daughter. She might not have lived a long life, but she lived well. She touched the lives of all of those she met. She has given me the greatest gift, in her passing. She would have been an incredible mother if she had been given the chance. Travis will never get to know the beautiful person his mother was, inside and out, but I will remind him of that each and every day. She lives on through him, as her memory lives on through us. Please, light a candle tonight for my daughter, Savannah."

The speech was short, but it was all that he could manage. He returned to his seat next to El and watched as Savannah's coffin, draped with hundreds of white tulips, was lowered into the ground. They left the building together, thanking the guests for their prayers and commiserations. In the car on the way home, El turned her attention to Mick so quickly that he thought something was wrong.

They'd been living together for the past week. Since Savannah's death. El had taken up residence in the spare bedroom in the attic of his house. Savannah's childhood bedroom had become Travis's room.

"I have to tell you something. But I don't know if I should."

"Do I need to pull over?"

"I think it would be better if you kept going."

"You've got me worried, El. What is it?"

"I took Savannah's phone from the hospital when we collected her stuff together. I managed to figure out the password. It was your birthday, by the way. Anyway, she left her Facebook logged in, and so I looked through the messages. I know it was a betrayal of trust, but I needed to feel closer to her. I needed to know more. I'm sorry."

El stopped talking, expecting Mick to intervene. He wasn't sure how he felt about El going through Savannah's phone, and so he wouldn't speak on it until he'd sifted through his feelings.

"Anyway, I read her messages and there were some to her baby's father."

"I thought she didn't know who the father was? A one-night stand!" Rage sparked within him. At Savannah for lying, and at El for keeping her secret.

"She knew his name. I don't know how. But it's Cameron Nicholson. He didn't want anything to do with her. I thought she'd decided that was okay, and that she was going to do it alone. It turns out that on the day she gave birth, she messaged him asking him to be there and allowing him the chance to be a part of the baby's life."

Mick didn't know how to react. There was no "typical" way to react to that kind of information. Biting his lip to keep his emotions in check, Mick asked a question he wasn't sure he wanted to know the answer to.

"And what did he say?"

"He didn't answer. He read it, but never answered." She paused. Mick could tell there was more to the story and so he remained quiet. "She messaged him before that too. Telling him that she was pregnant and that she planned to keep the baby. That if he wanted to be involved in Travis's life, he could be."

"Let me guess. He didn't answer that either?"

"Bingo."

"What the hell is wrong with that guy? What kind of a creep ignores a girl who tells him she's having his baby? Who the fuck raised him?" The anger within him felt insurmountable. There was no way to keep it in check. The way El looked at him, forehead lined with concern, told him that she was uncomfortable.

"I shouldn't have told you. I'm sorry."

"Why are you sorry? You have nothing to be sorry for."

Mick scraped his hand through his hair and sighed loudly.

"I just didn't know what to do. I'd thought you'd want to know…"

"You were right to do that. But that fucker ruined my daughter's life and now he gets to go and live his own life like nothing happened?"

"I know, it's not fair at all."

"He should pay for what he's done to her."

"Don't be stupid, Mick, there's nothing you can do. What's done is done. Let him live his own miserable life, and we can live ours. Look what we have that he doesn't." El gestured to Travis, bundled up in a blanket in his car seat.

He understood her logic, but it didn't ease the pain he was feeling. It felt like the universe was laughing at him. Somewhere out there, this Cameron, would have a lovely life and never think about the consequences of his actions. He'd essentially killed Savannah with his own selfish desires. The worst part was that there was no way to know just how many other girls he'd hurt the same way he'd hurt Savannah.

Mick smiled at El, hoping it would convince her that he would let this slide, getting on with his life and focusing on Travis. At that moment, he made a pact to himself that there was no way Cameron Nicholson would have a normal life. He would do everything in his power to make sure that didn't happen.

Cameron

Cameron ran. He didn't know which direction Hopwood Road was, but he needed to be moving. Pulling his phone out of his pocket, he typed the address into the maps app, trying to keep his momentum going. Five miles. The edge of town. He was in neither his running shoes nor gym shorts but didn't have a choice other than to keep running. He knew from experience that his shins would be on fire and his legs chaffed from the jeans he was wearing by the time he arrived at his destination, but none of that mattered. He had to find Liz. She was the sole thought in his mind as his feet pounded against the pavement, his arches already aching and protesting.

The house was nondescript. He hated that phrase, and always told his students not to use it in their writing, but it was true of the terraced house he'd arrived at. Had the number not been placed upon the door, then there would be no chance of deciphering which was the correct one, other than the fact that the door had been left ajar. Each house was the mirror image of the rest. Paint curled at the bottom, peeling away from the wood beneath.

Cameron pushed the door open. No sound came from within. Quickly arguing whether it would be better to make his presence known, or enter the building in silence, Cameron decided on the latter. If there was somebody there who wanted to hurt him, which he had to assume was the case, the element of surprise might be the only tool in his belt.

The house smelled of must and damp, the way houses that have been abandoned, left unloved by previous inhabitants, so often did. Three doors led off the downstairs hallway. He reached out for the first handle. Locked. He crept to the second. Locked. The third was also locked. Turning back on himself, he looked up at the staircase. His only option was to head upwards, the prospect of which was not appealing to him in the slightest. There was a rule in every horror film he'd ever watched, and that was to never go upstairs. Or into the basement. Because then you're trapped and would certainly die. But this wasn't a horror film. This was his life.

He expected the stairs to creak as he ascended, but they lay silently below him. The hallway was almost completely dark. There was no window, and the three doors were closed tightly. Unlike downstairs, the first door he tried swung open. The light was blinding at first, knocking him backwards. This room wasn't silent. There was a drumbeat, slow and steady. Muffled. Once his eyes adjusted, he saw that there were photographs littered across every surface. The walls, the bare floorboards, the table leaning against the corner of the room. At the very centre of the room was a wooden chair.

The wooden chair. He was not sure whether the fact that Liz wasn't tied to it was a good thing or not. Perhaps the torturer had finished with her, casting her aside like rubbish. The chair was immaculate. Under the strip lights above his head, it gleamed. There was no sign of blood upon it. No sign that anybody had ever been tortured there. Not Liz. And not Cameron. Nothing made sense. The photographs showed that he had been tortured right there, but his body showed otherwise.

He needed to find Liz. Making his way to the open doorway, a photograph caught Cameron's eye. In each one was the same person. Somebody he vaguely remembered, like a face in a dream.

A floorboard groaned on the landing, and somebody entered the room.

Cameron

"I'm sure you're not surprised to see me here, are you Cameron?" The bald man stepped towards him as he spoke. Slowly. In time with the gentle heartbeat that filled the room. He was not surprised, of course. He'd been right all along. The sense of fulfilment at being right was overshadowed by immense fear. The man before him was clearly dangerous, unhinged even. At least now there was a chance he would finally get some answers.

"Where's Liz?" His voice sounded stronger than he felt.

"All in good time. Don't worry, what's done is done."

"Is she okay?" Cameron pushed. Once he knew she was okay, he'd be able to breathe easier. At this stage, what happened to him was secondary to her well-being.

"As I said, we'll get to that later. First, I wonder if you've been able to figure out who I am yet? I gave you plenty of clues. Look around you." The man gestured to the walls, lined with photographs. A girl, the same girl, at different stages in her life. Until the age of twenty, perhaps.

"I don't know her," Cameron said, walking around the room. The girl was beautiful. Whoever took the photographs of her clearly loved her.

"You do, Cameron. You killed her."

Something hit Cameron hard across the back of the head. It sent him sprawling forwards onto the floor. Stars erupted across his vision as his world swam to black.

When he awakened, his body wasn't laid down like he anticipated it should be. He was upright. Attempting to move a hand to the back of his head to check the damage, Cameron found that he was bound to the chair tightly with blue rope.

"Why?" he managed to choke out.

"Keep up for god's sake. You killed my daughter." The smile grew across the man's face as he circled Cameron, like a great white shark playing with its prey.

"You've got the wrong person. I've never killed anybody." Cameron blinked, trying to rid himself of the headache that pounded through his skull.

"Don't play stupid with me. I know who you are. I know what you did. I've been waiting for this moment for a long time, Cameron. Years and years of waiting for the right moment to strike. The right moment when you were vulnerable enough to allow me to tear your life apart. I am going to hurt you, Cameron. It will be worse than the photographs. Worse than anything you could possibly imagine. I will make you beg for death."

The snarl curled at the corner of the man's lips. The white button-down shirt and grey trousers looked like he'd come straight from a board meeting.

"I don't know your daughter. I never killed a person. Ever. I'm a fucking teacher! I'm as boring as you can get. You have the wrong person; I promise you that. If you let me go, I won't tell anybody. Hell, I'll even help you find the right person." Cameron bumbled his words as he spoke. Nonsensical ideas poured into his head about how he could convince the stranger in front of him that he was innocent.

"You killed my daughter. You may not have placed your finger on the trigger, or your hand around the knife, but you signed her death warrant." The man's eyes flashed with anger as he spoke.

"Who was your daughter? The girl in the photos, right? I don't know her. Please, don't hurt Liz, and let me go. We have nothing to do with this."

The man's laugh raked across Cameron's consciousness. It was cold and callous.

"There is so much you have yet to learn. Allow me to tell you a story. It starts at university. My daughter, Savannah, was the sweetest girl you could ever hope to meet. She was smart, and beautiful, and so creative. She had her problems, but she got through them. She was on the right path when she met you."

Heat slid down Cameron's temples as he thought back to his university days. He'd been with so many girls that he couldn't even begin to count them. How was he supposed to remember Savannah? And how could he have been responsible for her death if he had no idea who the fuck she was?

"I don't remember her."

"Do you think that makes things better?" The man screamed at him, pounding his fist onto the wooden table. Cameron couldn't see it, but he heard it splinter.

"I don't know. I don't..." Cameron's breath came in ragged judders.

"Shut the fuck up and let me speak."

Cameron forced his mouth into a tight seal.

"Thank you. Anyway, as I was saying. My daughter met a man, and I use that term loosely, in a club and made the idiotic decision to go home with him. Now, I can't very well blame her for that. She was following her base desires, you know how it is. The man she went home with, she'd actually had a crush on for quite a long time, so her roommate told me. This guy took her home, despite her being inebriated, and had his way with her. He was gone when she awoke the next morning and she never heard from him again. It transpired that he gave a fake name and did all he could to be avoided on campus afterwards."

Cameron felt the fear tearing at his skin. This was something he used to do. Sleep with girls and give fake names. What student didn't? Nobody wanted the awkward encounters the next morning, or the awkward dates after that. He certainly hadn't been the only one to do that. Yet, something about this story struck him as familiar. The more he looked at the photo of Savannah, the more he recognised her. But there was something else. Something he was missing, that he wasn't quite remembering.

"My daughter was in no fit state to give consent. The man who slept with her, raped her. That man was you."

"Your daughter killed herself because she was raped?" Cameron couldn't help himself. The words were out of his mouth before he could stop them.

"No. My daughter died because whoever raped her, got her pregnant. She died giving birth to your bastard child."

Realisation dawned upon Cameron at the mention of the pregnancy. He remembered Savannah, but the story wasn't at all as the man had told it. The Savannah he remembered was no innocent little girl who Cameron had hurt. Quite the opposite was true.

Mick

The sight of Cameron in the chair in front of him sent shivers of pleasure down his spine. This moment had been building for so long. It had taken so much careful planning and patience, and now it was finally before him, spreading out with infinite possibilities. He hadn't lied to Cameron; he certainly didn't plan on making anything short and sweet. The box of torture instruments propped outside of the door was a testament to that.

At this point, he had hoped that Cameron would have begun to apologise for what he'd done, admitting his mistakes, and pleading for forgiveness. That wasn't the case. The bastard was still feigning ignorance. No matter, Mick had plenty of tricks up his sleeve to force a confession out of him. It wasn't easy to look at Cameron if truth be told. He found it difficult. The man was the spitting image of Travis, who he loved more than life itself. In fact, it was because of Travis that this whole thing was happening.

"After my daughter died in childbirth, because of the baby you forcibly put into her," Mick continued his tirade as Cameron sat and looked blankly at him. "I raised the baby. He's absolutely incredible, despite your genes. He's grown up to be the kind of human being everybody hopes that their children will become."

Cameron didn't speak, clearly having learned his lesson, and so Mick was able to continue this trip down memory lane, leading up to the big reveal. "When I first found out about you, I'll admit, I wanted to kill you. But Travis centred me. He made me calmer than I'd ever been before. A better person. I suppose I have you to thank for that, in a way. I forgot about you for years, concentrating on doing my best to raise my grandson. As luck would have it, you stumbled back into our lives."

The look on Cameron's face suggested that he didn't know what Mick was talking about. Which caused excitement to bubble within him. He couldn't wait for the realisation to batter Cameron.

"Travis came home from school one day and told me all about his cool new English teacher, Mr Nicholson. The name rang a bell instantly, as you can imagine. I asked Travis if he knew your first name. Of course, he did. All of the cool teachers tell the children their real names. And there we had it. There you were. Do you know what the worst part of it is?"

Mick leaned closely to Cameron, so close that he could smell his own breath refracting from Cameron's face.

"The worst part is that you were happy. You were doing well. Travis said that all the students liked you. Can you imagine that? All of the students liking a rapist? I wasn't sure whether to tell Travis who you were. When I spoke to El, she's Savannah's old roommate and has been a much-needed female figure in his life, since you killed his mother, El said to tell him. She said that we weren't the kind of family that kept secrets from each other.

"I didn't expect him to be able to hide it from you. I thought he'd want to go in there, guns blazing, and demand that you be a part of his life. Instead, he looked at me with this quiet resignation that read as 'Oh, it's a shame Mr Nicholson didn't want to be my dad. I quite like him.' I couldn't let you hurt my boy again. Your life was going so well that it didn't take much to throw it out of whack. A little bit of gentle stalking, the odd text message here and there, that was enough to ruin your life. Don't you think that's funny? You can build this life for yourself, and it only takes something minute to throw it off track completely."

Mick took a break from speaking and paced around the room. He wanted Cameron to snap at him. Or, at the very least, to admit to what he'd done.

"It was hardly something little. You made me think I was crazy. I don't understand the photographs. Were they of somebody who looked like me? How did you take them? Did you drug me? What about the ones where you cut off limbs or stabbed me? How do you fake that?"

Now the questions were flowing. What Cameron didn't realise was that part had been simple. Perhaps the easiest of the lot, for Mick at least. He'd had help in that department. His secret weapon. The one person who he could rely on. Who had stuck by him since

Savannah's death. El. She and Travis had made his life worth living after his daughter's death. If they hadn't been there, who knows what he would have done?

"I have a visual artist who is amazing at doctoring images. It wasn't easy, of course. She needed some original photographs to work with, so it had to be somebody fairly close to you, especially for the more intimate photographs." He smiled the smile he knew sent Cameron into a frenzy.

"I don't fucking understand!" Cameron pushed against his bindings. Mick prayed a silent prayer that they would hold. This was the first time he'd ever had to tie a human being up. His prayers were answered as Cameron slumped back into the chair, panting. Sweat shone slick across his skin.

"Did you never feel like you were being watched?"

"Of course, I did, you bastard. You were following me!"

"I'm sorry to say it was somebody closer than me." Mick smiled, watching thoughts race by Cameron's eyes.

"El, why don't you come in here and introduce yourself."

Mick's smile grew as Cameron's face contorted into anguish as she walked into the room.

Cameron

When Liz walked into the room, Cameron breathed a sigh of relief. She was alive. She was okay. For the briefest of seconds, he thought that everything would be okay. And then he saw the look painted onto her face. The look of derision, of disgust, unlike anything he'd ever seen mar her beautiful face before.

"Liz, what are you doing? Be careful! He's dangerous." Cameron had so many thoughts he wanted to say but these were the only ones he could dredge to the surface.

"Cameron, I want you to meet somebody. This is El. Savannah's roommate, and the woman who helped me raise your child." There was no hint of irony in the man's voice.

"What the fuck are you talking about? This is Liz. My girlfriend. Fucking hell. I don't understand what the fuck is happening to me right now." Once more he attempted to push against the ropes that bound him. They sliced into his already delicate wrists, making him grimace in pain.

"You know me as Liz. My name is Elizabeth. I used to go by El. I really hate the name Liz, by the way. Can we stick to El now that you know who I really am?"

"You were this girl's roommate? Liz, come on, you have to know I'm not the kid's father. I never even slept with her that night. Why the fuck didn't you just ask me? Why go through all of this shit? I could have just fucking told you it wasn't me!"

Cameron watched as the two of them smiled back at him, condescendingly, and shake their heads. They didn't believe him.

"I swear. I took her home, yes. But I never slept with her. She was wankered. I couldn't have even if I wanted to. She was a dead weight. I'm not into shagging corpses for fuck's sake." He watched as Liz's expression flickered slightly. It didn't last and the mask of contempt was placed back over her perfect features.

"We know the truth, Cameron. We know you raped her. That you got her pregnant, and that you refused to be a part of the baby's life." Liz's voice was soothing, the way it was when she asked him to take his pills or gave him a hug.

"This is fucked up, Liz. I never had sex with her. I never got her pregnant. I don't know how the fuck to prove that to you, but it's the truth."

"We don't believe you, do we Micky?" Liz laughed, smiling at the bald man. She'd known his stalker all along. She'd been a part of this since the start. Why? Because she thought Cameron was to blame for killing her friend, when he'd had nothing to do with that, other than ignore the crazy girl's Facebook messages?

"We know what happened, Cameron." Mick, the bald man, confirmed.

"So, what's your part in this?" Cameron turned to Liz, knowing that she was his only hope in getting out of this alive.

Mick answered on her behalf, cutting her off as she began to speak. "She's my digital artist. You knew she had a degree in art, and that she worked in Photoshop for a magazine, which isn't strictly true. Well, it turns out that she's crazy good at manipulating photographs. All she needed were some stills of you in various situations, and she could put together a torturous little image to send to you. I'll forever be in awe that she learned to do all of that, while raising your child. Crazy, right?" Mick smirked at him and winked at Liz.

Cameron wanted, more than anything, to jump out of the chair and punch the man straight in the throat. He loved Liz. Loved her? He didn't know how he felt anymore. All he knew, for sure, was that he was used to thinking of her as his girlfriend, and the way Mick was acting was straight-up disrespectful.

"All this time you were just pretending?"

"You killed my best friend, Cameron." Liz's voice was as hard as stone as she spoke.

"You have to know that isn't true." Cameron pleaded with her to see reason. There was nothing more frustrating than trying to convince someone that you were telling the truth when you couldn't prove it.

"You were the only one she slept with, Cameron. She told me that. You were the only one."

"I didn't sleep with her! I took her home that night and laid her in my bed. She could barely lift her own head up. I put a sick bowl there and slept in my roommate's room. There were four other guys in that house. If I didn't sleep with her, and she got pregnant, there were plenty of other candidates."

He didn't want to throw his old roommates under the bus, but at this point, it was him or them, and he was going to choose himself every single time. Back in college, they'd all slept with their fair share of women. As much as he loved his friends, he wouldn't put it past any of them to have taken advantage of Savannah when she was in that state.

"I've had enough of this. I want an apology from you, Cameron. Before I kill you. I want you to say you are sorry for killing my daughter, and for not being there for her, or for Travis. You had the chance to be a good person, and you chose the wrong path." Out of his pocket, Mick pulled a penknife. He slid the tip up and crouched before Cameron, placing the cold tip of the blade against his cheek.

"Are you ready to apologise?" Mick's face was an inch from his own. Cameron wanted to spit, or to headbutt, but there was still a chance he could get out of this.

"I'm sorry this happened to you. I really am. This shouldn't happen to anybody. I'm sorry your daughter died. And that her baby had to grow up without a father, but it wasn't me. I didn't do it." Tears began to leak from his eyes. Blinking against it, he continued to beg for his life. “She bumped into me, once, and told me she was pregnant. I told her then that the baby wasn’t mine. She acted crazy. Then she found me on Facebook and sent messages saying that the baby was mine and that she had all these plans for it. I honestly thought she was mental. I wasn’t going to answer that, especially when I’d never slept with her. I’ve been with my fair share of mental women, and it never ended well. I wasn’t going to risk that again.” It was strange how life forced memories further into the recesses of your mind. How he’d forgotten that this Savannah girl had existed until today. A mere anecdote that was easily pushed aside and never thought of again. Other than being weird, and stalker-ish, there had been nothing about her that seemed worth remembering. A notch on somebody else’s bedpost, not even his own.

Mick remained where he was, his face a practised mask.

“Please. I didn’t sleep with her. The baby isn’t mine.”

Deliberately, the blade pushed against his cheek. When it broke the skin, there was a brief moment of relief, and then the scorching sensation began to tear through him as the knife sliced to his jawline. He could feel the flap of skin hanging open, the cool air burning the flesh inside of him.

“If you continue to lie to me, this will only hurt more than it has to. I’m going to kill you anyway. Whether I do it quickly, or very, very slowly, is entirely up to you.”

“I didn’t,” Cameron forced the words from his mouth. With each syllable, the slash across his face felt like it tore further.

“Wrong answer. El, my toolbox please.”

Without any argument, or even a glance at Cameron, Liz followed Mick’s orders. The robotic way she moved flooded Cameron with dread. How could she be a part of this? How could he have fallen for her act?

“I’m sorry she died. It wasn’t me!” Cameron stuttered. “Liz, please, tell him I wouldn’t do that.”

“Savannah didn’t lie, Cameron. Not about something like this. I’m sorry, but this is the way it has to be. You broke her heart and then killed her.” She handed Mick the pliers without her face changing expression.

“What if she thought it was me?” Cameron said desperately. He watched their movements stutter, before they continued with their tasks. “Please. My roommates, it had to have been one of them. It wasn’t me! I’m not saying she was lying, but she was off her tits drunk.” He pushed against the bindings, a futile attempt, but he had to do something to show that he was serious.

“Take off his shoes please,” Mick commanded her, completely ignoring his explanations. She bent to her knees and complied.

A wry smile creased across Mick’s face as he placed the pliers around Cameron’s little toe. He could feel the steel against his skin, but his view was obscured by Mick’s hunched shoulders.

"Ever since El created this photograph, I've been desperate to give it a go."

The pain was unimaginable. There was the sound of a gunshot as his bone snapped. Unconsciousness washed over him, and his world went mercifully blank.

Cameron woke to the sound of hushed voices. When they saw he had stirred, they looked at him. Their expressions were unreadable. Mick asked the question Cameron was unable to answer as he would like.

"Are you ready to tell the truth?"

"I've told you the truth all along," Cameron said through clenched teeth.

"That's the wrong answer. What do you say, El? A tooth or a fingernail this time?"

"Why not both?" Liz tilted her head, waiting for a reaction from Cameron. He wouldn't give her one. He contorted his face into stone and fixed his eyes on hers.

Mick passed a thin screwdriver to Liz and fished out some kind of metal instrument from his toolbox. The device was forced into Cameron's mouth, holding it open. He gulped, flailing, and tried to breathe without swallowing his tongue.

"Please," he tried to say. The word was unintelligible.

"Ready?" Mick asked. Cameron wasn't sure whether it was directed at Liz, or him. Not that it mattered, the outcome was the same either way. The screwdriver was plunged under the nail of his ring finger at the same time the pliers were clamped around his tooth. Agony fired through him as he tried to fight against the pain, forcing the perpetrators away from him. It was no use. He couldn't move. But it was his body's natural response to the agony firing through every nerve within him.

Liz took the screwdriver out and sliced it under a different nail. The pain clouded his judgement, and he couldn't tell which one. There was a gentle clunk as his tooth fell to the floor and the taste of copper filled his mouth.

"We need to do something more substantial," Mick said to Liz. "Something that shows him we mean business." From the toolbox, Mick pulled a scalpel.

He teased it across Cameron's throat. Then down his chest and to his abdomen. The space where the ribs ended and the body descended into fatty tissue, was where Mick stopped. Through his shirt, Cameron felt the blade. No longer was Mick teasing. He plunged it into Cameron's side and drew a line towards his navel. Again, the pain was erased as Cameron was pulled from consciousness.

Mick

He hadn't anticipated how uncomfortable it would make him feel to watch El strip the naked prostrate form of Cameron. To see her handling another man, after their decade together, sent him sick to the core. Of course, he knew that she'd been intimate with him in the past. It was all part of the plan. Without sex, alarm bells would have sounded in Cameron's head, and they wouldn't have gotten to this point. But that didn't mean he had to see it firsthand. As he watched El peel off Cameron's underwear, annoyingly clean boxer briefs, he almost pushed her out of the way to do it himself. Almost.

Mick stood to the side until Cameron was stripped of his dignity, and then helped El pull his sleeping form back into the chair, securing his wrists and ankles once more. When that was done, they simply had to wait for him to wake up.

"Almost done," El said to him. She walked towards him, a sad smile on her face. Together, they had done something they wouldn't ever be able to take back. From this point on, they'd be killers. It was a price both of them were willing to pay. Savannah deserved her chance at revenge, even if she didn't get to administer it herself.

"I know." Mick pulled her close to him. Her scent was as familiar as his own. Planting a kiss atop her head, they waited for Cameron to swim back into consciousness.

The front door clicked open. After a second, it latched shut again.

"He's here," El said, looking to the closed door of the repurposed bedroom they were currently in.

Footsteps creaked up the stairs, slowly.

Travis entered the room, still in school uniform. It always brought a hitch to Mick's throat to see his grandson looking so grown up in his senior school uniform. It felt like moments ago when he was a babe in arms, relying on Mick for every little thing. And now, he stood there, practically a man.

Travis's mouth formed the shape of an "o" as he looked at Cameron, his father, strapped to the chair at the centre of the room. Bruised and bleeding.

"You actually did it?" Travis's eyes widened with elation. This was his idea after all.

"We'd do anything for you," El said, pulling the boy into a hug. He was at that age where he would usually resist, but today, he allowed it.

"Thank you," Mick heard him whisper to El.

"He's all yours now son," Mick said as Travis separated himself from El.

Travis stepped forward and slapped Cameron hard around the face. His head snapped backwards and lolled to one side precariously, teetering. An uncomfortable sensation prickled through Mick as he watched Travis.

When Cameron didn't wake up, Travis looked to his granddad and said, "Did you bring the cattle prod I bought?"

It was a curious feeling when your child asked for an instrument of torture, especially one they'd bought themselves online in anticipation of this moment. Mick picked up the cattle prod from within the recesses of the toolbox. The red stick looked mundane. The electricity that flowed within it when the terminals pressed against the skin, especially skin as slick as Cameron's, caused the most intense pain. A jolt could be both disorientating and long-lasting. The perfect tool of torture, one might argue.

A grin grew across Travis's face as he walked over to his father. There had always been something different about Travis. Mick blamed Cameron for that, of course. A child born of rape would never be "normal." A child whose mother died bringing them into the world, even less so. Mick watched as he pressed the cattle prod against Cameron's ribs, just above the gaping wound left at Mick's hand. There was a small spark as the man threw himself against his bindings repeatedly. A low moan escaped from his throat. His eyes blinked open.

Cameron

Pain wracked through his body, pulling him from the blackness before he was ready. He expected to wake up and see his tormentor, Mick, staring at him, tapping his foot, and waiting to continue with the torture. The sadistic bastard was definitely enjoying it. It wasn't just an instrument to get Cameron to tell the "truth." But, as his eyes blinked open, the pain slicing through his cheek, protesting the action, the face was not what he anticipated.

"Reese?" his voice croaked. The combination of pain and exhaustion made him feel like he was on a different plane of existence. His eyes betrayed him. He could barely keep them open. The desire to fall back into the blissful blackness overwhelmed him.

"Try again," the voice said. The voice was familiar. But he couldn't quite place it. He forced his eyes open again. Not Reese, but Travis. Travis. His own student. Screwing his eyes shut, he prayed that this wasn't real. The feeling of disgust rose in his stomach like bile. The storyline was knitted together in his head. Each fragment formed to make a clear picture. It made perfect sense now. The assumption that he was Travis's father, after Savannah, that mental case, had convinced everybody that he'd gotten her pregnant.

"They've got it wrong. I'm not your dad, I'm sorry." Adrenaline shot through him as he tried to think of some way to save Travis. There was no way a child should be involved in this sick, twisted game. What kind of a sick fuck convinced a child to witness this? He looked from Liz to Mick, trying to make sense of why Travis had been brought here, before him, and why the fuck there was a cattle prod in his hand.

"I knew you'd say that. Do you think I'm thick or something?" Travis's voice cut across him. He'd never heard the boy speak this way before.

"No. I know you're smart. You've been brainwashed. I never slept with your mum. There's no way you're my child. I'm sorry. You've got the wrong person." Travis shot a look at Mick and El, who both stood by like proud parents. It made Cameron feel physically sick. Bile ballooned in his stomach, threatening to force its way out of him. He managed to swallow it down. But only just. The bitter taste bit at the back of his throat.

"I told you he'd say that, didn't I? They'll always deny it if they think it means they'll get to live. It's just the way human beings are. Die an honest man. Never." Mick leaned back against the table, crossing his ankles and eyeing Travis, hungrily. A dare.

"You killed my mother. Not only that, but you pretended she didn't exist after you used her. What kind of a sick, twisted bastard does that? She begs you to be in her life, to be in my life, and you vanish. You leave her to die. You deserve this."

Cameron's teeth clamped together as the shock coursed through him. The pain filled every fibre of his being, so much so that he couldn't tell where the instrument made contact with his skin. His body felt white hot. Flashes of colour spurted in front of his eyes like neon signs telling him to give up. How could a child be responsible for causing so much pain?

The pain stopped as abruptly as it started. He was shattered. His head hung to his chest, sweat pooling where the skin made contact. He couldn't pick it up, and so he closed his eyes and tried to steady his breathing. The fist, or foot, slammed into this cheek. Agony like nothing he'd ever experienced hit him like a brick. Whatever body part smashed into him aimed for the knife wound on his cheek. His head ached deeply, a thumping pulse that caused him to lose his breath.

His head remained where it snapped. No muscles in his body would cooperate with his instructions. He had no energy left within him to move a muscle.

"Cameron?" The voice wasn't Mick's, it was Liz's. "Just tell him the truth. Apologise for what you did. This will be over soon. Don't draw it out any further."

Any further? Cameron could barely understand the idea that this torture could last any longer than it already had. He wasn't sure how many more times he would descend into agony, only to be revived once more.

"Make them stop," Cameron whispered. It was the only way he could convince his mouth to move.

"Admit it," Liz said. She sounded disinterested, bored even. It hurt almost as much as the physical torture did.

The anguish was unbearable. He had two choices, as far as he could tell. Lie and die. Or tell the truth and be tortured to death. He would die, no matter his choice. Dying quickly seemed like the only logical action. The image of Reese forced its way into Cameron's mind. The child looked so much like him. The gentle slope of his nose. His eyes. The indecision tore him apart. Could he throw his friend to the wolves based on a hunch, when they likely wouldn't believe him anyway? He'd never touched Savannah, that much he was certain of. But he wasn't the only person in the house that night. Never mind the fact that Savannah could have slept with any person at any time. It had been really fucking easy to convince her to come back to his place. In his defence, he had hoped that she'd have sobered up by the time they got back to the student house. He would have loved to have fucked her. But he'd spoken the truth before. He wasn't into fucking people who were so drunk they couldn't even stand.

"You're right." Cameron couldn't lift his head to speak, and so spoke to the floor. Until that point, he hadn't realised he'd been stripped of his clothing. He didn't care. He had no remaining dignity. He was about to beg for death.

"Tell me more," Mick said, the smile audible in his voice.

"I slept with her. Then I left her. I ignored her messages even though I knew the kid was mine. I killed your daughter. I killed Savannah." The lie felt good on his lips. With it would come freedom. There would never be a chance to clear his name, but he knew he was innocent, and that had to count for something.

"Thank you."

Cameron's head was thrown back, and his eyes met Travis's. The cattle prod was no longer in his hand. It lay on the floor beside his feet. Instead, he gripped a bread knife, the kind with serrated edges that saws through thick, crusty loaves. Travis held the knife to Cameron's neck.

If this was the quick option, Cameron thanked fuck he hadn't continued telling the truth. His eyes pleaded for it to be quick. For Travis to push the knife in as deeply as he could, hitting whatever arteries or veins lived in the neck. Biology had never been his strong suit, and never would be now.

The first cut stopped him from breathing. It skimmed the surface, tearing at the skin.

The second cut, the back end of the sawing motion, dug deeper. The pain was intense, but nothing like he'd experienced already. The knowledge that it would be over soon made it bearable.

The knife went forward. Back. Forward. Back. For the briefest second, Cameron felt warm blood spurt out from inside of him, splattering over Travis's face and neck. After that, nothing but darkness.

Epilogue: El

The view was stunning, better than she could ever have imagined. The sunrise over the almost-blue sea brought a smile to her face. Life was perfect, for now, at least. It was on days like this that she was thankful for Savannah's death. In dying, Savannah had given El everything she could have ever wanted. A loving partner, the perfect child, a life of luxury. Micky's investments meant that she would never have to work a day in her life. She'd moved in with him the day Savannah died and had only left his side to perpetrate her part of the plan. God, she'd missed him when she'd had to live with Cameron. Who'd want an English teacher with a tendency towards depression when you could have a handsome property tycoon? She'd always been into older men; things had worked out for the best.

Micky walked out of the bathroom wrapped in a terrycloth robe. He kissed her on the cheek and took the seat next to her on the bistro set that adorned the balcony. He picked up the newspaper while she sipped her coffee. They looked like a regular couple, despite the age gap, but that was even becoming common now. When Travis walked by their side, they looked like the perfect family.

They'd made the front cover of the newspaper. Well, their actions had at least. Cameron's face, the size of a passport photo, was accompanied by the headline: MAN FOUND DEAD – TORTURED AND NAKED. A laugh escaped El. He'd forever be remembered as the man who was found nude and tied to a chair. The photograph of his naked corpse had already begun to make the rounds on the internet. The perfect revenge, she had to admit. The last thing she'd want was for people to see photographs of her naked, and dead, body.

"Do you think the paperboy knew who he was delivering the paper to? That he'd spoken to the killers?" El bit her lip. She found this whole thing exciting. The aftermath particularly. The build-up, and the torture itself, hadn't been her cup of tea. Now she was beginning to feel like Bonnie and Clyde.

"I hope he didn't," Micky joked. They both felt safe. They'd covered their tracks well. The house was rented under a false name. They'd cleaned up. There was nothing to tie them to Cameron's death. The police would always suspect the girlfriend, of course, but seeing how mental Cameron was, well, that put the ball firmly in his court. El had played the grieving girlfriend perfectly. The police had apologised for their questions and let her go free. Travis was on holiday from school, so they'd decided to take a minibreak to celebrate their success. Get out of the way for a week or two. After that, they'd return to their lives. El would go home, to the home she shared with Micky and Travis, and return to being a homemaker with a penchant for doctoring photographs.

“Micky?” El asked. She’d been waiting for the right time to bring this up. Given everything that had been going on, there hadn’t been the right time.

“Yes, sweetheart.”

“Do you think it was Cameron? You know, who Savannah slept with. If what he said was true, there’s the chance one of his roommates could be the father of Travis.” It had been playing on her mind. Cameron had been a lot of things, but he wasn’t a liar. And, as much as she would never admit it to Micky, Savannah had never been the most trustworthy person. Plus, she had been very drunk that night, by her own admission. Perhaps she had misremembered or dreamed Cameron sleeping with her. She had invented a boyfriend earlier that year.

El dug through her bag, trying to find something that she had wanted to show Micky for weeks.

“I don’t know. But it doesn’t matter. It was one of them. They’ll all pay for what they did.”

“So we’re going to do this again?” The thought of doing all of that again was draining. Start to finish it had taken months. Truly exhausting months.

“Well, not exactly the same. You’ve met some of the roommates, after all. It won’t be hard to gain their trust and eke a confession out of them. If none of them admit it, they’ll all have to die.” Micky spoke towards the sea, instead of looking at El. She’d hoped that this had been the end of the whole thing, but she'd had her suspicions there would be more. Once you killed a person, you changed. The idea of killing somebody was no longer abstract. Instead, it was plausible.

"And once they're dead?"

"Then we'll be able to get on with our lives."

Her hand clasped around the pregnancy test, the positive result taunting her. She stuffed it back down into the bottom of her bag. Now wasn't the right time. She'd wait for it to be over, however long that would be.

ACKNOWLEDGEMENTS

They say that it takes a village to raise a family, well, the same can be said for writing a book. I first have to thank my long-suffering partner, Danny, who, when I told him I was leaving my proper job with no back-up plan, gave me the space I needed to heal and gently guided me towards freelancing. He supported the both of us while I figured my shit out, and for that, I am truly grateful. He also let me get a rescue dog who has made our lives both far more incredible and far more challenging. It is to Buster that I dedicated this, my first official book.

It goes without saying that I also want to thank my mum and dad, Anita and Peter (yes, we know their names rhyme), who have always been there for me, no matter what. They encouraged me to always try my best and supported me when my best wasn't quite good enough.

For Joe, my brother, who I hated growing up and who is now one of my best friends. For Shannon and Alfie for putting up with my brother and becoming part of the family. For my Auntie Julie, proof-reader extraordinaire and (as she likes to joke) my *real* mother. Together she, and my actual mum, read Found You too many times to count and always offered honest critique and support. The book wouldn't be what it is without the two of them.

For my grandparents. And for family and friends, too many to mention, who didn't laugh in my face when I told them I was writing a book. Please know that I am truly grateful for each and every one of you.

And to a certain employer who ruined my mental health and accidentally set me on the right path in doing so.

To Susan Keillor, who did the final proofread of this book and found more errors than I'd care to admit.

A huge thank you to you too. I know that taking a chance on a new author can be daunting. Why waste your time on something you might not like, right? Whether you stuck it out to the end, or tapped out early on, thank you for giving my book a try. It means the world.

ABOUT THE AUTHOR

Sarah is a self-professed accidental hipster (who refuses to apologise for this). She holds a Master's Degree from the University of Huddersfield, in addition to a BA (Hons) and Qualified Teacher Status. After realising teaching wasn't for her, Sarah took to the internet to find a job that allowed her to stay home in her pyjamas, and stumbled serendipitously across freelance writing. From there, Sarah Jules Writing Services was born. She still can't believe how lucky she is that this is her real-life, adult, job!

If Sarah isn't working, you can find her with her nose stuck in a book, watching horror films, travelling the UK with her partner, and her rescue pup, or sweating it out in the gym. She is a mental health advocate, coffee-addict, and has too many tattoos (of which most of them are book related).

If you enjoyed this book, please do give it a review, talk about it on social media, or share it with your friends. If you didn't, well, please keep it quiet. Kidding! I truly do appreciate the time it takes to leave a review, good or bad. They can be a great help for new authors like myself. And please do reach out to me via social media or my website if you'd like to chat. I'd love to hear your thoughts first-hand.

Instagram: @sarahjuleswriting

Website: www.sarahjuleswriting.com

This manuscript includes a snippet of Philip Larkin's Mr Bleaney, 1955.

Larkin, Philip. *The Whitsun Weddings*. Faber & Faber, 2012.

Printed in Great Britain
by Amazon

10271687R00189